The Murders of Mrs. Austin and Mrs. Beale

by the same author

A Perfect Match
Gone to Her Death
An Evil Hour
The Stalking Horse
Murder at the Old Vicarage
Murder Movie

The Murders of Mrs. Austin and Mrs. Beale

Jill McGown

St. Martin's Press
New York

Library of Congress Cataloging-in-Publication Data

McGown, Jill.
  The murders of Mrs. Austin and Mrs. Beale / Jill McGown.
    p.   cm.
  "A Thomas Dunne book."
  ISBN 0-312-06422-5
  I. Title.
PR6063.C477M87   1991
823'.914—dc20
                                                    91-20466
                                                    CIP

First published in Great Britain by Macmillan London Limited.

First U.S. Edition: September 1991
10 9 8 7 6 5 4 3 2 1

My thanks are due to Chris and Tony
for providing Exhibit A, and to my niece
Katy for providing the title.

The Murders of Mrs. Austin and Mrs. Beale

One

'Just a bite to eat,' said Jonathan Austin, his casual tone at odds with the tight grip he had on the receiver.

'Fine,' said Gordon, sounding a little puzzled. 'Just me?'

Jonathan licked his lips. 'Yes,' he said. 'Business. The girls would be bored.'

'Business you couldn't discuss in the office?'

Oh, God. Jonathan's blond lashes closed. Trust Gordon to start questioning things now. He could always be relied upon just to do whatever he was being advised to do, by anyone at all, and by Jonathan in particular. But now, he had to ask questions.

'Well – it's a bit . . . sensitive.'

There was a silence.

'Gordon?'

'Sensitive,' Gordon repeated. 'More redundancies?'

Sort of, thought Jonathan, looking out of his rain-streaked office window, then back at the agreement on his desk. Sort of. 'No,' he said, trying to sound jovial. 'But I'd prefer to talk to you in private.'

Another silence. He held his breath. Gordon, Gordon. You are a nice man. But please, please carry on being obtuse, just for another few hours.

'All right,' he said, amiably.

Jonathan breathed again. 'Good,' he said. 'About eight?'

'Sure.'

'See you then.'

'You're the one who said that the deployment of manpower in this force was ridiculous,' said Sergeant Woodford.

Chief Inspector Lloyd grunted.

7

'And that a chimpanzee with some graph paper could do a better job,' added Woodford, with a grin.

Lloyd sighed. 'Yes. Well now we've *got* a chimpanzee with some graph paper,' he said, his Welshness relishing the phrase, as it presumably had the first time. He picked a bundle of bulky files out of his in-tray, and dumped them down on the blotter. 'Where do they get them from, for God's sake?'

'Give the man a chance. I think his ideas are quite interesting.'

Lloyd looked at Jack Woodford and wondered what it was like to have an equable temperament. 'Special squads for this and special squads for that,' he said. 'He'll be setting up a special squad for telling people the time next.'

Jack laughed. 'It might work,' he said. 'We've got to do something about the statistics.'

'The statistics,' said Lloyd, 'have improved overall in the last two years.'

'The ones people worry about haven't.'

'Jack, it doesn't matter what we do. If we catch more burglars, the local paper will say that violent crime has risen. If we catch more muggers, they'll say that car thefts have gone up. If we concentrate manpower on one thing, something else loses out.'

'I know, I know. But that's why he's juggling the manpower around.' Jack smiled. 'I thought that was what you wanted,' he said. 'Judy could hardly have gone on working here with you and she being . . . '

You and her. Lloyd corrected him mentally, automatically.

' . . . being an – item? Isn't that what you call it these days?'

'It's certainly not what I call it,' said Lloyd, and smiled. 'I'd like to call it marriage, but . . . ' He shrugged.

'I think you'd be best to wait for her divorce to come through,' said Jack, with a smile. 'I wonder how she's coping with her first day at Malworth.'

'Well – Bob Sandwell's her DS, so she's among friends. But I've no doubt some of the lads will object to taking orders from a woman.'

'Ah – our new chief constable might have something to say about that,' said Jack. 'He's quite keen on getting women into the higher ranks.' He inclined his head a little as he backtracked. 'Or maybe *a* woman into the higher ranks, to prove he isn't prejudiced,' he said. 'And if he does set up the rape squad, there's every reason to suppose that Judy could get further promotion.'

Lloyd opened the top file, and stared at it, not taking in the contents. He closed it again, and looked round the office. 'What do you think of it, anyway?' he asked.

'Very nice,' said Jack. 'Compact, but nice.'

The new extension was finished at last, bar the painting, and for the first time in years, Lloyd had an office to himself. 'It's a relief not to have to put people wherever there's desk space,' he said.

'It's a relief not to have electric drills whining all day any more. But we did need an extension.'

'Yes, yes. He was right about that too,' said Lloyd. 'I'm not so sure we needed another detective sergeant, though,' he added.

Jack shook his head. 'If they hadn't filled the gap with another DS, you would have been climbing the walls,' he said. 'What is the matter with you today?'

Lloyd looked up from the file. 'I'm frightened of Sergeant Drake,' he said.

Jack grinned. 'He is keen, I grant you,' he said.

'Keen! The man is obsessed with police work.' He leant across the desk. 'He is obsessed,' he said, 'with *paper*work. They come back from a job, and he's there at his desk typing out reports while all the others are still hanging up their jackets and getting coffees from the machine.'

Jack moved forward slightly. 'Lloyd,' he said, 'as acting head of Stansfield CID, don't you think you ought to find that commendable?'

'I find it incomprehensible,' said Lloyd.

'I seem to remember a certain keen young detective constable practically turning cartwheels because he was going to be a keen young detective sergeant in the Metropolitan Police, no less,' said Jack. 'Twenty-seven, about to carve out a career for himself in the big city. With hair, even. Not unlike young Drake, I'd say. Not as tall, of course,' he added wickedly.

Jack's long friendship with Lloyd had been used many times to tone down Lloyd's more excessive prejudices. 'I was a bit cocky,' he admitted.

'You were. But here you are, back amongst us provincial

folk, with the rank to prove that cockiness works and height isn't everything.'

Lloyd smiled. 'I joined straight from school,' he said. 'He's been in the job – what? Four, five years? Do you know how long it took Judy to make detective sergeant?'

'Ah, but she fell at the first hurdle,' said Jack. 'She had the lack of foresight to be born female – a mistake that young Drake didn't make.'

'You're a poet, Jack,' said Lloyd wearily. 'I'm forty-five – are you running a book on when Drake's going to catch me up?'

'Well, he's guaranteed inspector next year. Let's see . . . he'll be twenty-five then – definitely before he's thirty, I'd say,' said Jack, getting up. 'Yes, I'd be nice to DS Drake if I were you.' He turned. 'Of course,' he said. 'You weren't here when he was here before, were you?'

'No. When was that?'

'He did the second of his probationary years here,' said Jack. 'You'd never have believed he'd last the course,' he said. 'He was nearly kicked out at one point. That was what – not four years ago. I think he realised that you had to take the job seriously or not at all.'

'He doesn't do things by halves, does he?'

'He's all right. He's just not Judy, that's all that's bothering you. He could be a considerable asset to— '

He broke off as there was a knock on the door.

Lloyd hoped the soundproofing was good enough as Drake appeared in the doorway. 'I'm just off, sir,' he said.

For an awful moment, Lloyd had no idea what he meant. 'Oh – yes,' he said, with relief, as it came back to him. 'The Mitchell Estate flats.'

'Yes, sir.'

'Now remember – it's observation only. I don't care who you see, I don't care how long we've been after him. You observe, and radio in anything of note. All right?'

'Sir.'

'And you're only being paid until eleven,' Lloyd reminded him. 'So don't stay there all night.'

Drake had had to fight to get that much overtime; there was considerable scepticism about his tip-off that an empty flat there was being used by squatters to manufacture crack cocaine.

10

For one thing it was unheard of in Stansfield, and for another the Mitchell Estate area seemed an unlikely place for it to start. They had to have something to go on other than an informant's word if they were to mount an operation, Lloyd had said. But Drake had just spent some months with the force drugs squad at Barton, and swore his contact was rock solid; Lloyd had been impressed by the young man's persistence in argument, and had finally agreed to let him watch the place until eleven, to see if he could pick up anything more definite that would warrant mounting a raid. For three nights only, he had warned.

Drake left, and Lloyd smiled at Jack. 'I am being nice to him,' he said. 'I'm the only one with any faith in his tip-off.'

'You couldn't even remember where he was going,' said Jack, with his usual accurate aim. 'Isn't it time you were off?' he asked. 'You're dying to know how she got on. You just don't want anyone to know that.'

Lloyd smiled a little as he thought of that morning, when Judy had been so nervous, losing everything. Convinced that she was going to start her first day at Malworth with dripping hair, no tights and one shoe. Making him leave early because he was laughing at her. She had doubtless arrived on time, dark hair shining, dressed with her usual flair, looking cool and composed; not a hint of the panic would have been allowed to show. And yes, he was dying to know how she had got on.

He looked at the clock. 'Good God, Sergeant Woodford, I've been setting the world to rights in my own time.' He put the bundle of files back into his in-tray, and smiled.

As he went out into the warm, wet June evening, Jack Woodford's words came back to him. He walked across the now tiny car park, along the windows of the new extension, making for his car. Another promotion? Well – yes, Jack was right. Not easy, for a woman, but given the new chief constable's apparently enlightened views, further promotion wasn't out of the question. And once she'd jumped *that* hurdle . . .

WPC Alexander hooted him out of his reverie as she passed him on her way in; he waved, and got into the car.

Damn it all, he didn't know *what* he wanted.

Pauline watched as Gordon got ready to go out. His new suit lay on the bed as he shaved unnecessarily.

'You're going to a lot of trouble just for dinner with Jonathan,' she said.

He switched off the razor. 'Sorry?' he said.

He had heard her; she didn't repeat the question.

He patted on aftershave. 'Are you going to stand there and watch me dress?' he asked.

She looked at him in the mirror, and shook her head. 'Sorry,' she said, and went back through to the sitting-room.

He was dressing up for Lennie, of course, not Jonathan. She knew that; there was no point in trying to make him admit it. And she didn't really think she had anything to fear. Lennie had thus far remained true to the vows she had made through clenched teeth, and it seemed unlikely that Gordon would be the one to persuade her to break them; Lennie's taste, when it was given its head, was for the hard, muscular type who could defend her with his bare hands if the need arose. Gordon's fair, fat and forty appeal was lost on her.

Pauline had met Gordon when he was still holding out hope of Lennie; he had been the friend that Lennie had invited to dinner to make up the numbers, and Pauline had been the solo woman who had messed them up in the first place.

It had been obvious to everyone, with the possible exception of Lennie herself, how Gordon felt about her. His eyes would follow her as she moved, like some large trusting dog waiting to have its head patted. Pauline wondered if Lennie did know, had ever known, of Gordon's devotion to her. She was used to men falling in love with her; she had them queuing up, unlike Pauline. She probably had never even noticed Gordon in amongst the others.

They had both met Jonathan at that same dinner. Jonathan, Lennie had told them, had been adopted as the prospective parliamentary candidate for Stansfield, and had just moved to the area. Jonathan was a chartered accountant, with a business flair that had led to his being on the board of several companies, and worth a bob or two, unlike Gordon or any other of Lennie's male friends. He certainly wasn't Lennie's type; there really was only one inference to be drawn from her flamboyant production of him to the more respectable of her rather startled friends. It had come as no surprise to anyone but Gordon, then, when Lennie had announced her engagement.

It had been difficult for Gordon to accept her marrying

Jonathan, of all people. Stiff, starchy Jonathan. He could have understood it if he had been unsuitable, like most of her boyfriends had been. But Jonathan was so eminently suitable, so much what every middle-class mother would dream of, and so very unlike anyone that Lennie might have chosen. 'Why Jonathan?' he had kept asking. 'Why Jonathan?'

No accounting for taste, Pauline had said. Jonathan, because Jonathan wasn't in love with her, and she had no intention of staying in the marriage any longer than she could help, that was why Jonathan. Jonathan needed a wife – prospective members of parliament did. Lennie needed money. It was a marriage of convenience. But Gordon would have been shocked, and Pauline hadn't said all that. Just no accounting for taste.

Lennie had asked him to give her away, apparently unaware of the irony; Gordon had agreed. The wedding – exactly the opposite of what anyone would ever have expected of Lennie, with its marquee and champagne – had taken place, and Gordon had, as far as other people were concerned, at last given up.

The friendship between Pauline and Gordon which had begun on the night of the meet-Jonathan dinner party had slowly turned into a romance, and marriage. She had always been aware of her status as consolation prize; it hadn't bothered her.

And Gordon had even forgiven Jonathan sufficiently to take him into his business first as an adviser, and then as a full-time director. It had made a difference: the firm was healthier than it had ever been, and she and Gordon had moved into one of the Malworth riverside development flats as soon as they were finished, on the strength of it. As a business venture, it had been more than successful, but Pauline still wondered about Gordon's reasons for welcoming Jonathan into the business the way he had.

But now Pauline was pregnant, and with the pregnancy had come an unexpected turning off of sexual desire, which the doctor had assured her was temporary and not unusual. Gordon had been understanding at first, then impatient, then indifferent.

But he was tarting himself up in the bedroom, he was still in love with Lennie, and it bothered her now.

'Leonora?'

'Yes.' Cold, as she always was with him. It wasn't deliberate;

13

the spirit manifest in all her dealings with other people died when her husband spoke to her.

'Look – Gordon's coming round this evening to talk to me about something.'

There had been a silence then, as though he had expected her to supply the request as well as comply with it.

'So can you come home? I've promised to feed him.'

'I've got Mr Beale here,' she said, looking apologetically at Mr Beale, her best customer. He would prefer patron, she was sure. She flicked the blonde hair from her shoulders, and smiled at him.

Beale smiled back, a fat cat smile, but pleasant enough. He wanted her to do something for his head office, and was here to discuss it. He had bought off-the-peg paintings for his flat, one of the luxury flats over her studio, but this was a special commission. He looked a little like a gangster, she thought. Every time she sold something to him, she half expected him to pull out a bankroll. But he just paid by cheque, and she was very grateful that he did. Plus, his wife had recently joined the board of Jonathan's company; that should have made him important in Jonathan's eyes, but apparently not.

'He can wait, can't he?' said Jonathan. 'He only lives upstairs from the studio, for God's sake.'

The fine summer rain still fell, turning the sky and the river grey. She flicked on the desk lamp, and turned her attention back to her husband.

'So does Gordon,' she reminded him. 'So he might as well give me a lift,' she said. 'I'll make us something when I get there.'

'No – I'd rather it was a proper meal. Gordon's fond of his stomach. He isn't coming until about eight.'

'But— ' It was useless to protest. She would stop what she was doing and go home.

'It's important, Leonora.'

He was the only one who called her Leonora. The only one of all the people she had known, ever met in her entire thirty years on this earth. There was something Victorian about Jonathan that she would never get used to; she was almost surprised that he didn't call her Mrs Austin.

'All right.' She put the phone down, and sighed.

14

'Have I come at an inconvenient time?' Beale asked, in the over-polite tones of one who knew how to talk proper when he had to.

'No, of course not,' she said. 'It's just – well, I've been called home, I'm afraid.'

He looked concerned, his eyebrows rising above his rimless glasses. 'Nothing wrong, I hope, Mrs Austin?'

'No,' she said, a little grimly. 'Nothing at all.' She smiled. 'Perhaps we could have a chat about the sort of thing you're looking for some other time,' she said, packing things into the desk drawer.

He held up his hands. 'Say no more, Mrs Austin – I understand domestic problems. With two sons-in-law, a wife and an ex-wife, I should.'

She walked with him through the studio, and he ran a little way ahead of her to open the door.

'No car?' he said. 'May I offer you a lift?'

'It would be rather out of your way,' she pointed out, smiling.

'Secret of success, Mrs Austin. Know who your friends are. And don't make them wait for buses.'

She lifted an eyebrow. 'I know who my friends are too, Mr Beale,' she said, with a sigh. 'Thank you.'

They walked through the misty rain along the row of craft shops and studios to the private car park at the rear of the Riverside Complex, which was how it had been described on the estate agents' literature, and the only way in which the residents thought of it. It was actually called Andwell House, after the river. Two spaces to each flat; Beale's Rolls took up both of his. Those who rented the shops and studios parked in a side-street, or they knew all about it when a resident found his space occupied.

Beale reversed with difficulty in the tight space, then glided out on to the quiet road with a warning toot of the horn. Rain beaded the window, and the silent wipers flicked back and forth every fifteen seconds.

'Do you think we'll have a summer this year, Mrs Austin?'

Other people had independence; so had she, once. But the money necessary for independence had gone into a dream. A dream of using her talent, instead of letting it fester. A dream that she couldn't afford, but she had done it, anyway. And then along had come Jonathan. Solid, dependable Jonathan. 'I've got

15

this enormous flat and no one to share it with,' he had said. 'You're in a bedsit that you can't afford. Why don't we get married, Leonora?'

Before that, she had somehow survived years of juggling credit cards, of begging sceptical bank managers for loans; years of writing apologetic, determinedly optimistic letters to creditors, of persuading the council that she really would pay the back rent on the flat and the studio at the end of the month; years of breadline economics.

And now, two years of marriage. Jonathan's offer of security, of a roof over her head that wouldn't actually cost her money, of three meals a day and a constant free supply of toothpaste, tights and Tampax had been an offer that she couldn't refuse. But it had not been she who had accepted it. It had been some woman called Leonora.

The little river along which they drove was moving slowly today, its surface flecked with the fine rain. Beale turned right, on to Stansfield Road, leading out of Malworth and – not unnaturally – to Stansfield, and Jonathan's flat. Leonora kept Jonathan's flat clean, washed his clothes, ironed his shirts and cooked his food. Leonora slept with him, come to that, for there was a strange formality about even Jonathan's lovemaking to which Lennie could never have conformed. So Leonora had taken over there too, a dutiful Victorian housewife, lying back and thinking of England.

The car slowed to a halt, opposite the darkened windows of a shop that had turned into a doctor's surgery; through the car window, in the darkened plate glass, she could see her reflection. It made a curious double image that seemed all too appropriate.

Beale was chatting, all the time; Lennie was supplying appropriate answers, and not listening to a word.

'I can't go on calling you Mrs Austin,' he said. 'I feel we're old friends by now. What's your first name?'

She looked at him. 'Lennie,' she said.

'What?' He inclined his ear slightly, as the in-car CD played James Last.

'Lennie.'

'That's a boy's name.'

'It's my name,' she said firmly. 'Do I get to know yours?'

'Lucy,' he said, his face entirely serious.

16

She laughed.

The car moved off, past the open fields and hedgerows, into the light industrial estates which fringed the town in place of the now demolished Mitchell Engineering, down towards the big roundabout that guarded the entrance to the old village that had once been all there was of Stansfield. Mitchell Engineering had been a pre-war enterprise, cloaked in secrecy, plonked down beside an Elizabethan village that had barely altered with the centuries. After the war, it couldn't find enough people to employ, and her father had come looking for work in the fifties, like so many others. They had made him redundant, in the end, when electronics and microchips took over, and the days of heavy industry were past.

Beale turned left, away from the village, passing the old post office building, now closed.

'What is it really?' she asked.

'What's what really?'

'Your name.'

'Frank,' he said, and glanced at her. 'What's yours, really?'

'Lennie.'

The sleek car turned into the Mitchell Estate, and entered the thirties housing with which she had grown up while what had been countryside had turned into a new town; it looked different, now, with the smoke and dust of the heavy engineering works gone, and the side-streets blocked off from traffic by bollards.

'Thank you,' she said, as he smoothly pulled up outside the two new blocks of flats which had risen on the edge of the pleasingly elderly houses, aping their architecture. 'That was very kind of you.'

'It was a pleasure.' The car slid to a halt. 'And don't forget – I still want to talk about business some time. I don't want domestic crises stopping me investing in you. You've got real talent.' He paused, almost hesitant. 'As a matter of fact, I've got a friend who's into art exhibitions and stuff like that. I could have a word with him for you.' He leaned over her to open her door, and winked. 'Lennie,' he said.

Lennie smiled. 'That would be very nice of you,' she said, getting out. 'Mr Beale.'

He smiled, shrugged philosophically, and drove off. She

watched the car go; Leonora could perhaps have put up with Mr Beale. She couldn't.

She took out her key, and pushed open the door to the flats, letting herself into one of the two on the ground floor.

She rang the garage as soon as she got inside. The car, she was assured by the youth who answered the phone, would be ready in about half an hour; it was just being valeted. There would be someone there until seven if she wanted to collect it.

'Of course I can't,' said Jonathan as, her hand over the mouth-piece, Lennie had asked if he could run her to the garage later. 'Gordon's coming. I have to have paperwork ready for him.'

'It'll only take quarter of an hour,' Lennie argued, but she knew she wasn't going to win. 'I can't get there for seven,' she said, once more addressing the youth. 'Is it possible to leave it somewhere I can pick it up later?'

'I'll have to ask the boss,' he said, and the phone clattered down.

'I probably still won't have time later,' said Jonathan.

Lennie didn't reply, as the phone was picked up again. 'He says he'll leave it in the yard with the key under the seat, but to tell you that it's at your own risk.'

'Fine,' said Lennie, slamming down the phone, and relayed this information to Jonathan, who seemed less than interested. She went into the kitchen where, presumably, she belonged.

Gordon arrived, and the meal was eaten with barely a word exchanged between his hosts.

'That was lovely, Lennie.' Gordon pushed away his empty plate, and plonked unpretentious elbows on the table. 'Jonathan, I hope you know what you've got in this girl.'

'I've always appreciated Leonora,' he said, with a smile. He was handsome. Lennie had called him her fair-haired beauty, in the days when she had still been making an effort. But her efforts never seemed to please him, and she had long ago given up.

'She looks good and she cooks good,' Gordon said, putting his hand over hers and giving it a squeeze. 'You can't beat that for a combination.'

Gordon Pearce was the son of friends of Lennie's family, and she had known him almost all her life. He had followed her hope-fully around until she married, but he had only recently taken to chatting her up, and then only in front of Jonathan.

Jonathan glanced at her, his fair lashes closing for a moment

18

before he spoke. 'I'll give you a hand to get this lot loaded up,' he said.

As they loaded the dishwasher, he asked her if she could find something to do so that he and Gordon could talk.

'I beg your pardon?'

'We've a lot to get through,' he said. 'And I'd rather you weren't distracting him from the matter at hand. I want him to keep his mind on business, not on your legs.'

She was glad that she had changed out of her jeans; she almost hadn't, since it was only Gordon.

'You brought me home just to cook a meal? I've to retire to my room and do my embroidery? Read an improving book?'

'I really don't care what you do,' he said. 'Just don't do it in the same room as us.'

In her time, she had been irritated by him, annoyed by him, angered by him. Sheer blind rage was new.

'Right,' she said, going into the living-room. 'Sorry, Gordon,' she called over her shoulder as she walked past him. 'I'll have to love you and leave you.'

Gordon, halfway through easing his well-fed frame into an arm-chair, stood up again. 'Oh,' he said, with mock-disappointment. 'You're the only reason I came.'

'Sorry,' she said again, picking up her jacket, walking quickly to the door.

She turned and treated Gordon to a dazzling smile. 'I might be late back,' she said. 'So I probably won't see you. Tell Pauline she must come with you next time.'

'How did your first day go, ma'am?' asked Lloyd.

'Oh, don't!' She twisted out of his arms. 'I'm never going to get used to that – it makes me feel like the Queen Mother.'

'Now there's someone who knows a bit about promotion,' Lloyd said.

She smiled.

'How come you haven't said anything about it?'

'How come you're such a great cook?' Judy asked, the button at the waist of her jeans wishing that he wasn't.

'I learned at my mother's knee,' Lloyd said, sitting down beside her. 'Come on,' he said. 'What's up?'

'I thought Welsh mams waited on their menfolk hand and

19

foot,' she said, leaning back, eyes closed, drawing her legs up and resting them on his knee.

'They do,' he said. 'Real Welsh mams. Don't change the subject. What's wrong?'

'Nothing.' That was no more than the truth. Nothing was wrong. Malworth, once a busy market town, was now a haven for successful, middle-aged, middle-class businessmen; winner of the Best Kept Town competition three years running in the eighties, clean and neat and tidy.

Real shops and businesses had given way to estate agencies and twee craft and gift shops. Nothing was wrong, and it looked as though nothing ever would be. And the sad fact was that police officers really rather preferred things to be wrong. Malworth did a roaring trade in parking offences, and its officers lurked in lay-bys with radar guns to catch the motorists who failed to observe its thirty-mile-an-hour speed limit as they went through; others waited by the traffic lights to catch the ones who didn't obediently and unnecessarily wait on red late at night.

She smiled to herself. Bob Sandwell had solemnly assured her that one of these well-appointed houses with the manicured lawns was a brothel, but even he hadn't found out which, so it obviously kept itself to itself if it was. She half believed that he'd made it up to make her feel better.

'Bob Sandwell is very supportive,' she said.

'Does he have to be?' Lloyd asked, his voice concerned.

Well. Judy didn't answer. She seemed to have acquired some sort of reputation as a women's rights activist which had preceded her to Malworth. She had sensed a good deal of hostility, though none of it was overt. An over-punctiliousness, perhaps. Too much emphasis on her rank, which was after all newly achieved and the bottom rung of middle management. She supposed that they were being defensive; they were having to get used to a new sergeant and a new inspector. Perhaps it was more wariness than hostility.

'I did hear that you might run into some male chauvinist piggery,' said Lloyd.

'I run into that all the time,' grumbled Judy. 'Sometimes from a source not a million miles from where I'm sitting.'

Lloyd looked hurt, but that had long ago ceased to fool Judy.

'Do you *really* want to know how my first day went?' she asked.

'Yes.'

Well, he'd asked for it.

Gordon Pearce stared at Jonathan Bolton.

'You'd get a salary, of course,' Jonathan said, pouring him another whisky. 'That's probably a blessing, with a baby on the way. You don't need uncertainty with another mouth to feed.'

He had known it wasn't going to be good. He had known, from the tone of Jonathan's voice when he'd asked him over. Pauline thought that his careful preparation had been for Lennie, but it hadn't. He had known, had wanted to feel on top of things. He picked up the whisky, and stared at Jonathan. He had known it wouldn't be good. But this.

'Salary?' he said, his mind still unable to take it in.

'It's a good deal, Gordon,' said Jonathan. 'I wouldn't recommend it if it wasn't.'

Gordon's mouth opened. 'Recommend it?' he said. 'You *drafted* the bloody thing!'

Jonathan shrugged a little, and sat down again. 'The board drafted it,' he said, in reasonable tones.

Gordon's mouth opened and closed again as he tried to dredge up the words. 'But this isn't . . . ' he began. 'We . . . *I* didn't . . . '

'Come on, Gordon,' Jonathan said, his voice full of comradely encouragement. 'If there's something about the agreement that bothers you, just say. We can be flexible, surely? We're friends, aren't we?'

Gordon didn't know which point to counter first. 'Agreement?' he repeated. '*Agreement?* I haven't agreed to anything – I haven't . . . ' He finished in a spluttering cough, and drank some more whisky.

'I know,' said Jonathan. 'But you have to agree, Gordon. If you don't sign this, then . . . ' He sighed. 'Then you'll simply be voted out altogether. No job, no salary. No dividends for at least five years – Gordon, you've just taken on that flat. You've got a baby on the way. Pauline won't be working – you've got commitments. Yes, I drafted it! Christ, Gordon, I *fought* to get this agreement!'

'Fought?' Gordon knocked his drink over as he got to his feet. 'The board was your idea – your friends. There was no board until you came in!'

Jonathan mopped up the coffee table with tissues, and shook some drops off the bundle of papers. 'Gordon,' he said, 'you are an engineer. Not a business man. The figures speak for themselves. Until I came in you were going downhill. The board feels that you should . . . ' He sighed again. 'They think you should stick to what you know best, and let business brains run the company.'

Gordon sat down heavily. 'A moment ago they wanted me out altogether,' he said. 'You want to get your story straight.'

Jonathan replenished Gordon's glass. 'All right,' he said. 'I'll be straight. Your expertise isn't what's needed any more. What's needed now is someone with the right attitude to take the company into the nineties. Into Europe.'

'1992 and all that.' Gordon shook his head.

'Yes!'

'And you're it, are you? Tomorrow's man? The business brain?'

'No,' said Jonathan. 'Obviously, I hope to be elected whenever the general election happens, so I won't be involved at all after that.'

Through the hurt and the anger sudden clarity presented itself to Gordon. 'Rosemary Beale,' he said.

Jonathan went slightly pink.

'Your fancy woman's going to run *my* company!' roared Gordon.

Jonathan's eyes widened.

'Do you think people don't know?' Gordon gulped down his drink. 'A woman! A woman running an engineering firm? Whoever heard of – what the hell does she know about it?'

'She . . . she knows the market-place. She knows about beating off the competition, about reaching the winning line first.'

'She's a crook,' said Gordon, indistinctly.

'Oh, don't start all that again.'

'She's a crook! She and her husband are the biggest crooks this side of prison bars! And I let you talk me into giving her a seat on the board. What's she want with my company? I asked. And you said we were going to be big. Big, big, by the end of the century, and she recognised a good thing when she saw it.'

'We are.'

'Damn all I'll get out of it!'

'You're still a major shareholder!'

22

'But it's *my* company,' Gordon said weakly. 'I started it. I built it. I . . . '

'You would have seen it into bankruptcy. I've got it where it is now, Gordon. I've trebled the profits – I've got lorries with *our* name on them taking *our* products to six Common Market countries, and further. The Middle East – maybe even eastern Europe when things settle— '

'And what's Mrs Beale done for us? I'm not denying what you've done. What's *she* done?'

Jonathan didn't speak.

'I'll tell you,' said Gordon. 'Nothing. But she's going to, isn't she? She's going to be prepared to cook whatever books she has to to make it look as though you're complying with the obligation to give up your interest if you get into parliament. Right?'

Jonathan looked horrified.

Gordon shook his head. 'You're getting rid of me because I'm too honest for you,' he said. 'Isn't that what it's all about?'

Jonathan sighed. 'You have to think of Pauline,' he said. 'And the baby. If you won't sign, then you'll be in trouble. Unless you've more savings than I think you have.'

'My savings are my business,' said Gordon.

'I know, I know. But this way you've got a salary. And you'll get dividends too, as soon as we can pay them out again. In the long term, you can afford to stand on your dignity. But in the short term, you simply can't. Unless you think that you can get a job somewhere else, and at the kind of salary you'd need . . . '

'So I'm to be employed by my own firm,' said Gordon, heavily.

'We're all employed by it. It's a limited company now.'

'Don't split straws! You'll go public, won't you? That'll be the next thing.'

'Maybe – that'll make your shares worth even more.'

'Oh, sure. But I won't have any say in the running of my own company. As soon as I sign that, you'll be laying more people off, you'll be— '

'It has to be done. We have to be competitive.'

'You're going to force a strike. Aren't you? Aren't you? We want to cut back on production, so when better? Force a strike, get rid of the union . . . I know you and your lady friend – you're hatching something.'

Jonathan sighed. 'It's nothing like that,' he said. 'I just . . . '

'Why didn't she do her own dirty work anyway? Why you?'

'It was thought best that I should talk to you because you're a friend of the family, that's all.'

Gordon frowned. 'What family?' he demanded.

'Leonora's family. Me.'

'Oh, yes,' said Gordon. 'It's her I've got to thank for this.'

Jonathan closed his eyes. 'Please, Gordon, don't blame my wife for anything you think I may have done to you.'

'Your wife got me into this. "Let Jonathan have a look at your problems, Jonathan understands about business, Jonathan would be an asset to you, Gordon." I can hear her now. You wanted into my company, and she made sure you got in.'

'I could see that you had a business that could take off, or go down the drain,' said Jonathan. 'That's all.'

'Oh, she worked hard for you, Austin. I hope you do appreciate her. She always knew how to get round me. She used me – she always did.' He made a sharp noise, a cross between a sob and a laugh. 'I met Pauline because she was using me. I'd come and make up the numbers – she could always count on me doing what she wanted. She just had to flutter her eyelashes. She did a lot of eyelash fluttering for you, Austin.'

'Gordon – Leonora had nothing whatever to do with any of this. I'd rather you left her out of it.'

'I only let you in because she wanted me to.'

'She wanted to help you out!'

'Yes, well – she's helped me out all right. Right out of the bloody door!' He got to his feet.

'Gordon – you're wrong. Leonora has done nothing to you – your friendship is important to her. To both of us. I hope we're not going to lose it just because—'

But Gordon walked away from the words, from the talk, from Jonathan's smooth demolition of his life.

'I'll see myself out, friend,' he shouted.

In the hallway, he almost stumbled over the joke present he had brought. He picked it up, and went out, slamming the door as hard as he knew how.

The slammed door, plainly audible through the glass of the entrance door, made Mickey look up, and he watched with interest as the man strode to the car parked directly outside, slamming its door too. It was the heavily built man with thinning light brown hair whom he'd seen arrive two hours earlier. He didn't drive off; he just sat there, rather like Mickey himself.

Ten o'clock. There was a great deal more happening in Flat 2 than there was in the one he was supposed to be watching. First Frank Beale, and now this. He had noted the number of the Rolls when it arrived to drop its passenger off, though he had a feeling it was probably the only brand-new Roller in the county, never mind in Stansfield. Frankie Beale was always interesting.

She had left the flat too, later on – also, he fancied, less than happy with life. He had watched as she had walked quickly through the brightening evening, taking the shortcut to the main road through the alleyway. The husband was still in the flat.

A movement in his wing mirror caught his eye, and Mickey swivelled round in time to see a jacket disappear round the corner, out of the garage area in which he was parked, into the alleyway through the old houses. But for someone to be reflected in his mirror, they had to have *passed* the corner, he reasoned. So someone had changed his mind about where he was going.

He frowned. He had been spotted. That wasn't someone just changing his mind, or realising he was going in the wrong direction. He had a sixth sense about these things. He had been spotted. Who knew him? He hadn't been back in Stansfield long, and he had been in uniform the last time he'd been here. Who knew to duck out of sight just from his back view in a car? Perhaps he ought to think about that. His previous stint in Stansfield was a little hazy; other things had seemed much more important than being a police officer.

And perhaps they were, he thought. Perhaps they were.

Steve Tasker pushed open the door of the pub, his dark, handsome face wincing as fifties rock bounced off the walls at him. The fifties was his era, but the music was never meant to be amplified on state-of-the-art equipment. He made his way to the bar, and indicated what he wanted by pointing to the pump and holding his hands a pint distance apart. He took his drink, his mind still on the ominous police presence that he had just discovered, and turned from the bar, his free hand catching, and knocking over, someone's drink.

'Oh, sorry, love,' he said, stooping to pick up the empty glass as it rolled to his feet. He straightened up, and smiled broadly. 'Lennie!' he said. 'Fancy meeting you here.'

'Are you following me around?'

Not quite, he thought, signalling to the barman for a replacement. This was a happy accident, unlike the other times.

'Don't try chatting me up,' she said, as they sat down, and the music stopped.

He grinned. 'Listen, sweetheart, if I see a good-looking blonde, I chat her up. If I see a good-looking blonde I used to be very friendly with, who's on her own in a pub' – he looked pointedly at her left hand – 'minus her wedding ring – I reckon it's my lucky night.'

'Well, it's not.'

Conversation became impossible that close to the speakers; he watched as she tapped her glass in time to the music which was drowning them again, and bent his head close to hers. He knew Lennie. 'I reckon if the music's this loud, all you can do is dance to it,' he shouted.

'No thank you.'

'Come on, Len! I'll bet that stuffed shirt doesn't take you dancing, does he?'

She shook her head.

'Come on, then. You need cheering up.' He put down his glass and stood up, holding out his hand.

She gave a little sigh, then took his hand, and went with him to the dance-floor.

The music of his youth pounded in his ears; she hadn't even been born. But they had discovered something primeval when they had discovered rock; something that made your blood beat faster through your veins, something that produced a need to move to the rhythms, something sexual; it was timeless, ageless. And it had always worked like a charm on Lennie, which was its chief appeal.

Out of breath, they made their way back to the table. Steve let his knee press against hers as they sat down.

'Forget it, Steve,' she said.

Steve picked up their glasses, handing hers to her. 'Drink up,' he said. 'I'll get you another.' Gin had always had a pretty good effect too.

He worked hard for the next few minutes; he even managed to

get his arm round her shoulders without her objecting. Or noticing might be nearer the mark, he conceded. She seemed to have other things on her mind. Whichever, it was good. His hand strayed to her breast; she reacted, but she didn't stop him.

'It's getting late,' whispered the DJ, his lips too close to the mike. 'So let's get romantic.'

He led her on to the floor again, and took her in his arms as the slow ballad began. The DJ, with a shattering lack of empathy, uttered again. 'Not much you can do to this last batch but smooch,' he said. 'That's the word, isn't it?'

His hand moved from her back to her waist as he drew her closer to him. 'What do you say, Len?' he whispered, clasping his hands behind her; her arms were round his neck as they moved together.

His lips brushed her face.

'Please, Stevie,' she said.

He grinned. Stevie was good. 'Please Stevie what?' he murmured, and nibbled her ear.

'Please stop.'

His hands slid lower, applying gentle pressure; she caught her breath as his mouth found hers, and their shuffling footsteps slowed to a halt, only their bodies moving to the slow, slow music, until the final chord died away.

She drew her lips away from his, and smiled at him.

'Can I walk you home?' he asked.

She looked at him for a long time, then gave a little sigh. 'No,' she said.

Another soulful ballad; Steve smiled. 'Let's get some air,' he said, and they left the dance-floor, picking up their things en route to the door.

In the shadows of the pub car park, he kissed her again.

'Stevie,' she said, pushing him off.

He lifted up her left hand. 'Where's your ring?' he asked.

She drew in her breath, then let it out again. 'I threw it away,' she said.

'When?'

'Tonight.' She looked up at him. 'I was angry,' she said, as though he had demanded an explanation.

There was nowhere as silent as Stansfield at night, Steve thought. He was a London boy, and had never got used to it;

27

there was traffic somewhere, rumbling along the dual carriageway; there was a slow, muffled heartbeat from inside the pub, but that only heightened the silence round them.

'Are you throwing him away too?' he asked.

'No.' She leant back on the wall. 'I wasn't angry with him,' she said.

'Who then?'

'Me. Who else?'

If he had somewhere to take her, she would come with him, he was sure. But he lived in digs, and his landlady would not take kindly to his bringing a woman home with him. He pushed her gently against the wall, his lips at her ear. 'Let's go somewhere,' he whispered.

'Stevie, *please*,' she said, closing her eyes as his lips touched her face. He was winning.

'Stevie, please what?' He pressed hard against her as a car came out of the main road, its headlights sweeping them, slowing almost to a stop as it passed them.

She pushed him away, and watched it go. 'Just leave me here,' she said nervously. 'Someone will see us.'

'Oh, forget him,' he said, smiling, taking her in his arms. 'Don't let that put you off.'

'Stevie, *please*,' she said.

'Stevie, please what?'

'Just please,' she said, kissing him.

Two

Gordon Pearce pulled the car into the kerb, almost unable to see because of the tears in his eyes.

He had caught them in his headlights. Just a courting couple, he had thought, until he had really seen what he was looking at, and he had stared transfixed. Lennie. It *had* been Lennie. He had told himself that he had been mistaken, that it *couldn't* have been. She wouldn't behave like that – she wasn't . . . He sniffed, and searched for a handkerchief. He had a good mind to go straight back and tell Jonathan what she was up to when his back was turned. That would wipe the smug look off his face.

Not that Jonathan was behaving much better, but at least it wasn't in public. She had been wrapped round that . . . that – he blew his nose noisily as his brain failed to come up with an adequate description of her companion.

He knew him. He knew his face, from way back. From before Lennie had married Jonathan. Was he the one she had been trying to avoid, when she had used him, as she had always used him? 'Oh, Gordon, save my life, there's a love. If you're with me, he'll just go away.' And he had done as she had asked, as he had always done.

He had been so pleased to be of assistance, so eager to prove himself worthy to her. And she had smiled, and kissed him, and said she didn't know what she would do without him. He had believed her, when she had presumably just been playing hard to get, and using him to do it. She wasn't playing hard to get now.

He had been there, if she had needed someone. But of course, there was Pauline. Even if he had known that Lennie was . . . well, available, there was still Pauline.

He'd only married Pauline because Lennie had got engaged.

29

And if she hadn't wanted Jonathan at all, then why? Why? What sort of a marriage was that? You were meant to stay faithful to your vows – my God, look what was happening to him. He wasn't grabbing at anything that passed just because Pauline wouldn't . . .

He rubbed his eyes, and started the car. They had screwed up his life, between them, Lennie and Jonathan. Damn them. Damn them both. Damn them all. Jonathan and Lennie, Rosemary Beale, Pauline. All of them. All screwing up his life.

Damn them all.

Jonathan didn't want to stay in the house, with Gordon's animosity still thick in the air. It had been the hardest thing he had ever had to do; he genuinely liked Gordon. In an odd way, he would have felt better if it hadn't been true, but the company could function without its founder. It could function just as well with him, but his usefulness had long since been overtaken by the company's own momentum. And, left to Gordon's devices, it was entirely true to suggest that the whole thing would have slid into bankruptcy. All true, and none of it made him feel any better.

He wasn't looking forward to telling Leonora what they had been discussing, either. But that wouldn't be as awful. She would be angry, and demand reasons which he couldn't give, but he could handle that. Gordon's bewilderment, his hurt confusion, was much more difficult.

Where was Leonora, anyway? He glanced at the clock. Ten twenty-five; it was getting late. He would have expected her to have been home by now. Perhaps she was staying at the studio for the night; she had done that on other occasions when she had been angry with him. But she had told him, those times. She was just staying out as long as she could to worry him, he told himself. That was all. Or she had got wrapped up in something that she was doing. He didn't pretend to understand Leonora's work, but she did seem to be very highly thought of by those who mattered in the art world, and she could forget everything when she was working.

He wished he could. More than anything, he wished he had some overriding interest in something, something in which he could lose himself and let the rest of the world go to hell. But facts and figures were his forte, and they concerned the rest of the world too much to let him forget it. Leonora's painting was more important to her than anything; it was why she had married him, Jonathan knew that. He wished, really, that she hadn't. He wished he had never asked her. She could have had his financial backing without marrying him; he might not understand what she did, but he understood investment in art, and Leonora was a good investment.

Where had she gone, anyway? She had never left without telling him where she was going. His heart suddenly sank as he realised that she might have gone to keep Pauline company. She might be hearing about it from Gordon even now. He closed his eyes. This was a nightmare. The whole thing was a nightmare.

He had opened the floodgates deliberately, but he hadn't really been prepared for just how insecure Judy felt.

'It's only the first day, love,' he said, his arm round her, patting her. 'It'll get better. It's bound to.'

'It couldn't get much worse.' She sounded so down.

He sighed. At least she wasn't crying. He realised with a little jolt of surprise that in all the time he'd known her, and all the trauma that their relationship had been subjected to, he had never seen her crying. She'd be fine once she had been there a couple of days, he knew that. Judy hated change, hated anything which removed her from whichever rut she was in, whether she liked being in it or not. She hadn't enjoyed being married, but it had been a long, painful haul before she had finally left Michael. She had almost cried that night, he remembered. Almost, but not quite. She had *been* crying, that much had been obvious; but not in front of him. He wasn't sure he liked that, and had said so. She had told him that it was the job that had taught her how to check tears. It was one thing a six foot six burly copper shedding manly tears over a particularly sad accident; it was quite another to have some damn female blubbing all over the show.

But she hadn't been crying tonight. And in a way, this was tougher than leaving her dead marriage, because she had loved it at Stansfield. All that was wrong with her, Lloyd knew, was that she was in a new place with new people and new routines to which she would almost immediately become accustomed, and then that would be where she felt comfortable. No point in telling her all that, of course. She never believed him when he tried, so now he just made encouraging noises. And if it occurred to him that no one would be having to perform this service for DS Drake, it was merely a passing thought on human nature, on the different personalities with which one had to deal on one's daily round. It wasn't a male chauvinist thought on *la différence*. Of course it wasn't.

'For some reason,' she went on, 'they've got it into their heads that I'm some sort of tub-thumper for Women's Lib.'

'It'll settle down,' he said. 'Eventually they'll realise your sterling worth.'

'Stop making fun of me,' she grumbled, but she was smiling. She closed her eyes and leant against him.

'*Vive la différence*,' he dared to say aloud as he gave her a cuddle, and escaped a telling off because she had just done the slowest double-take in history.

'Yours wasn't a real Welsh mam?'

He shook his head. 'She was only half Welsh,' he said.

'What was the other half?'

There was a tiny silence before he spoke, and Judy opened her eyes. 'Well?' she said.

'I've just given you a clue, as it happens,' he said.

'What? What did you just say? I wasn't listening.'

'You never do. I said, "*Vive la différence*." '

'*French*?' Judy looked at him suspiciously. 'Your mother was half French? Is this true?' she demanded.

'Yes.' He smiled. 'French. My grandma Pritchard was French.'

Judy blinked. 'So you're part French,' she said.

He nodded.

'Which part?'

'You tell me.' He kissed her.

'I'll tell you later.'

'You know something?' said Lloyd, as they got up from the sofa.

'What?'

'I've never made love to a detective inspector,' he said.

She smiled. 'I have,' she said. 'I can recommend it.'

'He doesn't make you feel like this,' Steve said. 'Does he?'

She shook her head, her eyes closed. 'You can walk me

home,' she said, after a moment, relenting a little. 'Well – some of the way, anyway.'

Rock 'n' roll, walking a girl home. It was the fifties, thought Steve, as they walked up from the pub, arms round one another's waists, crossing the railway bridge as a train thundered under them.

'If this *was* the fifties,' said Steve, going over to watch the train, 'there would be smoke and steam everywhere now.'

'I don't remember steam trains,' she said, joining him.

He smacked her playfully. 'Don't rub it in,' he said, looking over the edge of the bridge as the train snaked off into the distance, its red tail lights blurring with the speed. 'I loved them. Even then – it's not just nostalgia. They were big and noisy and smelly – I don't know. They had personalities. I didn't want them to go.'

They spent a few more minutes on the bridge, until Lennie decided people might see. They walked on slowly, past rows of shops.

'If this was the fifties, we'd be ducking into a shop doorway,' he said. 'People wouldn't see then. There aren't any now,' he added wistfully, looking at the plate glass doors, flush with the windows, covered in their safety mesh.

'Neither there are,' she said, surprised. 'There used to be. When I was little. When did that happen?'

'Search me.'

They left the shops behind, and passed the empty spaces where Mitchell Engineering's buildings used to be. Some had been redeveloped, mostly by small factory units let out to various businesses; Lennie's husband's new, custom-built factory still stood alone, but it was surrounded by ground marked out for others.

They crossed over the silent, empty traffic roundabout, and walked towards the old post office. Pedestrian street-lighting was not a priority here, where the combustion engine reigned; dark slashes of shadow were pooled here and there by watery light. They took advantage of the privacy, and made slow progress through the shadows, stopping for minutes at a time, then moving on a few feet before stopping again. She wanted him, Steve knew that.

She drew away from him as they came up to the old, empty post office, stepping into the deep shadows of the building. 'You'd

33

better not come any further,' she said. 'I don't want anyone on the estate seeing us. Let's say goodnight here.'

Steve had no intention of saying goodnight; she was as eager as he was, and he made the most of it.

'Oh, Stevie, please stop. Please,' she said, after long, agonising moments. 'Please don't do this.'

'We'll find somewhere to go, Lennie.'

'No – no.' She tried to twist away from him; he pulled her back roughly, his tongue teasing hers into a would-be reluctant kiss as headlights swept them again, this time remaining on them as the car pulled to a halt a few feet away.

Steve looked over at it after a moment. Was it the same car? It had to be, but he couldn't make it out; it was just an indistinguishable dark shape behind its glaring headlights.

'What the hell is he up to?' he said angrily. 'I'll sort him.' He walked purposefully towards the car, which drove off as he came up to it, heading down towards the village.

He walked back to Lennie. 'Where had we got to?' he asked, slipping back into the shadow with her.

'Steve – stop it. I'm going home. Now. I'm not going to get involved with you.'

He stood back a little and looked at her. 'You want to,' he said. 'You know you do.'

She took a breath, and nodded. 'But I'm not going to. I've made promises, Steve.'

He laughed. 'Marriage vows?' he said. 'Who takes any notice of them?'

'Jonathan does.'

Steve shook his head. 'Why did you marry him, Lennie?'

'Security,' she said.

'Security,' he repeated.

'Yes,' she said hotly. 'Three meals a day. Not being frightened to open my mail in the morning. Security. Precious little of that I'd get from you.'

'I'm not asking you to give that up!' He took her in his arms again. 'A nice, old-fashioned affair, that's all.'

'And a nice, old-fashioned scandal. Candidate's wife in love-nest with pusher.'

Steve smiled, and pulled her closer to him. 'All right,' he whispered. 'A nice, old-fashioned one-night stand.'

34

She shook her head. 'It might not be a match made in heaven,' she said. 'But he sticks to his part of the bargain, and I'm sticking to mine.'

Steve let her go, and put his hands in his pockets, looking at her. He hadn't been going to say anything. None of his business. But Austin didn't deserve Lennie. 'Is that what you think?' he asked. 'That he sticks to the bargain?'

She frowned. 'Yes,' she said warily.

Steve shook his head.

Mickey Drake drove slowly past the Austin-Pearce factory; a car had come out of the service road a few minutes ago, and it was an odd time of night for anyone to be in the area. He looked across, watching for any signs of life that shouldn't be there, but his mind was still on the couple.

They *were* a couple; he was sure of it. She wasn't being molested, as he'd thought might have been the case, when she had seemed to try to pull away from him.

He picked up his radio. 'Delta Sierra to Delta Hotel,' he said.

But it wasn't either of the men who had been at the flat earlier, and it wasn't Frankie Beale, who had dropped her off there in the first place.

The factory logo was lit up at night, though they had stopped working nightshift. It made the police's job a little easier, lighting up the corrugated grey wall like a fluted cinema screen, against which any miscreant would clearly be seen. Lorries were scattered round the car park, and he watched carefully for signs of life behind them.

He shook his head slightly, wondering why architects wanted new factories to look like old Nissen huts, and why it was suddenly fashionable to have all the paraphernalia of servicing a building picked out in red paint instead of boxed off neatly, out of sight.

'Delta Hotel,' said Jack Woodford's voice. 'I thought you were off watch, Mickey?'

'I am. But I thought you ought to know that I haven't seen the panda car.'

She must have been with him, all the same; she hadn't tried to get away when he came towards the car. Though she might have been too frightened, if she was being assaulted. But she wasn't.

It had looked, for a moment, as though she was resisting, but she wasn't. She was with him. She was.

There was a silence, during which he knew that Woodford was sighing, or mouthing to someone. 'He's checked in, thanks Mickey,' he said. 'Everything's OK.'

Maybe she was frightened to run, in case that got him angry, he thought. Maybe he should have got out of the car and found out for himself what was going on.

'It wasn't him I was worried about,' he said.

'No, well – you wouldn't have thanked him if he'd scared off your courier. He'd be keeping clear.'

The sarcasm wasn't lost on Mickey. 'Or sitting up a side-street eating fish and chips,' he said.

He drove through the old village. Chief Inspector Lloyd lived here. He glanced at the flats as he passed, on his way down to the dual carriageway; he'd heard that he lived with Judy Hill, but he was disinclined to believe station gossip. People usually had the wrong end of the stick. And he was inclined to think that it was their own business, if it was true. The force didn't own your soul. But she wasn't divorced from Mr Hill; he knew that.

'That's a possibility,' said Woodford, after another long silence. 'But I'll tell you what, Mickey. You worry about your job, and I'll worry about mine. All right?'

Mickey had found DI Hill to be pleasant to look at, and talk to, but he'd only worked with her for a couple of weeks before she went off on a course prior to taking up her inspector's duties at Malworth. He'd have to reserve judgement on her, and on the rumours. Though he certainly wouldn't kick her out of bed.

He shrugged at the radio. 'All right,' he said. He liked Jack Woodford, but he really didn't check up on his beat men often enough.

She was with him, he was sure. She *was* with him. She was with him, she wasn't resisting.

He drove along the dual carriageway, to where there was a break in the central reservation. Then he executed an illegal U-turn on the empty road, and headed back the way he had come.

Pauline Pearce sat in the darkness, looking out of the window at the still, quiet street, and the dark river. Some noise, something had attracted her attention; it was unusual to hear anything after the shops had closed. She had switched off the lamp, and gone to the window, but whoever it was had gone. Across the road on the other side of the river was a children's play park; the moon, high and round and full, sat hazily in the dark blue sky, lighting the swings and slides standing silent in the night. It was such a beautiful night now, after the drizzle that had fallen all day; she would have been able to see if there was anyone across there.

A dull glow lit the pavement outside one of the shops below her, and it was this that Pauline was looking at, had been looking at, for ages. It was coming from Lennie's studio, directly beneath their flat. And why would Lennie be working at this time of night? It could hardly be burglars; they surely wouldn't put a light on. And she hadn't heard anyone breaking in – though it could have been someone forcing the door, she supposed, but it hadn't sounded like that. It couldn't be Lennie working, because it wasn't the studio light itself; that would make a much brighter splash of colour. It was the light in the back room. She closed her eyes briefly, and tried to recall the noise.

More like *trying* the door, she would say, when she was asked to remember everything she could about this moment. But right now, she didn't know to commit it to memory. It was just a strange noise, down there in the street.

Perhaps Gordon had carried out his threat; she had thought he was joking, but he might not have been. He had come in from the bedroom, smelling of aftershave, still in his bathrobe.

'How about some afternoon delight?' he had said. 'Well – early evening delight, anyway.'

She had wanted to say yes. She could have said yes; she had done that before. But that had just made him angry, because she didn't know how to simulate desire. So she had said no.

'Oh, well, I'll just have to go and make another pass at Lennie,' he had said.

Now she was being silly. Jonathan was there too; if she did have anything to fear from Lennie, it wouldn't be tonight. But he had said that; *another* pass. Just a joke? Or a slip of the tongue? Or an oblique way of telling her that if she couldn't bring herself to . . . She was being silly, she told herself. But it was late. Quarter past eleven was late, especially in Jonathan's book, and Jonathan never encouraged visitors to stay late. And Gordon wasn't home. And she had heard someone . . . doing what? *Opening* the door to the studio? Someone was in there. Someone had been in there a long time. And why would Lennie be working?

She turned from the window, and was still sitting in the dark when she heard a car drive away; too late, she looked out again, but it was gone. She jumped as the door opened.

'Why are you sitting in the dark?' Gordon asked, switching on the light.

'Where have you been?'

Gordon sat down. 'You are beginning to sound exactly like a wife,' he said, and the words were slurring.

'I *am* your wife. I've been worried.'

'So you are. I knew I'd seen you somewhere before.'

She felt guilty. 'Have you been drinking?'

'I've been for a drink. I thought you were going to bed?'

'I was. But I heard this noise.'

'Noise?'

'Someone. I think— ' She stopped. She mustn't. If it had been him, this wasn't the time to tackle it. If it hadn't, he wouldn't want to know.

'What?'

'I think I must have been hearing things.' She went over to him, kneeling down beside him, her head on his knee. 'I'm sorry about earlier,' she said.

She could feel him curl her hair round his fingers. 'It doesn't matter,' he said. 'You can't always be in the mood.'

This was how he had been about it at the start. That bothered her a little, rather than comforted her. She planted a little kiss on his knee and looked up at him. 'The doctor said it would pass,' she said.

'I'm sure it will.' His eyes were closing, and he looked pale and upset. 'It doesn't matter. Nothing matters.'

'What?' she said. 'What's wrong? Why have you had so much to drink?' He didn't drink, not as a rule. Just the odd pint. She had never seen him drunk.

He gave a shrug.

'You didn't drive home like that, did you?'

'Yes. I drove home like this.'

His clothes, with which he had taken such care, were dishevelled. There was a strange smell.

38

'Where have you been?' she asked. 'What's happened?'

His eyes were closing. 'To my own funeral,' he said, indistinctly.

'What? What do you mean? Gordon, tell me!' She shook his arm.

'Your friend Lennie,' he said. 'And our delightful next-door neighbour. They've . . . ' He opened his eyes with difficulty.

She sniffed. 'Can you smell burning?' she asked.

He sat up. 'No,' he said. 'I'm out, Pauline. I'm out of my own company. They wanted me to sign some . . . some agreement, but I'm – I didn't. So I'm out. No money. No dividends, even. No money, no flat.'

'Lennie wouldn't do that to you!'

'Don't you believe it. She's fallen in with thieves, Pauline. She's no better herself. Used me. Only ever used me. And that Beale woman – she's nothing but a . . . ' The words were slurring, and his eyes weren't focusing. 'I've really done it now,' he said, and fell back. He closed his eyes, and was dead to the world.

Pauline sniffed again, and went to the window, shielding the reflection with the curtain. She couldn't see anything on fire. The studio light was still on. She remembered the noise, and looked again at the light from the studio. No. No, he wouldn't have done anything like that.

She picked up the door key, and looked at Gordon, lying back, his mouth open.

He wouldn't.

The champagne cork didn't shoot up and break the light fitting; Lloyd was very proud of his prowess at opening bottles of bubbly. He poured it neatly, without spilling any, into two glasses, then topped them up as the fizz subsided.

He sat on the edge of the bed, and handed Judy hers. 'You were right,' he said, clinking his glass with hers. 'DIs are OK.'

She sat back on the pillow, her legs across his knee. 'Just OK,' she said. 'And I get champagne. What do I get if I'm great?'

'The champagne is to celebrate your new job, which you *will* like, believe me.'

Lloyd had made her feel better. The champagne was going to make her feel better still. One day, she would tell him how lucky she was to have him, but not right now. It would just make him unbearably smug.

'How on earth did your grandmother come to be French?' she asked.

'I imagine it was being born in France that did it,' he said.

She hit him. 'How did she come to be living in a fishing village in Wales?'

'Ah, well . . . ' Lloyd smiled. 'It's a very romantic story. It'll be wasted on you.'

There was something malevolent about the telephone, she thought, as it punctured the mood. These days it did it almost politely, purring quietly at them; it was an improvement on harsh bells, but that was all. Its effect was the same, she thought, as Lloyd picked it up.

'Lloyd.' He listened. 'Yes, she is. Just a moment.' He held the phone out to her.

She sighed. If something was going to happen in that dead and alive place, why did it have to be now, for God's sake? She glanced at the bedside alarm. Twenty past eleven. A burglary, she thought.

'DI Hill,' she said.

'Judy?'

She frowned, then recognised Jonathan Austin's voice.

'Oh, yes – sorry, Jonathan. I thought it would be work.'

'I'm sorry to call so late,' he said. 'I just wondered if Leonora was with you.'

Judy frowned. 'No,' she said. 'Sorry, Jonathan. Should she be?'

'What? Oh – no. That is, she didn't say she was going to see you or anything. It's just that she's not home yet.'

Judy imagined that she must be the last desperate hope in a long series of phone-calls. Lennie had lots of friends, all of whom she had known longer, any of whom would be more likely than she was to receive an unannounced visit.

'I haven't seen her,' she said. 'Are you worried about her?'

'No, no. She probably did tell me where she was going. I was a bit preoccupied this evening.'

It was so patently a lie that Judy was at a loss to know what to say next.

'Look – she isn't just telling you to say she's not there, is she?' he said.

'Of course not,' Judy said.

'No. Sorry.'

40

'It's not all that late, Jonathan. She's probably on her way home now.'

'Yes. I expect so. I'm sorry to have bothered you.'

Judy looked at Lloyd, and shrugged. 'What's worrying you?' she asked Jonathan. 'Have you had a row or something?'

'Well, to be honest, I don't think that's— '

'You're quite right,' Judy said quickly. 'Curiosity is an occupational hazard, I'm afraid.' In the background, she could hear the rise and fall of a siren in the distance, and an illogical cold shiver swept over her. 'Jonathan – everything is all right, isn't it?'

'Yes,' he said. 'I'm sorry, I – yes, we did have words. Nothing spectacular, but she wasn't very pleased with me. She's probably at the studio. I can't think why I didn't try there. I'm sorry to have bothered you.'

Judy put down the phone, concerned about Lennie.

'Who was that?' asked Lloyd.

'His name's Jonathan Austin. He's married to a friend of mine.' She shrugged a little. 'He seems to have lost her.'

'Does he think something's happened to her?' asked Lloyd.

'It's hard to say. I don't think he has reason to think that,' she said. She swung her legs off his knee, and sat up, the better to address the situation. 'They've had a row, and she hasn't come home yet, that's all. It's not late, not really.' She smiled. 'By your standards this is late afternoon,' she said.

'Do I know her?'

'No. I met her when I was the crime prevention officer at Stansfield. She had a studio flat on Queens Estate. We got quite friendly. After she got married, she and Jonathan used to visit me and Michael now and then.'

'Maybe she's got a boyfriend. Used you as an alibi, and you've just blown it.'

Judy shook her head. 'She's not like that. Oh – I don't mean that their marriage is too solid, or anything. Just that she'd walk out rather than cheat, I'm sure.' She flushed slightly. 'She's not like me,' she said. 'She's got a lot more courage.'

'Well – maybe she has walked out.'

'Yes.' Judy nodded. 'She's not a bit like herself with Jonathan, you know. She's like . . . that film. You know? Where all the women do exactly what the men want?'

'*Stepford Wives*,' said Lloyd, and laughed. 'Maybe her wiring's

41

gone wrong.' His face sobered. 'It's bothering you, isn't it?' he said.

'Yes, though for the life of me I don't know why,' said Judy. 'I just don't understand why he rang me. I saw her today, so we arranged to have lunch once I'd got settled in. And I gave her this number, and told her about you. But we're not all that close – I mean, I hadn't told her about you before, for instance. And we don't *pop in* on each other.'

'Maybe your number was written by the phone, or something,' said Lloyd. 'First one he saw.'

'No. Jonathan was dropping her off at the studio, and she got him to take a note of it.' She pulled a face. 'Jonathan has a Filofax,' she said. 'Of course.'

'Well, that's probably why he rang you,' said Lloyd, putting down his glass and getting back into bed. 'If you saw her this morning, and your number was to hand. Stop worrying about him. Worry about me instead.'

She smiled. 'And why do I have to worry about you?' she asked.

'I'm lonely. And I've got a frightening detective sergeant.'

'Poor Mickey,' said Judy. 'He's all right.'

'He's like a recruitment film.'

'Oh, leave him alone!' She laughed. 'And you say *I* don't like change! Anyway – he's frightened of *you*.'

'No one's frightened of me.'

'He is. He told me you'd probably heard terrible reports about him from Jack Woodford. I think he's trying to impress you, not frighten you. He needs a good report from you.'

'Mm,' said Lloyd, not looking much happier. He put his arm round her. 'What do you say we forget about Drake, and your friend and her husband?' He kissed her.

Judy tried to forget. But she wished, all the same, that Jonathan hadn't rung. It wasn't like Lennie just to go off and worry him. She was straightforward, direct. The phone-call had unsettled her, and Lloyd wasn't getting her full attention.

'Hey,' he said. 'I'm still here, you know.'

She made a determined effort to push the phone-call out of her mind. 'Sorry,' she said. 'I'm all yours.'

But she just hoped that wherever Lennie was, she knew what she was doing.

* * *

Lennie walked briskly through the Mitchell Estate roads while she listened to Steve, not caring much who saw them. Then she realised that that wasn't sensible. Why kill the goose?

'All right,' she said slowly, measuring her words. 'But we're not going to advertise it.' She smiled. 'You come to the studio tomorrow. At lunchtime.'

'Just to get your own back?' He smiled. He didn't care why she was doing it, just as long as she was.

'No,' she said seriously. 'To get you back. Now, I'm going home.' She started to walk away.

He caught her up, catching hold of her arm. 'I'm not letting you walk up there alone,' he said.

'It's five hundred yards! You can see the flats round this corner.'

'I'm not leaving you alone with that weirdo in the car,' he said.

Lennie frowned. 'Do you think it was the same car both times?' she asked.

'I hope it was. Or there are two weirdos in cars. Come on.'

As they rounded the corner, Lennie could see that the flat was in darkness. 'That's odd,' she said.

'He's gone out,' said Steve, and smiled. 'So I can see you safely in.' He paused. 'Maybe I shouldn't have told you,' he said.

'But you have,' said Lennie. And it was the truth; she knew that. When does he go there? she had asked Steve, just in case. Wednesday, he had said. Jonathan's chess evening, at a club in Barton. And she had believed him, wished him luck – asked him how he had got on, week after week. And she had been made a fool of, week after week.

'Are you going to say anything to him?'

'No.' No. But she would have a separate room in future. Not that that would worry Jonathan. And she would do exactly as she chose, but discreetly.

They could hear the muffled ring of the telephone as they pushed open the door to the flats. With an urgency that only the telephone can produce, Lennie scrabbled for her keys, and opened the door.

She went into the sitting-room, lit only by stray beams from the flat entrance light, and Steve followed her in, beating her to the phone and putting his hand on it as he caught her, turning her round.

43

'Leave it,' he said, pulling her into yet another kiss, which she never wanted to stop. All the time, the phone rang, over and over and over, demanding that she answer it, telling her that this was not discreet. If she was embarking on a truly double life, she should plan it, not let this happen.

She pushed him away. 'Go,' she said. 'I'm in. Safely. Go.'

'You can't leave me feeling like this,' he said.

'How do you think I feel? Go. I'll see you tomorrow.'

He held up his hands in surrender, and waved as he went back out of the room; she turned, and picked up the phone.

'Hello?'

There was silence. Not total silence, but no one spoke.

'Hello, who's there?'

She could hear sounds; unidentifiable, fuzzy sounds. 'Who's *there*?' she asked again, feeling a little alarmed. 'I know there's someone.' But no one spoke.

She replaced the receiver, and glanced at herself in the mirror; even in the dim light she could see the little bruise developing on her lower lip. She examined herself for further proof of her evening's activities, in order to disguise them before he came home. She had never had to be duplicitous, but if she was going to be, then she would do it well. She sat back a little, and looked at her back-lit reflection, smiling a little as she thought of tomorrow, and Steve.

That was when she saw the figure in the mirror.

Three

Gordon opened his eyes, and immediately shielded them from the overhead light. Then he tried to get to his feet, and staggered slightly as he became upright.

He'd say he was drunk. He didn't know what he was doing. He had known, of course. He had been horribly aware of what he was doing, aware that it was wrong. Aware that the only way in which it would change things would be that he would go to prison if he got found out. He shook his throbbing head. Can't blame the drink, he told himself, as he stumbled through to the kitchen. You didn't have enough. Still. You can try.

I was drunk, m'lud.

Were you, Gordon? Oh, well, that explains everything. Don't worry about it, old son, could have happened to anyone. Don't give it another thought. If you were drunk, you were drunk.

Thing is, m'lud, I think I was intending suicide. But I got frightened, and ran away instead.

Suicide? Well – no wonder. I mean, here you are, no bloody use to anyone. The only worthwhile thing you ever did was to develop an engineering process so obscure that no one knows what it was you did anyway. And then you couldn't even cash in on that without help. And you were too stupid to see that people don't do anything for anyone but themselves in this world, that everyone is out for what he – or she – can grab. Your wife doesn't want you, your fellow directors don't want you, and the woman you would have jumped off a cliff for was practically having it off against a wall with some ne'er-do-well of her acquaintance. No wonder you were contemplating suicide.

Gordon finally got the childproof top off the aspirin bottle, and knocked three tablets into the palm of his hand.

45

Go on, Gordon. You can still do it. Where's Pauline? In bed? Well – she won't mind. She'd get the insurance.

Would she? Where did she keep the policies? He should check that. Make sure there wasn't an exclusion clause. He chewed the aspirin and groped his way back into the sitting-room, pulling open the drawer in the bureau where Pauline kept important documents.

Will. You haven't made a will, Gordon. You should have. You've a baby to consider now. Still. Doesn't matter. It'll go to Pauline and the baby anyway.

He scrabbled amongst the envelopes and folded A4 sheets, but he couldn't concentrate.

Sorry, m'lud. Couldn't kill myself, couldn't find the insurance policy. Scared to, anyway. What if it's true? What if you're damned?

Damned if you do, and damned if you don't, Gordon. Prison. You weren't drunk, you weren't unaware of what you were doing, you knew the difference between right and wrong. No option but to send you to prison, old son.

Might as well, m'lud. Better than a funny farm. Better than everlasting hell.

Of course, Gordon, we have to prove that it was you. No proof, no prison. Did you leave evidence, Gordon?

I don't know, m'lud. I just left.

He pushed the drawer, trapping paper in the runners; he tried to ram it shut, but it wouldn't work. Sighing, he straightened up, and held on to his head, moving slowly through the room, out into the hallway, and into the bedroom.

No Pauline. Gordon frowned, and focused with difficulty on the alarm clock. Twenty-five to twelve.

'Pauline?' he called.

He went back out into the hallway, and knocked on the bathroom door. 'Are you in there, Pauline?'

Panicking a little, he tried the door, which opened immediately. No Pauline.

'Pauline!' he called again, uselessly. The other rooms were open; she wasn't there. But he went from one to the other, calling her name. Where was she? Where had she gone? Why had she gone? He ran back into the bedroom, and opened the wardrobe doors. Her clothes were there. But they would be, he told himself. It was only in films that people removed every item

46

of clothing when they left the marital home. Real people didn't do that.

Real people just left. When things got too much, they just left. She hadn't wanted him before; now he had told her what they had done, she just wanted out. She didn't even know what *he* had done, and she had gone. Which was all he deserved. What had he done for her, other than give her a standard of living which he had just told her was about to take a nosedive? Nothing. He had married her because Lennie had deserted him, and she knew that. He hadn't appreciated what he had got, so envious was he of what Austin had. She knew that too. She had accepted it; even let him make jokes about it. They weren't jokes, and she knew that too.

Not surprised she's quit the happy home, old son. All you deserve, really. So – you don't have to worry about going to prison, do you?

A car slowed down outside, and pulled into the car park. The police. It was bound to be the police.

Perhaps he shouldn't have told her. He hadn't been going to; for one thing he was a very strong believer in minding his own business, and for another Rosemary Beale would be less than pleased if she found out that he'd told anyone. Steve shook his head slightly, as he waited for the kettle to boil. Mrs Sweeney didn't know he had a kettle; he hid it when he went out. Very hot on use of electricity, was Mrs S.

He wasn't sure why he *had* told her; true, it had entirely altered her stand on fidelity, but he hadn't known that it would. And risking Rosemary's wrath for a bit of nooky was far from sensible, even if it was with Lennie. Telling Lennie had been pure madness. But he had told her, out of some long-dormant sense of the fitness of things. Seeing her there, holding her, knowing how much she still felt for him – not just physically, either – watching her determination not to give in to these feelings, however tempted, because of loyalty to Austin . . . it had just got too much for him. Austin had no right to that loyalty, no right to use Lennie as he had.

At first, when he found out, his only thought had been that it served her right. Marrying that prat while he was in prison, and in no position to talk her out of it. But the first thing he'd done

47

when he got out was find out where she was. Then he'd hung about in the hope of catching sight of her. He had; she hadn't seen him. And he hadn't been prepared for the shock of seeing her again, after so long.

She looked the same; she hadn't altered. She wore jeans and a sweatshirt, and walked to the same car that she had been running when he knew her. It was as if nothing had happened. Then Beale had offered him a job; chauffeuring Rosemary around, plus. Plus reporting back to Beale if she was taking too much interest in any member of the opposite sex. It was while gainfully employed in this fashion that he had found out about Austin, and he had wanted to tell Lennie then. Tell her what a mistake she had made. Tell her it served her right. Next time he found himself at the Mitchell Estate flats, he had let her see him; he had spoken to her. But he didn't tell her.

The kettle sang louder and louder, then the sound died away, and steam poured from the spout. Steve splashed water on the coffee, and looked at the clouded dressing-table mirror.

He hadn't told her because he hadn't wanted to hurt her after all, and that's what the knowledge was. A weapon. A weapon that he didn't want to use. But when all he had hoped for a was a roll in the hay for old times' sake, when all it looked like he was going to get was the frustration of a teenage heavy petting session, and he was prepared to settle even for that, he had told her. There she was, vulnerable and alone; the perfect time to hurt her. But he hadn't done it to hurt her; he had handed her the weapon hilt-first. Because it seemed to him that she needed it more than he did.

So that was why he had told her. He wiped away a patch of steam, and looked at himself. A funny time of life to find your self-respect. But he must have found it, to feel so strongly about Lennie's.

He hoped Lennie used her weapon wisely – for his sake, he admitted to himself – not hers. Because if she blew the whistle on Austin, Rosemary would not be pleased.

And that would be bad news for Steve.

Pauline moved quietly along the corridor, and put her key in the lock, jumping as the door swung open, just as the Beales' door had.

Slowly, cautiously, she stepped inside, her heart beating too fast, her breath too shallow. She walked along the hallway without making a sound, and pushed open the sitting-room door. The room was empty; her heart beat painfully fast.

'I heard your car.'

Gordon's voice made her start; she closed her eyes with relief.

'Sorry,' he said. 'I opened the door when I realised it was you. I thought at first it was— ' He stopped speaking, shook his head, and went back into the kitchen.

She licked her lips, took a deep breath, and followed him in. 'You thought at first . . . what?' she asked.

'Nothing,' he said. 'Forget it.'

She frowned. She had expected him to be still slumped in the chair, sleeping it off. 'Are you sober?' she asked.

'Not really,' he said. 'I've put the kettle on for black coffee. That's what you're supposed to drink, isn't it?'

'If you're trying to sober up,' she said.

'Well, that's what I'm doing, isn't it?' His voice was hard-edged, unhappy. Not like his voice at all.

'If you were ever drunk in the first place,' said Pauline.

He looked puzzled. 'I don't do it often,' he said. He smiled, a brittle, unhappy smile. He made coffee. 'Where have you been?' he asked, taking his into the sitting-room.

Pauline stiffened slightly. He was supposed to be unconscious in the armchair; he wasn't supposed to know that she had been anywhere. 'I went for a drive,' she said.

He looked at his watch. 'At quarter to midnight?'

'I just wanted to think,' she said, picking up her mug, and going in.

Gordon sat on the sofa, hunched up, with his hands round the mug.

'Are you cold?' she asked, sitting beside him.

He shook his head.

They drank the coffee in silence.

'And . . . what were you thinking about?' Gordon asked.

'It doesn't matter.'

'No.' He put his mug beside hers on the table, pushing it over until they touched. 'Nothing matters any more.'

'Stop *saying* that!'

'Why? It's true.'

49

'No,' she said.

He looked bleakly at her, and she touched his cheek. He turned his head to kiss the palm of her hand.

'We'll be all right,' she said, as he buried his face in her shoulder. 'We'll be all right. You'll see.' She kissed the top of his head. 'It'll be all right.'

The call had come about twenty-minutes after Jonathan Austin's call to Judy. A woman had been murdered at Flat 2, Mitchell House. Lloyd had tried to talk Judy out of coming, but to no avail. She sat beside him in the five-minute journey round the corner from the old village, her face tense.

'There's all sorts of reasons why you shouldn't be here,' he said. 'It's not your division, you're probably going to have to give us a statement about that phone-call – which makes you a witness – and you – ' He took a breath. 'You're personally involved,' he said.

'I don't know her all that well,' said Judy, defensively.

No, thought Lloyd. But you're none too keen on dead bodies that you don't know at all.

'And I can give you an immediate ID,' she said. 'Don't worry, I'll keep out of your way.'

The car swept round the roundabout, leaving the old village. 'You'll keep out of *Austin*'s way,' said Lloyd.

'I just want to see for myself what's happened,' she said. 'I won't go for him, don't worry.' She gave a bitter little laugh. 'And you said *she* was using me for an alibi,' she said.

Neither of them spoke until Lloyd had made the turn into the Mitchell Estate.

'You seem to have already decided what's happened,' he said, turning into the garage area, bringing the car to a halt behind Drake's Chevette. From there they could see the side and the front of the flats. A police car sat outside, and another joined it, siren blaring. A small crowd had gathered.

'Why ring me?' said Judy. 'I *don't* know her well. Why ring me unless it was to have a police officer confirm . . . ' She shook her head.

'Confirm what? That he was in the house minutes before the neighbour raised the alarm? That he was upset about her not having come home?' He sat back. 'As alibis go, it isn't much

50

cop, is it? Isn't it more likely that she came in after that and they had a row that got out of hand?'

Judy closed her eyes in a brief nod, and they got out of the car. As they entered the flats, a tough young constable was standing in front of the open door of Flat 2.

'Sir,' he said. 'Ma'am.'

'Do we have any witnesses?'

'Well, sir, the lady next door – the one who rang? WPC Alexander's with her. I don't think she saw anything, though. Sergeant Drake's inside, sir. He was here first.'

Lloyd smiled, and nodded his thanks. He paused at the threshold of Flat 2, looking through the open door before he entered, to make sure he didn't disturb evidence.

Slowly, carefully, he and Judy went into the hallway, and looked into the room. The mirror which had been on the wall behind the telephone was shattered; splinters of glass had been showered on to the table and the floor, and twinkled in the light. Broken furniture lay scattered, and the girl lay dead amongst it. A freestanding chromium ashtray of the kind used in office receptions lay close by, its recent use all too apparent. A box of tissues had been torn open, and its contents strewn over the floor.

'That's her,' said Judy, looking away immediately.

Drake, his face pale and grim, picked his way carefully through the devastation towards them as the scene of crime officers arrived. He looked at Lloyd as he joined them in the hallway. 'I was watching these bloody flats all night,' he muttered.

Lloyd looked through the door again, and noticed the open doors on to the balcony. Though it was a ground-floor flat, it had a balcony like the upper floors; it opened on to a public grassed area with young trees. Cover, means of entry, on the ground floor. Architects never thought things through. But the glass was intact, and the door didn't appear to have been forced; not from where he was standing at any rate. The fingerprint man was working on it.

Judy was almost certainly right about what had happened, even if Lloyd had his doubts about her theory.

'Was the balcony door open when you entered?' he asked Drake. 'Or did you open it?'

'It was open, sir. So was the front door. I ran out on to the balcony, but I couldn't see anyone. Then I . . . ' He tailed off.

51

'Yes?'

'I had to pull all the stuff off her. I tried . . . I tried to revive her, but – ' He looked down at himself, at his clothes streaked with her blood, and his hand flew to his mouth.

Lloyd sighed. Another one like Judy. A few more years on the beat would have taught him how to cope with this like they had taught her; in Lloyd's opinion high-flyers were more trouble than they were worth. Too much theory and not enough practice. 'Outside,' he said, pushing him towards the door. 'Right out, into the air.'

Freddie, tall and thin, appeared at the front door. 'I thought the lovely Inspector Hill wasn't based in Stansfield any more,' he said, as Judy greeted him with a brief smile of acknowledgement before taking advantage of the diversion to slip into the room.

'She's not,' sighed Lloyd. 'It's a long story. How come you're here already? Were you camping out on the doorstep waiting for a body to examine? She's only been dead half an hour.'

Freddie gave him a smile, the only clue his appearance gave to his true nature. In repose, his face made him look a bit like everyone's idea of an undertaker. Or death itself, even, thought Lloyd. Thin, serious, almost sad. But the smile was really Freddie.

'I'll be the judge of that, DCI Lloyd,' he said. He smiled again. 'I was in Stansfield, visiting friends, your honour,' he said to Lloyd. 'Jack Woodford knew that because I had rung him up earlier in the evening to check on my date for the squash tournament, and I left him the number. I have not yet taken to murder as a means of remaining on the Home Office books.'

'Just get on with it, Freddie,' groaned Lloyd. 'Oh – and Judy was friends with this woman, so no wisecracks, all right?'

Freddie's face sobered. 'Oh.'

'Looks like a row that got out of hand,' said Lloyd. 'The husband seems to have taken off.'

'Sir,' said a voice.

Lloyd turned to see Drake, some colour back in his face.

'I saw her earlier, sir,' he said. 'With a man. I thought she might be in trouble . . . that is – I couldn't be sure. I've given his description to control,' he said. 'Such as it is. It was dark – I didn't get that good a look at him.'

Freddie gave Lloyd a look of sympathy, and went off to begin his examination.

Lloyd took Drake back out again. 'Right,' he said. 'From the beginning.'

Hazy stars were appearing; midsummer day, and a short night. That was good, whoever and whatever they were looking for.

'I was watching the flats,' said Drake. 'And I saw this lady being dropped off at about teatime. By Frank Beale, as it happens.'

'Who?'

The young man looked a little surprised. 'Frank Beale, sir,' he said. 'He's well known in Barton. Used to live there, but he's moved to Malworth now. All his business interests are in Barton,' he added.

'Right. Go on.'

'Later on she went out alone, leaving her husband with a visitor. The visitor left at about ten – that is, he left the building. But he sat in his car for about twenty minutes. The husband left the flat about half past ten. I went off watch a few minutes after eleven, and I was passing the old post office building when I saw her again. With a man. Not the husband, or the visitor.'

'Or Frank Beale, presumably,' said Lloyd.

'No, sir. Five ten, regular features, dark hair. Jeans and a leather jacket.'

'What time would that have been?'

'About ten or quarter past eleven, sir. I thought for a moment that she was trying to get away from him, so I stopped the car. But then I thought I was mistaken, and I drove off. But it bothered me a little, so I turned round and came back. There was no sign of them, and I came back up here. The flat was in darkness, but the front door was open. I was just on my way to investigate that when Sergeant Woodford asked me if I was still in the area, because they'd had a 999.'

'Did you see anyone enter or leave the flats?'

'No, sir.'

'Right. Did you talk to the next-door neighbour?'

'I sent WPC Alexander to take her statement, sir, now that she's calmed down a bit. The neighbour, that is, not WPC Alexander,' he added in an heroic attempt at a joke. 'I couldn't talk to her myself, not looking like . . . ' He looked down again at his clothes, and fought the nausea. 'She was very upset, sir,' he said.

Lloyd nodded, then smiled for what may have been the first

53

time ever at Drake. At last, the man seemed human. 'She's not the only one,' he said.

'No, sir. Sorry, sir. It was just— ' He shook his head. 'If I'd acted on my first instinct, maybe I could have stopped it. It just suddenly got to me.'

Lloyd shook his head. 'There's a very fine line between crime prevention and downright interference. We can't always get it right.' He looked up at the still distraught young man. 'Anyway, I'm not sure it's the boyfriend we should be looking for.'

'Sir?' He didn't look any happier at that; just puzzled.

'Her husband came back after you left,' said Lloyd. 'So where is he now?'

Drake frowned. 'How do you know that, sir?'

'Because he rang me. Well – not me but . . . ' He sighed. 'I just know, all right?'

'Sir.'

'I think you should go home and change,' said Lloyd. 'Then come back here.'

'Yes, sir,' said Drake, visibly pulling himself together.

Judy came out of the room, her face controlled and calm.

'Are you all right?' he asked.

She nodded.

'Let's talk in the car,' he said.

She lit a cigarette as soon as they were outside. She had almost given up, too. She hadn't had one for days, as far as Lloyd knew.

'Are you sure you're OK?' he asked, as he got into the car beside her.

'Yes,' she said.

'Sergeant Drake's thrown a bit of a spanner in the works,' said Lloyd. He gave her the description of the man with Mrs Austin. 'Does it mean anything to you? One of her friends?'

Judy shook her head. 'I don't really know her friends. I think she prefers to keep it that way. I don't think too many of them are all that keen on the law.'

'So,' said Lloyd, pulling the door shut on the fresh breeze. 'The phone-call. What did he say to you?'

'He asked if she was with me. He seemed to think I might just be saying she wasn't. He said they'd had words. Then he just suddenly said she was probably at the studio, and he didn't know why he hadn't thought of that in the first place.' She looked at him. 'Neither do I,' she added drily.

'What do you mean?'

'I just felt as though he was acting,' she said. 'Something. Something about his manner.' She sighed. 'But I really don't know him at all. He might always sound like that on the phone. Some people do. They can't talk naturally to a piece of plastic.'

'So it sounded unnatural?'

She nodded. 'In fact,' she said, after a moment, 'it sounded as thought he knew perfectly well where she was.'

Lloyd looked through the narrow entrance to the garages at the normally quiet street, now awash with police vehicles and flashing lights, and neighbours who had given up hiding behind net curtains to stand at their doors and watch.

'Are you saying you think she was already dead when he rang you?'

Judy didn't answer, and he looked at her. 'And then he made all the noise that alarmed the neighbour?'

The boot was on the other foot for once. It was Judy who was sitting there having to account for a theory that didn't really hold water while he demolished it. Somehow, that made him feel uncomfortable. He was the theoriser, the scenario man. Judy just took notes and looked at the facts. But then, she wasn't part of this investigation. She was on the other side of the fence; her friend had been murdered, and she had been unwittingly involved.

'Well,' said Lloyd. 'Let's look at what we know. She was with this man at the old post office, at about ten past eleven. We know that her husband was out of the flat from about ten thirty and back again by eleven twenty. Ten minutes after that the neighbour heard noises which alarmed her, and by eleven thirty-two she was dialling 999. The message went to Drake at eleven thirty-five.'

'I didn't like that call,' she said again.

'It doesn't make sense, Judy,' Lloyd said gently. 'What good would ringing you do him? What would be the point of making such a commotion that the neighbour rang the police if he'd already disposed of her quietly?'

'I don't know,' she said. 'I just know that that call disturbed me.'

It had. This wasn't hindsight; Lloyd had seen that it had

55

worried her. But it didn't make sense. And it hardly mattered.

'If he'd been trying to establish some sort of alibi, he'd have pretended he was somewhere else altogether,' he pointed out reasonably. 'Isn't it more likely that he went out for whatever reason, came home – she still wasn't in, and he rang you because you were the first person who came to mind, since she'd seen you this morning? She comes in, they have a row. It gets out of hand, and he takes off the back way.' He put his arm round her. 'Either way, there isn't much doubt,' he said.

But Judy had twisted round, and was looking out of the rear window, her eyes widening.

'That's him,' she said.

Lloyd saw a tall, fair man walking slowly past the car, towards the flats. One of the officers stopped him, and there followed a short conversation.

Lloyd saw Austin's reaction when the officer told him what had happened, and glanced at Judy.

'He's still acting,' she said firmly.

But Lloyd wasn't so sure.

'Mr Austin?'

Jonathan looked at the man who emerged from the garages, and walked into the light.

'Detective Chief Inspector Lloyd, sir. Stansfield CID.'

'He won't let me see her,' said Jonathan.

The chief inspector took his arm. 'You will have to make a formal identification, Mr Austin,' he said. 'But it doesn't have to be now.'

'I *want* to see her! How do you know it's her – how do you know you've not . . . ' He broke off, looking again at the flat, its aspect suddenly altered by the police activity, by the urgency, by the pall of death.

'DI Hill has . . . ' began Lloyd.

Judy Hill stepped forward, and Jonathan saw her for the first time. 'Judy?' he said, his mind trying to cope with too many things at once. 'Is . . . is Leonora really dead?'

She nodded, and turned away, getting into a car.

'I want to see her!' he said again.

Lloyd led him into the house, and Austin nodded briefly when they asked if it was his wife.

'Is there another room, Mr Austin?' asked Lloyd. 'Where we could talk?'

Jonathan took him into the kitchen, and sat down at the breakfast bar.

A young man wearing very casual clothes came in; he and the chief inspector had a hurried conference just out of his hearing. All Jonathan found himself doing was wondering why the young man looked as though he was going out for an evening run. A track suit, or jogging suit or whatever. He never knew the difference. It said 'Morocco' across the front, and there was a palm tree on the breast pocket.

He reached into his pocket for his cigarettes, and lit one, his hand shaking. Jonathan hated himself for smoking. It was anti-social, it was unhealthy, it was expensive, and dirty. It was proof of his lack of willpower. Leonora hadn't wanted him to smoke.

They sat down with him at the breakfast bar, and the young man was introduced. It was he who asked the first question; that surprised Jonathan. He would have expected the senior man to make the first move.

'You rang Mrs Judy Hill at twenty past eleven, didn't you?'

Jonathan nodded.

'So what happened after that?'

'I . . . I went out. To look for Leonora. I was worried.'

'What about?'

'It isn't – wasn't – like her. Going off without saying where. Staying out.'

The sergeant nodded, and looked at the chief inspector.

He, in his turn, took a slow, deep breath, and stood up. He walked round the room, pausing to pull back the blind and look out of the window. There was nothing to see; just the reflection of the neat kitchen. 'Where did you look for her, Mr Austin?' he asked.

'Just . . . about. I went through the alley behind the garages – it goes down to the main road. I thought . . . ' He shrugged.

'Had you already been out looking for her?'

'No,' said Jonathan.

'But you had been out before?'

Jonathan frowned, and didn't answer.

'You left the house at ten thirty, and you hadn't returned by eleven o'clock.'

Jonathan stared at him. 'How do— ?' He shook his head. 'How do you know that?'

Chief Inspector Lloyd smiled. 'All in good time, Mr Austin,' he said, his Welsh accent becoming more evident. 'But it's true, isn't it?'

'Yes. But – but, no, I wasn't looking for her. Not then.'

'Perhaps you won't mind telling me what you were doing?'

'I . . . my wife's car was in being serviced,' he began.

And he had thought that maybe it would help if he collected it. Stop her being angry with him. Put her in a better mood before he had to tell her about Gordon. What did that have to do with them?

'Go on,' said the chief inspector.

Jonathan realised that he hadn't actually said any of that. 'She'd asked me earlier if I could run her over there to collect it, and I'd said I didn't have time,' he said. Of course he had had time. He just hadn't wanted to be distracted from his preparations for breaking the news to Gordon.

He looked at Lloyd. 'She had arranged for it to be left out for her, and I thought . . . I just went to collect it.'

'What made you decide to pick it up for her?'

Jonathan put out his cigarette on a saucer, and lit another. 'I thought it might make up for my being short with her earlier,' he said.

'Short?'

'I had a very difficult business meeting. I had asked her to leave.'

Lloyd sat down again, and looked at him, his face a little puzzled. 'So she left the house in a huff?'

Jonathan sighed. 'Sort of,' he said. 'She didn't like being asked to leave – and as I said, I had been a bit short with her.'

He looked more puzzled than ever. Too puzzled. He should try to curb the over-acting.

'Did your wife normally attend business meetings, then?' he asked.

'No, but this was with a very old friend of hers. And I don't normally have business meetings at home.'

'Ah,' said Lloyd. 'That would be the gentleman who left your flat at about ten o'clock?'

'Look, what is this? Have you been *watching* me, for God's sake?'

'No, no, sir. The flats. One of the flats in this building. Nothing whatever to do with you. But the officer did notice all the comings and goings from the building, naturally.'

Jonathan flushed. If he had known someone was out there, watching . . .

'Could I have this friend's name, sir?' asked the sergeant.

Gordon? They couldn't think that . . . Jonathan remembered how angry, how hurt Gordon had been. Blaming Leonora. 'Gordon Pearce,' he muttered.

'Your co-director,' said Sergeant Drake.

'One of them. There are a number of directors now.'

'Ah yes,' said Lloyd. 'You've expanded very rapidly, haven't you? New factory – much larger premises.'

Jonathan could contain himself no longer. 'If someone was watching the flats, then he must have seen Leonora come back,' he said.

But the chief inspector was shaking his head. 'It was Sergeant Drake who was watching the flats,' he said. 'He went off duty at eleven o'clock. Just before you returned from your first trip out, apparently.'

They didn't believe him, obviously.

'You went straight to pick up the car?'

'Yes.'

'Where is this garage?'

'It's one of the factory units on the old Mitchell Engineering site. Quite close to the Austin-Pearce factory.'

Lloyd nodded. 'And you went on foot – how long would you say it took you to get there?'

'Twenty minutes or so.'

'And what – a few minutes' drive back?'

Jonathan closed his eyes. 'I didn't drive back,' he said.

'Oh?'

'The car wasn't there. She must have picked it up herself. I walked back.'

'It hadn't occurred to you that your wife would have picked it up herself?'

59

'No. It's a much longer walk by the roads – I took the shortcut across the Mitchell Engineering land. I didn't think she would have done that – it's very lonely.'

'So you came back, without the car. Then what did you do?'

'I went out to look for her! Does it matter? Isn't it what Leonora was doing that you should be concerning yourself with?'

Lloyd frowned very slightly. 'What do you think she was doing, Mr Austin?' he asked.

'I thought she was at her studio,' he said. 'In Malworth.'

'You said that to Mrs Hill,' said Lloyd.

'Yes.'

'But you didn't think that when you rang Mrs Hill in the first place,' he pointed out.

'No.' Jonathan desperately tried to sort out his thoughts. 'I did think that, earlier. Or that she'd gone to visit Pauline Pearce. But then I remembered she hadn't got the car, and I dismissed the idea. That was when I went to get it for her. But when I was talking to Judy I suddenly thought that if she had the car after all, that was where she would have gone,' he said.

'So why did you go out to look for her, if that's what you thought?' asked Drake.

'I . . . I just went out. To see if I could see her car coming.'

'And you returned a few minutes ago, at midnight,' he said. 'By which time your wife had come home.'

Jonathan closed his eyes.

'Where would she park?'

'In the garage area,' said Jonathan. 'Her car isn't there,' he said, anticipating the next question.

They took the make and number, and the sergeant went into the sitting-room again, leaving the door open. Someone got on to the radio about it, what seemed like hordes of people moved around, flashbulbs went off now and then. People spoke to one another, called to one another. A group of them *laughed*. Lloyd looked angry, and got up to close the door, but the sergeant came back in.

'Is your wife on the phone at the studio, sir?' he asked as he came in, closing the door behind him.

'Yes.'

'Did you ring there when you were looking for her?'

'No. She doesn't like to be disturbed when she's working.'

'Does your wife normally wear a wedding ring, Mr Austin?'

Jonathan frowned. 'Yes,' he said. 'Yes, of course.'

'And she was wearing it this evening?'

Jonathan was bewildered. 'I – I imagine so,' he said.

'She isn't wearing it now, Mr Austin,' said Drake.

'Did you kill your wife, Mr Austin?' asked Lloyd, his voice gentle, belying the harsh question.

'No,' said Jonathan, turning back to him, unsurprised at the accusation. 'No.' He looked from one to the other. 'Why?' he said. 'Why would I kill her?'

Lloyd sat back a little, apparently at ease. 'Would anyone want to kill her, Mr Austin?' he asked.

'There was . . . ' His voice trailed off.

'There was what?'

'A few weeks ago. She told me some man was pestering her. She – she was quite worried.'

That made the chief inspector sit forward. 'A man?' he said.

'Just before I met Leonora,' Jonathan said slowly, 'she was seeing some man. He . . . he was becoming a nuisance. I think one of the reasons she married me was to make it clear to him that there was no future in it. It was him. That's all I know.'

'And you don't know his name, or what he does for— '

'That's *all* I know!'

'Why did your wife tell you about him?'

Jonathan shook his head. 'Why shouldn't she? She was worried about him – I've *told* you that.'

'I mean – did she want you to do something about it?'

'No – she . . . ' Jonathan sighed. 'I have been adopted as the parliamentary candidate for the Conservative Party in the next general election. My private life has to be free of . . . well, you know. He had been here, apparently. Once or twice. She said she thought he would have grown out of it by now, but he was just as persistent, and she thought he might cause some trouble. She was warning me.'

He had been prepared for scepticism, but they seemed to be taking it seriously. 'You should be finding out what Leonora was doing,' he said, emboldened by that. 'Not what I was doing.'

Lloyd sat back again. 'We do know something of your wife's movements,' he said. 'We're trying to discover more.'

Jonathan frowned. 'What? What do you know?'

61

'I saw your wife as I left the estate,' said Sergeant Drake. 'At about ten past eleven. Were you waiting for her when she got home, Mr Austin?'

Jonathan couldn't grasp it all. 'No,' he said. 'I wasn't *here* when she got home.' He looked up at them, bewildered.

'When I saw her,' Drake said slowly, watching Jonathan's face as he spoke, 'she was with a man.'

Jonathan frowned. 'What do you mean?' he asked. 'What do you mean, *with* a man?'

The young man looked a little uncomfortable.

'Well? What *do* you mean?'

Drake coloured, and looked away.

Jonathan stared at him. 'She *wasn't* with him, was she? He was accosting her, wasn't he?' he shouted. 'Wasn't he? When you saw her? He was accosting her, and you did nothing!'

'I – I couldn't tell if . . . '

'You did nothing, and now she's dead! Why aren't you looking for him? She was afraid of him, she told me! Why are you wasting your time with me, instead of looking for him?'

'We are looking for him,' said the chief inspector, his voice still gentle, still soothing. 'Did your wife tell you anything more about him?'

Jonathan was still glaring at Drake, who stared unhappily at the formica. Slowly his gaze turned to Lloyd. He knew the name. Lloyd, Lloyd . . . wasn't that the man that Judy Hill had left her husband for? So he must have answered the phone.

He shook his head. 'I've told you all I know about him,' he said, and looked back at the sergeant. 'Ask him,' he said. 'He saw him molesting her, and he did nothing. And now she's dead.'

The sergeant got up abruptly, and left the room.

It wasn't my fault.

That's all that went through Mickey's head as he came out of the kitchen into the sitting-room. The doctor was dictating notes to his assistant, the photographer was still snapping away at the devastation, and he thought he was going to be sick again.

'I've given Mr Austin a brandy,' said Lloyd, closing the kitchen door. 'He's going to go to the Derbyshire.' He looked at the doctor. 'I'd rather she wasn't still here when he leaves,' he said.

'I won't be much longer,' said the doctor.

Lloyd squatted down beside him. 'I think he'd just taken off when Drake got here,' he said. 'How much can you tell me now? Anything that would help?'

'She's been dead less than an hour,' said the doctor. 'But then, you told me that.'

Lloyd grunted.

'Death due to a single blow to the temple, probably from behind.'

'Just one?'

Mickey looked at the mess it had made of her. He felt sick again.

'Just one. One very savage blow. There doesn't seem to have been a struggle, as such. The indications are that she was trying to get the furniture between herself and her attacker, rather than trying to fight him off.'

Lloyd got to his feet. 'Look at this lot,' he said.

The leg of one chair was broken off; a shelf unit had been broken almost in two. The coffee table had a deep indentation in the middle, and the corner was smashed away. One of the scattered tissues clung to the ragged edge; it was folded into a square, unlike the others. Mickey took a closer look, and could just see that it was slightly discoloured. He bent down and sniffed. 'Whisky,' he said, looking up at Lloyd.

'Gordon spilled some,' Jonathan Austin said, and Mickey turned to see him standing in the doorway. How long had he been there? 'Sir, do you think you should— ?' he began.

'It's my house,' he said, and looked again at his wife. But then he went back into the kitchen, closing the door.

Lloyd looked at Mickey. 'You didn't hear anything, I take it?' he said.

'No, sir. It was quiet.'

The doctor straightened up, and looked at the smashed furniture. 'She ran out of protection, and he found his target,' he said, with the cheerfulness of a football commentator.

Mary Alexander came in. 'I've spoken to the next-door neighbour, sir,' she said. 'I've said someone will be back to take her formal statement. All she knows is that she heard screaming, and' – she looked at the shattered furniture – 'all this,' she said. 'And someone shouting "whore", over and over again. A man's voice, she thinks. It was hysterical – she couldn't be certain.'

'Which means she can't identify it.'

'No, sir.' WPC Alexander looked at Mickey. 'Are you all right?' she asked.

Mickey nodded, praying that he wasn't going to be sick again.

Lloyd glanced at him. 'If you think you're going to throw up, go out,' he said.

'I'm all right, sir.'

'The neighbour's phone is by the window, sir. She says the noises were still going on when she was talking to the station, and that she stayed there, watching. She didn't see anyone at all.'

Lloyd nodded. 'She wouldn't,' he said. 'He went that-a-way.' He pointed to the balcony. 'By the looks of things.'

Mickey watched as the murder weapon was carefully bagged.

'Ask Austin where that ashtray was normally kept,' Lloyd said.

Mickey got the feeling that he was just giving him an excuse to leave the scene, but he was glad of it, and escaped back into the comparative normality of the kitchen, where Austin sat, sipping his brandy, smoking.

'Mr Austin,' he said, sitting down at the breakfast bar. 'Can you tell me where the tall chromium ashtray was usually kept?'

Austin looked blankly at him.

Oh, God. Mickey took a breath. 'Did you keep it in the sitting-room, or in here, perhaps? Did you have it in the sitting-room tonight, for instance?'

Austin frowned. 'What ashtray?' he asked.

'About two feet high,' said Mickey. 'With a heavy metal base. The kind you find in banks, and— '

Austin was shaking his head. 'I've never seen anything like that here,' he said.

Mickey stared at him. 'But— ' he began.

Realisation dawned in Austin's pained features. 'That's what he used, isn't it?' he said.

Mickey nodded briefly, and got up. 'Just . . . just wait here, Mr Austin,' he said.

He went back out and told Lloyd, who raised an eyebrow, and turned back to the doctor. 'Anything else you can tell me?' he asked.

'There are indications of a fairly enthusiastic amorous encounter,' he said, beckoning Lloyd to join him.

With some reluctance, the chief inspector crouched down again.

64

'This,' said the doctor, indicating a mark on the curve of her neck and shoulder, and another on her breast. 'The usual sort of thing. Small bruise on her lower lip. But the underclothes are intact, and there's nothing to suggest assault.' He looked up from the body, and beamed at Lloyd. 'But maybe the lady wouldn't let him go any further, and that upset him.'

'Mm.' Lloyd got to his feet again. 'He'd hardly call her a whore in those circumstances,' he said, and looked at the closed kitchen door. 'Her husband might if he caught her at it, though. And Mr Austin reckons he's never seen the murder weapon,' he added quietly, almost to himself.

'Her blouse was unbuttoned,' said the doctor. 'Not all the way, just more than modesty would usually permit.'

'Could that have happened while she was trying to get away from him?'

'Doubt it. I think the buttons would have had to have come off. I think – for what it's worth before I've done a proper examination – that she called a halt, or they were interrupted.' He frowned, and looked round. He nodded to a piece gouged out of the plaster in the wall. 'But this was a ferocious attack, Lloyd,' he said. 'With a weapon from the word go. There are no manual blows. I'd have thought her husband would have grabbed her, if he'd been that angry. I'd have expected some signs of a struggle. But there's nothing. Just that,' he said, indicating the terrible injury that had killed her.

Mickey looked, and fled.

Outside, he was sick again. He took deep breaths of fresh air. He was having to make a fool of himself, in front of Lloyd of all people. As if it wasn't bad enough being back in Stansfield without having to make himself look like a prize idiot into the bargain. It wasn't his fault. It wasn't. But the two images kept swimming into his mind: one of her and the man, one of her lying there. Minutes. Just minutes. It wasn't his fault. If it was anyone's fault, it was her own. Because she had been with him, she had been encouraging him. She wasn't trying to stop him – the doctor was wrong. He wasn't accosting her, she wasn't frightened of him – Austin was wrong. He had seen a couple, not someone being assaulted.

And the jogging suit. Oh, God, the jogging suit. Everything else he possessed was sitting in the washing machine, soaking wet. He'd missed the jogging suit, which was just as well, really.

If only he'd missed a sweater and jeans. But no, he had to come back looking as though he was on holiday. He'd seen the look that passed between Lloyd and the doctor.

It wasn't his *fault*. The colour drained from his face again, but he fought it this time. God damn it, she was with the bloody man, and Lloyd wasn't even going after him. And if he thought Austin had done it, why was he letting him go to a hotel, instead of taking him into custody? He couldn't make him out. Sometimes during the interview, he had been convinced that Lloyd thought Austin had killed her; at others he seemed to think he had nothing to do with it. He'd heard about Lloyd's tactics. Lull them into a false sense of security. Their guard will slip. No point in treating murderers like common criminals. They're not. They're uncommon criminals. He was used to Barton, with its hard core of crooks, like Beale. Softly softly was no good there. But this was different.

He decided he was all right, and went back into the flats.

'Drake,' said Lloyd. 'OK now?'

'Yes, sir.' But he kept a discreet distance from the body this time.

'Chief Inspector?' One of the SOC men came back in, still carrying the murder weapon in its polythene bag. 'There's something in here,' he said, shaking it slightly. Something rattled in its depths.

'Probably a ring-pull,' said Lloyd. 'Let's find out.'

A sheet of paper was placed on the floor, and the end of the bag opened. As the ashtray was upturned, and after much careful shaking, a plain gold wedding ring fell to the ground, rolling off the paper.

Lloyd stood up, looking grim. 'Bag it,' he said.

Mickey looked expectantly at him, but Lloyd shook his head. 'Leave it,' he said.

'But, sir— '

'Oh, I know,' said Lloyd. 'The book says to confront them with evidence straight away and with any luck they'll break down and confess. I prefer to let them think they've got away with it,' he said.

Working with Chief Inspector Lloyd wasn't going to be dull, Mickey could see that.

'Oh – Sergeant. Mickey, is it?' the doctor said, looking up from the body.

'Yes, sir.'

'Call me Freddie. And – do me a favour, will you? Ring my wife and explain to her where I am, or she'll think I've wrapped the car round a tree.'

Mickey took a note of the number, and went to the phone. 'Has this been done?' he called to the fingerprint man.

'Yes, Sarge. Mind the broken glass.'

He picked it up, and was about to key the number automatically when he realised he didn't have a dialling tone. He frowned, and pressed the rest, but he couldn't clear the line. He listened, and tried again, then checked to see that the phone hadn't been pulled out. It was intact. And the line *wasn't* dead, he realised; he just couldn't get the dialling tone back. Despite the way he was feeling, a little tingle of excitement went through him. Something odd, something that had to be explained. It was why he had wanted CID work.

'Chief Inspector,' he said.

'Yes?' Lloyd came over to him.

'The phone's dead – at least . . . ' Mickey listened closely, anxious not to make a fool of himself again. But he was right, he was sure he was. 'I think the line's open, sir,' he said, handing Lloyd the phone.

Lloyd listened.

If the line was open, then someone had rung the Austins' number, and hadn't hung up properly. It would almost certainly lead to nothing, but it was interesting, all the same.

'I think you're right,' said Lloyd.

'Right, sir,' said Mickey. 'I'll get on to BT, get them to trace it.'

'You do that,' said Lloyd.

Mickey went out, sighing with relief. For one thing, he'd stayed in the room without feeling sick, and for another, he had actually done something which met with Lloyd's approval.

There was a wait, of course, but when he got the answer, it was worth it.

More than worth it.

Judy saw Sergeant Drake hurrying towards her, and stubbed out her cigarette for some reason.

He leant in the open window. 'Frank Beale – do you know him?'

'Who doesn't?'

'Chief Inspector Lloyd,' he said, with a grin.

'Oh, I don't suppose he does,' said Judy. 'He hasn't had him on his patch. I got told all about him before I even got to Malworth.' Sandwell had briefed her well about her new manor, as he insisted on calling it.

'Someone rang this number from his number some time this evening,' said Drake. 'We know, because the line's still open. The chief inspector says it's your pigeon. I've to drive you over there and you've to see what you can get from them.'

Judy smiled. This was Lloyd not allowing her to get involved. 'Right,' she said, getting out of Lloyd's car. 'Let's go.'

It had taken ten minutes for her to get from the village to Malworth that morning. It would take Sergeant Drake about two, at this rate.

'I think we could afford to slow down,' she said. 'It probably has nothing to do with it, anyway.'

Drake allowed the car to lose some speed. 'You never know,' he said.

'No,' said Judy. 'But Frank Beale's wife is on the board of Austin-Pearce.'

'Is she?' Drake sounded startled, as well he might. 'I'd have thought she was a bit . . . well, shady, for an outfit like that.'

'Isn't she, though,' said Judy. 'But she's on the board, nonetheless. And she probably just rang Austin about something.'

'Oh – of course. You know the Austins, don't you?' said Drake, apologetically. 'I'm sorry. This must be terrible.'

Judy smiled. 'It's all right,' she said. 'We weren't bosom friends or anything. It was a shock. But I'm much happier having something to do, even if it is a wild goose chase.' She wondered if mentioning it would be right or wrong, and just hoped that she was right. 'It was a bit of a facer for you too, I gather,' she said.

He went pink.

'I'm sure it is a wild goose chase,' he said. 'I think the chief inspector was just getting me out of the way.' He glanced at her. 'I was sick again,' he said.

'Don't be embarrassed,' she said. 'You're not the first, and you won't be the last.'

'God knows what Chief Inspector Lloyd thinks of me,' Drake muttered.

'Lloyd understands,' she said. 'He's none too happy with dead bodies himself. But he can make himself squint so that he doesn't really look at them. I don't know how he does it.' She took out her cigarettes. 'He was always thinking of useful things for me to do, too,' she said. She waved the cigarette packet at him. 'Do you mind?' she asked.

'No, no. Go ahead. I was a sixty a day man once.'

'How did you give up?'

'I found something else to lavish my money on.'

She laughed, and lit one. 'I had very nearly given up,' she said. 'But if I have three in one day, I think I'm chain-smoking, so I'm not too bad.'

'You're a non-smoker,' he said. 'You don't crave it.'

'No.'

'I couldn't have made a worse impression, could I?' asked Drake. 'I made a complete balls of it.'

'Don't worry about it. You did what you thought was right.'

He drove without speaking until they were entering Malworth. 'It wasn't my fault,' he said.

Judy looked at him. 'Lloyd said that Austin had blamed you,' she said. 'He was upset, Mickey. Of course you weren't to blame.'

'No. But he wasn't assaulting her,' said Drake. 'I'd have stopped him if he had been. He says she was afraid of him – but she wasn't.'

'But you did think she might have been in trouble?' Judy said. 'I mean, that's why you went back, isn't it?'

'Yes,' he said defensively. 'But – but it wasn't like Austin thinks. She was – she was *with* him. She *was* with him. I mean – I suppose she might have been saying no, but— ' He broke off, and slowed down as they passed the row of craft shops and studios. 'The doctor thinks that's why she got killed,' he added, in a low voice.

Judy noticed the light in the studio, as Drake signalled to turn into the small car park. 'Stop a minute, Mickey,' she said.

There was nothing to be seen through the window; just the empty studio, and the open door into the office, where the desk light burned.

'Austin said he thought she was here,' said Drake.

Judy listened to the story about the car, and tried the studio door. 'Do you think she was here with her boyfriend?' she asked.

69

'I didn't see the car anywhere when I saw them,' said Drake. 'They'd have been in it, wouldn't they?'

'Maybe not,' said Judy, as they got back into their car. 'If she was trying to get out of a tricky situation.'

'If you ask me, it was her own fault,' he said, as he pulled into a parking space in the private car park behind the flats.

'You don't mean that,' said Judy quietly.

'She could have got away,' he said. 'She could have got away, when I pulled up. He came towards the car. She could have got away then, and she didn't! It wasn't my fault!'

Judy knew what Lloyd meant; Drake wasn't ready for any of this. And they would promote him next year. She put her arm round him, instinctively comforting him.

'Don't keep blaming yourself,' she said. 'I think you saw exactly what there was to be seen. Someone who wasn't sure what she wanted. But whether that was what made this man kill her, or whether Austin killed her in a rage – it doesn't matter. We'll find out which – but don't whatever you do blame yourself. Most people wouldn't have come back at all. Wouldn't have found her, wouldn't have put themselves through all this. You're a good policeman, Mickey. I know you are.'

'Lloyd doesn't,' he said miserably.

She smiled. 'Give him time,' she said. 'And don't try so hard to impress him. He won't think any less of you because you were upset tonight – but you have to start being professional about it now. You couldn't stop it happening, but we can find out exactly what did happen.'

She gave him a little squeeze. 'Come on,' she said. 'Let's see if Mr Beale can help us with our enquiries, as I understand he's so often done before.'

She was rewarded with something approaching a smile. 'Yes,' he said.

But it wasn't as simple as all that, as they discovered when they were confronted with the Andwell House hi-tech security system.

'You have to have a card,' said Drake, wonderingly. 'And a PIN number.'

'My God, I'd never get in,' said Judy. 'I'm always standing at hole-in-the-wall machines having another stab at remembering my number and then watching it eat my card.'

Drake touched the sensor below the Beales' name, but nothing happened. He tried again. And again. 'We'll have to wake someone else up,' he said. 'Someone with more on his conscience than Frank Beale.'

Judy laughed. 'Try the . . . oh – the Pearces live here, of course.' She wasn't sure of the etiquette. Gordon Pearce was Austin's partner – they could hardly barge in there, if the Pearces didn't know what had happened.

'Pearce,' said Drake. 'He was at the Austins' house tonight. I think Mr Lloyd wants to see him.'

'Does he think he might be involved?'

'Well . . . he seemed to. He was the cause of the row, in a way.' He explained the nature of the row to Judy.

Judy made a decision. If it was the wrong one, she would hear all about it in due course, but for now, she was the man on the ground, so to speak. She pressed the pad under the Pearces' name.

There was a moment's wait, then a woman spoke. 'Who is it?'

'Police, Mrs Pearce. I'm sorry to bother you so late, but we have to come in. Could you open the front door for us?'

'Can I see your identification?'

Judy frowned. If she couldn't get in, how could she show her ID?

'There's a camera just above your head,' said the voice.

So there was. Self-consciously, Judy removed her warrant card and held it up to the lens. 'Is that all right?' she asked. 'Can you read it?'

'Could you move it back a little? Yes – yes, I can read it . . . Inspector Hill? Thank you.'

There was a buzz and a click, and Drake pushed open the door, and went in.

Judy was still taken with the camera, until she realised that the door was slowly closing again. She made it in just before it closed with a little world-weary sigh.

'Wow,' she said. 'How much do you suppose it costs for a flat here?'

'No idea,' said Drake. 'I'd feel a bit as though I was in prison.'

'Mm. Nice, though,' said Judy, looking round at the designer reception area, where chauffeurs and the like waited, by the look of things. A table, with magazines. A little fountain, switched off for the night. Plants. Real or plastic? She peered at them, then

71

realised that the ash on her practically unsmoked cigarette was dangerously close to falling all over the floor that looked suspiciously like real marble. There must be an ashtray. She looked round.

There was. A free-standing chromium ashtray, with a heavy metal base. She looked at Drake as she let her cigarette slip into its depths. He had gone pale again. 'Sit down,' she said.

He obeyed, and she sat down too, to work out how to approach the matter.

'Sorry,' he said.

'It's all right. Just take your time. I've got a lot to think about.' She sat back in the chair. 'All right,' she said quietly, after a few moments. 'We've got two lots of people upstairs who knew Mrs Austin. One was on the phone to the Austins, and the other was visiting them.'

Smoke curled up from the ashtray as she stood up again, and picked it up. The weight surprised her. 'It must have lead in the base,' she said, and understood how it had made such a mess of Mrs Austin. 'Right,' she said, briskly, in grave danger of emulating Drake. 'Mrs Pearce knows we're here, so we can't just disappear again, I don't think. We'll proceed exactly as we meant to – don't ask anyone about the ashtray. OK?'

'Keep them off their guard?'

She smiled. 'I see you've had the lecture. But if someone left here with one of those things in order to kill Mrs Austin, there's nothing to be gained by letting them know we suspect that.'

'No,' agreed Drake. He stood up.

'And if the subject arises, I don't smoke.'

They used the lift. It deposited them quietly and went back down with a well-bred whine.

Knocking on the Beales' door, and ringing the Beales' bell proved just as ineffective as the Beales' entrance phone had.

Judy sighed, rather like the entrance door. 'They're out,' she said.

'Or avoiding us. If that camera comes on when you press the pad, then Beale would see us, wouldn't he?'

Judy nodded, and bent down. 'When in doubt,' she said, 'look through the— ' The door swung open at her touch.

Rosemary Beale lay on the hall floor, the telephone receiver lying on her chest. Its cable was still tight round her neck.

Four

'Did you hear anything at all suspicious?'

Gordon was under instructions to let Pauline do the talking, which command had been given to him last night, when the entrance phone had buzzed.

'I think,' he had said, still feeling light-headed, still breathless from Pauline's urgent restoration of marital relations, still strangely removed from the guilt he should have been feeling, 'I think that might be the police.'

Pauline had already got out of bed, and was pulling on a wrap. 'Yes,' she had said, matter-of-factly. 'Just let me do the talking.'

It was like something out of a film. Except that he must have dropped off, or they'd put the reels on in the wrong order. She didn't know what he had done, but she hadn't been at all surprised that he had thought it might be the police, and calmness itself when that proved to be the case. She had pressed the button to admit them to the building, slipped off the wrap, and returned to bed.

The night had been interrupted by the alarms and excursions next door, and now the police were here, in the flat, asking questions.

'Did you hear anything at all suspicious?' DI Hill repeated.

'Gordon was out for the count,' Pauline answered. 'He wouldn't have heard if they'd dropped a bomb.'

The inspector smiled. 'I'm like that, given half a chance,' she said.

'Gordon's like that given half a pint,' countered Pauline.

Gordon wasn't sure who she was playing, but from the moment she had uttered the deathless line 'Just let me do the talking', she had been playing someone. Brittle, smart, unmoved by the tragedy

73

next door. Too coquettish to be Joan Crawford, he thought.

'Did you hear anything unusual?' asked the inspector again, almost as though she hadn't just asked twice before.

Nice-looking girl. Honest, open face. If he hadn't been ordered to say as little as possible, Gordon might even have been flirting with her. Flirting was all right, he thought, providing it was in the presence of one or other of the spouses. He had flirted with Lennie when Jonathan was there. Not any more.

'No,' said Pauline slowly, as though she were trying to recall. 'No, nothing. It was very quiet – it always is.'

Gordon hoped that the frown hadn't appeared, but from the sharp glance the inspector gave him, he felt that perhaps it had. But he had never known Pauline to lie before. About anything. He had teased her about it – she had a thing about the truth. And here she was, saying she had heard nothing unusual, when the first thing she had said when he had come home was . . .

'Have you remembered something, Mr Pearce?'

'No,' he said. 'I'm afraid I'd had a bit more than half a pint. I don't remember much at all. I'm still a bit woozy.' A very tall young man hovered at the open door, and the inspector went to talk to him.

That's not true, Gordon, old son. You remember everything about last night.

He smiled as she came back in, closing the door this time. 'Can we offer you a cup of tea or coffee or something?' he asked. 'You might want some breakfast – have you been here all night? You look a little tired.'

'Here or hereabouts,' she said, with a smile. 'I'd love a cup of tea, thank you.'

'I'll get it,' he said to Pauline.

You've lied to the police now, old son.

Yes. But I'm sowing the seeds. I remember nothing. That's what my defence will be.

I see. So you've gone off the idea of suicide?

I've got a baby on the way. Can't run out on Pauline like that, can I?

And you think this defence will work, do you? You remember nothing? That one's sharp, Gordon, old son. She isn't going to let you toddle off and make tea and let Pauline do the talking. It might work in old movies, but it doesn't work in real life. She's

74

going to ask you more questions, and you had better have answers,
because she won't be fooled by Joan Crawford in there.

He made three mugs of tea, and buttered toast. She must
want something to eat.

He went back in, and put the tray on the table, bringing
three chairs round it as Pauline answered the inspector.

'Not very well, no. These flats are very private, really. You
can't hear people through the wall, or anything. Not like our
old place.' She smiled a little. 'To be perfectly honest, I'm not
sure I didn't prefer the lack of privacy. At least we knew our
neighbours there. And we really don't here. We know the Beales
better than the others because Mrs Beale recently joined the board
of Austin-Pearce, but that's the only reason.'

Too much talking, Pauline, thought Gordon. Could even be
regarded as prattling. How very unlike Pauline it all was.

'You were here all evening?'

Hill. That was it. Gordon had been trying to remember her
name all night. Hill. Detective Inspector Hill. He had only heard
Pauline's end of the entry phone conversation; he had imagined
a large man with a five o'clock shadow, wearing a raincoat and
a trilby. He thought perhaps he ought to update his image of the
average police officer; his was Jack Hawkins or someone. Detective Inspector Hill did not in any way resemble Jack Hawkins.

'Yes. Well, I was in all evening. Gordon was out for a couple
of hours.'

'What time did you get home, Mr Pearce?' she asked.

Gordon looked at Pauline.

'Oh, no use asking him. It was after ten, I know that. About
quarter past, I think. Yes – *News at Ten* was just coming on
again.'

My God. Gordon could feel the frank brown eyes on him
again, and shiftily avoided their gaze. If Pauline was going to
take to bearing false witness, she might at least have let him in
on it. With a great effort he pushed the question of her reasons
to the back of his mind.

'Does that seem right, Mr Pearce?'

'If Pauline says so . . . I just came in and fell asleep in the
chair.'

'Were you celebrating something?'

'No – just having dinner with my partner.'

'We think Mrs Beale came home at about eleven o'clock. Were you still up then?'

The question was addressed to both of them; Gordon looked at Pauline.

'Yes,' she said. 'I was trying to get Gordon to go to bed, and he just kept falling asleep again. I wasn't exactly keeping track of the time, but I think it must have been about midnight before I finally got him to bed.'

This time Gordon knew the frown had appeared. That was true, of course. She was telling the truth as much as possible; covering herself. Covering him. She knew.

'Yes, Mr Pearce?'

He looked at the inspector. 'Sorry?' he said. 'Oh – look, I'm forgetting the tea. Come and get it.'

They sat round the table and drank cool tea and ate soggy toast.

'I thought you were going to say something,' she said, not letting go.

Gordon had given himself a few moments' thinking time. 'No,' he said. 'I just suddenly remembered Pauline telling me it was quarter to midnight.' He got up. 'Excuse me a moment,' he said.

He walked quickly to the bathroom. It wasn't an excuse. Suddenly, the deception, the guilt, the realisation of what he had done and what he was doing had hit home, and his bladder had reacted instantly. He sighed with relief, flushed the lavatory, and washed his hands.

Pauline knew. Somehow, she knew, and she was shielding him. And now, for the first time, Gordon was scared. Scared of an attractive young woman in a summer dress that showed off her very nice legs, who looked a little tired.

'Well,' she was saying, 'if you do remember anything – anything at all – just give me a ring.' She handed Pauline a card. 'Don't think it's too insignificant, or that you'll be wasting anyone's time. That's sometimes just what we need.'

She was playing someone too. There they were, the three of them, all playing parts fit to bust, and no one knowing the script.

'Oh – one other thing,' she said, on her way out. 'There's an ashtray downstairs in the foyer – were there two, originally?'

'Yes,' said Pauline, looking a little puzzled. Then her expression changed. She wasn't puzzled any more, but she wanted the inspector to think she was. Gordon was in no position to say how successful she had been; he only knew it hadn't fooled him.

'Where's the other one?' asked the inspector.

'Isn't it there?'

Isn't it there? Oh, Gordon, Gordon. What's the little woman doing, for God's sake?

The inspector shook her head.

'They were both there yesterday – weren't they, Gordon?'

Oh, dear God. Gordon looked helplessly at Pauline, then at the inspector. 'I . . . I wouldn't know,' he said. 'Sorry.'

'Well,' she said. 'Thank you anyway.'

'Why do you want to know?' Pauline asked.

There was a pause before she answered, and then it was evasive. 'We think it may have been used in the commission of a crime,' she said. 'Thank you for your help.'

Pauline showed her to the door, then shut it, both hands on the eye-level knob, her forehead resting on them.

'Pauline, I— '

'Don't say anything, please, Gordon.'

'I have to! I can't let you do this.'

She turned from the door. 'I've done it,' she said. 'We were here, together, from quarter past ten. And that thing was downstairs. All right?'

He shook his head. He didn't understand about the ashtray, and he didn't think he wanted to. 'They'll find out I wasn't home at quarter past ten,' he said. 'Anyone could have seen me – I was probably driving badly, and— '

She walked up to him. 'Then we'll cross that bridge when we come to it,' she said, putting her arms up, clasping her hands behind his neck. 'For the moment, that's our story, and we're sticking to it.'

Gordon licked dry lips. 'We'll both end up in prison,' he said.

She gave a quick shake of her head. 'They have to prove it,' she said, drawing him into a kiss.

Did you leave any evidence, old son? That's the question.

The smell was the hardest thing to take, and would probably be the most difficult thing to eradicate. The damage, mainly smoke

77

and water, was mostly cosmetic, except where the fire had started. But the office had certainly looked better before it caught light.

Mickey moved into the centre of the room, and looked round at the devastation. It could have swept through the whole floor; an open-plan office, there was nothing to stop the advance of a fire. But the sprinkler system had done its job, and the damage was limited to one small area. A potted plant, its leaves charred and thick with grime, sat defiantly on a wall unit.

Mickey walked over to it, and looked closely to see if it might survive its ordeal. He thought it just might.

'Whose office is this?' he asked.

'Mrs Beale's,' said the factory manager.

Mickey's back was to him; he carefully rearranged his expression into its previous professional blandness before turning back. The door of one cupboard was partially open, buckled by the heat at the seat of the fire. Mickey removed a pen from his inside pocket, and pushed it open further. Inside were bottles and glasses; two unopened bottles of wine, one unopened bottle of gin, and mixers. On the floor, behind the open door, its glass darkened by flames, lay a half full bottle of Scotch. A glass, cracked in two, lay on the floor in the middle of the room.

The flooring under the cupboard had been burned away in a semi-circle; elsewhere it was browned and distorted, but there it had burned away.

'Looks as if it started here,' said Mickey. 'It looks as though it must have been deliberate.'

'It was deliberate, all right.'

'Was it now?' Mickey Drake was interrupted in his conversation with the factory manager by the fire officer. He held out his hand. 'Sergeant Drake, Stansfield CID.'

'Alarm cut,' he said, giving Mickey's hand a shake as perfunctory as his conversation. 'Sprinkler system's on independent wiring. Came on, doused the flames before too much damage done, end of fire. Not discovered till morning.'

Mickey had to make an effort not to emulate the economy of speech. 'Er . . . good,' he said, with a smile. 'Would someone think that cutting the alarm would cut out the sprinklers too?'

The fire officer smiled. 'Good question. Probably would. Wires terminate in a junction box in the basement, and that's where

78

they've been cut. If you follow the wiring as it looks to the naked eye, if you get my meaning, you'd think you'd got both. But if you look at the wiring diagram . . . '

To Mickey's horror, he unfolded a sheet of paper. He couldn't even follow the London Underground map, but his question had apparently been astute enough to qualify him as an *aficionado* of wiring systems. He nodded and tried to look intelligent. The upshot was that the wires parted company in the junction box, and that only someone involved in actually wiring up the system would have any reason to know that. And since whoever did it *didn't* know that, it narrowed the field down to the rest of the civilised world.

'Well, thank you very much,' he said, and watched with relief as the fire officer went back about his duties. He turned back to the factory manager. 'Right – I think perhaps if we could go to your office . . . '

'I shouldn't by rights be doing this,' he said, as he reluctantly led the way. 'But none of the directors has come in this morning.'

No, thought Mickey. There's a good reason for that, as you are about to find out.

In the glass-panelled office, door closed, he told the manager why Mr Austin wasn't in.

'Oh, dear,' he said. 'Oh, dear, dear. That's dreadful – that's unbelievable. Nice woman, Mrs Austin. I didn't see her all that often, but she was always . . . oh, dear.'

Mickey took a deep breath, and told him why Mrs Beale had failed to discover the fire in her office for herself.

'Dear God.'

No instant praise for the dead this time. Just stunned disbelief. Mickey allowed the man a moment or two to gather his thoughts. 'I don't know if you're aware of the fact, but Mr and Mrs Beale live next door to Mr Pearce, so I shouldn't expect him in too early, either.'

'I wasn't really expecting him in anyway,' said the manager.

'Oh?' Mickey sat forward a little. 'Why was that?'

'Well – I think it's all a bit hush-hush.' He snorted. 'A lot of things are, these days. Not like when it was just Gordon Pearce.'

Mickey smiled. 'I don't think hush-hush counts any more,' he said.

'No. Anyway, I don't know what it was all about. It was just that Mr Austin— ' He broke off, and shook his head again. 'Poor lass,' he said. 'Do you know who—?' He finished the sentence with another shake of his head.

'No arrest has been made yet,' said Mickey.

'Well he came to me last night and said that Mrs Beale would be here on a more regular basis in future. She normally just comes in once or twice a week. And that if Mr Pearce wasn't here today, I had to refer anything that cropped up on transport to her.'

Mickey nodded. 'Transport – that's Mr Pearce's job, is it?'

'Well – there used to be a transport manager, but now each of the directors is responsible overall for particular things. And the managing director is labour and transport. So that he's on the spot if there are any major problems. The other directors just turn up for board meetings.'

'Isn't Mr Pearce an engineer?'

'Yes, but that side of it hardly involves him now. He employs people who know more about what we're doing here than he does himself. He got bogged down with running a company while techniques improved and production got slicker and faster, except here. When Austin came, he made a lot of changes. All for the better.'

'Does that mean he sacked a lot of people?'

'There was a rationalisation programme,' said the manager.

'He sacked a lot of people,' repeated Mickey.

'Yes, but you're not suggesting that someone would . . . come on!'

Mickey shook his head. But someone had set fire to Rosemary Beale's office, and someone had strangled Rosemary Beale. Someone was less than satisfied with something she had done. And the office suggested it was something she had done in her guise as an Austin-Pearce director rather than any other of her activities.

'Anyway,' said the manager. 'It was Austin did that – not her. I don't hold much brief for the woman. I'm sorry she died the way she did, but if half what I've heard is right, I'm not all that surprised. But she had nothing to do with the redundancies. That was all over with by the time she got involved.'

'How many directors are there?'

'Five – including Mrs Beale.'

80

'Austin, Pearce, Mrs Beale and . . . ?'

'Fred Mullen and Charles Race.'

'You're not expecting them in, are you?'

The manager shook his head. 'Though I'd better get on to them and tell them what's happened,' he said. 'Bloody hell.'

Mickey sucked in his breath in sympathy. 'It took me a long time to work out how to tell you,' he said.

'I'll bet it did.'

Mickey was about to leave, and had lifted himself off the chair a fraction when he caught a look on the other man's face. He sat down again.

'It's . . . ' he began, but looked at Mickey.

Mickey looked receptive, and he didn't speak.

'It's not something I'd normally talk about,' he went on. 'I don't encourage gossip, but you can't stop it. And you can't help hearing it, and you can't help noticing things yourself.'

Mickey continued to look interested.

'Men are worse gossips than women, you know,' he said. 'I know. I've worked in factories all my life – mostly with women. But men are worse.' He leant forward, and lowered his voice, unnecessarily, since not only was the room soundproof, but there was absolutely no one in the vicinity; they were all working diligently at desks with green screens on them. 'They reckon she only got on the board because she was sleeping with Austin,' he said.

Mickey stared at him. '*Rosemary Beale?*' he said, with a total lack of professional detachment. He knew the woman. She was a tart. Had been. Then Beale had employed her at one of his clubs, and she had married him, and become respectable. After a fashion. He didn't know Jonathan Austin, but from what he'd seen of him, of his house, of his manner . . . it seemed inconceivable.

And yet it didn't, now he came to think about it. In the last century, no one would have thought it at all odd. All the same, he argued with himself, it might not have surprised him so much if she had still been plying her trade. But she wasn't. Still, it did explain why she was on the board. It didn't, he thought, explain why she wanted to be.

'That's what *I* said. Someone like him and a woman like her? I thought they were talking rubbish, but then – well, you can't deny what you see with your own eyes, can you?'

Mickey looked round the factory, with its glass partitions everywhere in the office area, and none at all in the production area, from what he had seen of it. A vast warehouse of a place, as unappealing inside as it was out, in his opinion. He could see clear to the other end of the room. Not the sort of place to conduct an illicit romance, he wouldn't have thought.

'What did you see with your own eyes?' he asked.

'Them. Whispering in corners. Taking long lunch hours – sitting in the car park for practically the whole afternoon. Once, I caught them behind a lorry.'

Mickey tried and failed to see Jonathan Austin being caught in a compromising position behind a lorry. But it wasn't difficult to imagine Rosemary Beale in such circumstances, and if the man was involved with her, then she had presumably caused him to shed his inhibitions.

'I mean, they weren't doing anything . . . you know. Not then. But I've heard they had somewhere in Barton that they went to.'

'And you think that this might have something to do with what's been happening?'

'Well – someone might resent it,' said the factory manager, guardedly.

Pearce, thought Mickey. That had to be who the man was indicating. Pearce, being pushed out by Mrs Beale. He had seen Pearce briefly last night, when Judy Hill had been trying to contact her divisional DCI without success. Spoken to him. He hadn't said much; his wife had answered for him, saying he was still half-smashed from his evening out.

As he walked back through the factory, he passed Rosemary Beale's office, and stopped and looked. The fire officer was in there making notes; Mickey looked at the hole in the tiling, and the bottle at the door.

'Can I have a word?' he asked the fire officer.

'Come in,' said Jonathan to the handsome young man who stood at the door. 'You're the one who brought me here yesterday, aren't you?'

'Yes, sir. Sergeant Drake.'

'You're rather more formally dressed this afternoon.'

Drake looked a little embarrassed. 'Yes,' he said. 'I was caught a bit on the hop, I'm afraid.'

Jonathan offered him a chair, and sat down himself, reaching over for his cigarettes.

'No, thanks,' said Drake, to the proffered packet.

'Are you a bachelor, Mr Drake?'

He looked a little surprised at the question. 'Yes,' he said. 'Well – not really. Divorced.'

Jonathan lit his cigarette. 'An occupational hazard, I believe.'

Drake nodded briefly.

Jonathan thought of his own, prolonged bachelor days. No one to do your washing. Make your meals. He had got used to having someone to do that.

'Have you found him?' he asked. 'Is that why you're here?'

'Not yet, sir. We don't know much about him.'

Jonathan flicked non-existent ash from his newly lit cigarette. 'But you saw him,' he said.

'In the dark, sir. And I wasn't really looking at him with a view to recognising him again.'

'Why not?' demanded Jonathan. 'He was accosting my wife!'

Drake took a breath. 'Sir, I have to say that I got the impression that . . . his attentions were not unwelcome.'

'All I know about him is that she had an on-off sort of relationship with him. He was too possessive.'

She had told him about this boyfriend when he was still just a friend, someone who took her out occasionally, someone she eventually felt that she could confide in.

'She told me she was frightened of him,' he said. 'But presumably she felt something for him once. She may have resumed the relationship,' he conceded, reluctantly. 'I'm sorry for what I said. I know it upset you. I'm sure you did all you could.'

'There really was no reason for me to interfere with them,' said Drake. 'And . . . there isn't really any reason to suppose that he was responsible for what happened.'

Jonathan frowned. 'Do you still believe I killed her?' he asked, his voice belying the emotion he felt.

'Sir – the murder weapon. You say that you don't possess an ashtray like that.'

Jonathan shook his head.

'Where could he have got it from?'

Jonathan stared at Drake. 'Are you saying that someone went there with the *intention* of killing Leonora?'

'If the ashtray wasn't there to start with, then— '

'No one would want to kill her! It *has* to have been someone who lost control, just picked it up!'

'But you say it isn't yours, sir.'

It wasn't. Jonathan had never seen it in his life before.

'Is this your wife's ring, sir?' The sergeant handed him a small plastic bag.

Jonathan took it; through the plastic, he could read the inscription. 'Yes,' he said, but his voice had failed. He cleared his throat. 'Yes. Where did you find it?'

Drake looked at him for a moment before he answered. 'In the ashtray, sir,' he said, his voice expressionless.

'But – but I . . . ' Jonathan stared at it.

Drake took it back from him. 'Do you know how your wife's ring came to be in there, sir?'

'No.'

'Mr Austin, do you know of anyone who might have a grudge against you?'

'A grudge? No one would kill my wife because of a grudge! Is that what you came here to ask me?'

'No, sir. I've just been to your factory. There's been a fire there.'

Jonathan's mouth fell open. 'What?' he said. Perhaps it was a dream. His conscience playing tricks on him. 'How bad? Should I be there?'

'Not too much damage,' said Drake. 'Your factory manager is there, and Mr Pearce is being informed. I don't think there's any need for you to be there unless you want to.'

'How did it start?' Jonathan tried not to think of avenging angels and acts of God, because that wasn't rational, and he must remain rational, whatever was going on.

'It was deliberate, Mr Austin.'

Deliberate. No avenging angel, then. An avenging person.

'It started in Mrs Beale's office,' the sergeant went on. 'The damage was confined to that room.' He cleared his throat. 'When I was there, I became aware of rumours concerning you and Mrs Beale.'

Jonathan closed his eyes. Gordon had said that. Last night – my God, was it only last night?

'Are they true?'

'No.' He stubbed out his cigarette.

The young man stood up. 'It's very warm in here,' he said. 'Do you mind if I take my jacket off?'

Polite. Unusually so, in Jonathan's experience. He shrugged his indifference, and the sergeant took off the jacket, revealing a short-sleeved shirt, which looked odd with the tie. It must have seemed odd to him too; he pulled the tie loose, and put it in his jacket pocket. His arms were already tanned; he unbuttoned the button at the neck of the shirt, and sat down again. He was well built, well muscled. These loose running tops disguised body shape.

'The thing is,' Sergeant Drake said, his manner changing slightly with the removal of the formal trappings, 'it doesn't really matter whether or not it was true. What matters is that people believe it.'

'And you think all these things have happened just because someone dislikes me?'

'I know it sounds a bit unlikely,' said Drake.

'It sounds very unlikely. Why wouldn't whoever it was just kill me and be done with it?'

Drake shrugged. 'We're talking about a psychopath,' he said.

'Is that official thinking?'

'We're keeping an open mind, sir.' Drake's eyes were half shut against the sunlight streaming in the window; he held his hand over his eyes.

'I'll close the blinds,' said Jonathan.

He looked down at the busy shopping street, pedestrianised before its time, and a victim of such forward thinking. It looked old-fashioned now, and people went to more up-to-date shopping centres at the weekends. But during the week, it still bustled. Black London cabs formed a constantly moving U-shape at the hotel end of the street, where the pedestrian area met the ring roads. A queue of people formed and reformed. Others stood at the bus-stops. It was an odd mixture, Stansfield. Classless: buses, taxis, private cars – you travelled in the way that suited, not in a way dictated by your circumstances. Leonora liked to use her car. He could have gone to collect it for her when she asked. He could have. And if he had, then . . .

He remembered why he was at the window, and let down the blind, turning to check that he had remedied Mr Drake's problem. The chair in which he had sat was no longer in the sun's glare, but

Drake wasn't in it. He stood, looking at the painting on the wall, lost in thoughts of his own, his hands in the back pockets of his trousers.

'That's one of Leonora's,' said Jonathan. 'The hotel bought quite a few.'

'Restful,' said the sergeant.

Jonathan could see a strip of sweat down the back of his shirt. 'Would you like a cold drink?' he asked, opening the fridge.

'Thank you,' he said. 'I'll have orange juice, if there is some.'

Jonathan poured him his drink. 'So what is the official thinking?' he asked, handing it to him as he resumed his seat.

The sergeant hesitated before he spoke, then took Jonathan into his confidence. 'One possibility is that your wife may have overheard something on the phone – something that put Mrs Beale's killer at risk. We think it's possible that the fire in Mrs Beale's office was to destroy some sort of evidence.'

Jonathan sat down on the bed.

'So we're looking at the possibility of an Austin-Pearce connection.'

'And I'm it?'

'*Were* you having an affair with Mrs Beale, sir? You do understand that I have to know, if I'm going to get anywhere with the investigation.'

The very idea. Jonathan shook his head.

'But you were in the habit of spending long periods of time with her alone?'

Jonathan turned to look at him. 'You and I,' he said steadily, 'have spent a long period of time in my hotel room. Alone. You have even removed some of your clothes. What construction would you put on that, Mr Drake?'

He saw the muscles tense just a little, for just a moment, then the young man relaxed, and smiled. 'Point taken,' he said.

'We had confidential business to discuss,' said Jonathan.

'Would that have concerned Mr Pearce?'

It was Jonathan's turn to tense up. 'Amongst others,' he said.

'You said that your meeting with Mr Pearce was going to be difficult. Why?'

Jonathan didn't want to tell him what had happened at their meeting. It was ridiculous. Their theory was ridiculous. 'I had to ask him to resign from the board,' he said.

86

'And how did he take that?'

He would have to tell him. Gordon's bewildered anger, his accusations . . .

But Gordon would never have harmed a hair on Leonora's head. Never. He couldn't let them suspect Gordon. He didn't have to tell them everything.

He lit another cigarette.

'Not very well,' he said.

'How did you get on?' asked Judy, as Bob Sandwell emerged from the flats, and they walked to his car.

'I didn't. No one saw anything unusual, no one heard anything unusual. They all did the usual things at the usual times – this must be the most usual place in the universe.'

Judy smiled. 'Well, it is. Isn't it?'

'Yes,' sighed Sandwell. 'Well, it was.' He looked at her. 'You look all in,' he said. 'You should go home and get some sleep.'

'I know,' she said. 'But we have to go to Stansfield. Mr Allison wants a meeting, going on the assumption that all these incidents are connected.'

Sandwell started the car. 'After that you should go home,' he said.

'I feel all right,' she said. 'But I didn't really get any sleep the night before last either – I was a bit keyed up about starting this job.' She put her notebook, for once not used, into her handbag. 'Where nothing ever happens,' she added.

Sandwell smiled.

'Anyway – did you believe all your usual people?'

'Yes,' said Sandwell, a little hopelessly. 'I don't think any of them knew anything was going on at all.'

'I'm not so sure about the Pearces,' said Judy.

Sandwell raised his eyebrows. 'Do you think one of them's lying?' he asked.

'Oh, Bob, I think we were *all* lying,' she said. 'I hated not telling them about Mrs Austin. They say the ashtray was there yesterday.'

Detective Chief Superintendent Allison had told her she must interview them without reference to the other murder, but to find out about the ashtray; obviously the thinking was that Pearce was involved. But she still felt a nagging doubt about that phone-call.

'Beale's going back to his own flat today,' said Sandwell.

Judy wasn't looking forward to that. Beale, she had discovered, had been in, of all places, Malworth police station when someone was strangling his wife. There had been trouble at the Riverside Inn, and he and the man with whom he had been fighting had both been taken in to cool off. Rosemary Beale had walked home alone.

Beale had taken the news with apparent stoicism, but Judy knew his reputation well enough to know that that was for show. On being released from custody he had spent the rest of the night with friends, and she hadn't bothered him with questions. But the incident at the Riverside Inn was odd, for two reasons. One, it wasn't the sort of pub which had incidents of any sort, and two, if Frank Beale had trouble, he had lots of very unsavoury characters to cause it for him. He very rarely caused it himself. Except where Rosemary was concerned. He was jealous of Rosemary, and had reason to be, according to Sandwell. But she had to be careful; Frank held the purse-strings, and Rosemary knew which side her bread was buttered. So was the trouble about Rosemary? And had she really walked home alone?

'I'll have to talk to him,' said Judy. 'But I want to have a word with Mr Pearce first. Without his wife's ventriloquist act.'

'So much for getting some sleep,' said Sandwell.

Lloyd and Allison were deep in conversation when they got to the station. Judy's own divisional DCI was on holiday; she had rung his deputy last night to discover that he had been taken to hospital that afternoon, having been inconsiderate enough to fall off a ladder and break his leg. And the connection between the two murders was obvious; it all combined to put her in a very awkward position.

Judy hadn't seen the extension since it had been brought into use, and they all took a few moments off to discuss the merits and demerits, and the smell of paint. It seemed quite pleasing at first, then just made you want to run as the midday sunshine warmed it up.

Lloyd opened all the windows wide, and ordered coffee.

'All right,' Allison said, when they were settled with their coffee. 'Facts. Yesterday Mr Austin invited his wife to come home and cook a meal for him and Mr Pearce, in which enterprise Mrs Austin was assisted by Mr Beale, who gave her a lift home in his Rolls.'

Drake stirred his coffee thoughtfully, a slight frown suggesting that he was pursuing thoughts of his own.

'Sergeant Drake here saw Mrs Austin with a man shortly before she died, at eleven thirty. Mrs Beale died some time between approximately eleven p.m. and one a.m. and an arson attempt has been made on the Austin-Pearce factory, of which company Mrs Beale is a director.'

Why? Judy wondered if Beale could throw any light on Rosemary's sudden interest in engineering.

'Mrs Beale was apparently strangled while making a phone-call to the Austin house,' Allison went on, 'and so far we do not know at what time that call was made or to which of the occupants. Mr Austin denies receiving any call from Mrs Beale or anyone else at any time during the evening. Mrs Austin was hit with a heavy metal ashtray, and Mr Austin denies knowledge of any such object. Mrs Austin's wedding ring was found inside the ashtray. An exactly similar ashtray is in the lobby of Andwell House, where the Beales have their flat.'

Judy told them her findings on that, such as they were, and Allison sat down.

'Any suggestions?' he said, with more than a hint of humour.

'Someone with a grudge against the company, sir?' said Sandwell.

Lloyd moved his head from side to side in a gesture which indicated that he wasn't happy with that suggestion. 'It might explain – at a push – the factory fire and Mrs Beale's death, sir,' he said. 'But a director's wife seems a bit over the top, even for a homicidal maniac.'

'Wholesale insurance claim,' Judy ventured, not entirely seriously, but not entirely facetiously.

'Ah,' said Allison. 'Another fact. Mr Austin is not what you would call short of money. In fact – he's rolling in it.'

Lloyd frowned. 'Why does he live in the Mitchell Estate flats?'

'I thought the Mitchell Estate was quite middle-class these days,' said Sandwell. 'And it was always quite a nice area.'

'Still is,' said Lloyd. 'But it's very ordinary.' He smiled. 'Let's face it, I could afford to buy one of those flats.'

'Man of the people,' said Judy.

'Probably,' said Allison. 'I met him at a council dinner the other night. When I broached the subject – out of sheer nosiness, I admit

– he said that he had his eye on a property outside Stansfield, which he intends to buy when it comes on the market. Which, as far as I can gather, will be when the old lady who currently owns it has the decency to fall off her perch.'

'Anyone checked that she hasn't, sir?' asked Sandwell. 'Perhaps he was having a clear-out.'

They all laughed, even Judy. Laughter was one way to deal with it.

'Grudge against Austin, sir,' said Drake. 'I'm told that he and Rosemary Beale were thought to be having a fling. So he would deny getting a call from her, wouldn't he?'

Judy stared at him. 'Jonathan Austin and Rosemary Beale?' she repeated, incredulously.

He smiled. 'That's the story. The factory manager reckons he caught them behind a lorry. I checked, to make sure the man wasn't subject to delusions, and it is definitely a firm belief in the factory. He has denied it, of course, and I— ' He changed his mind about what he was going to say, and shrugged. 'A hundred years ago it was practically the done thing for men like Austin, of course,' he said.

Judy frowned. True. And Lennie had always said that he was like a Victorian. But Victorian women weren't exactly encouraged to be hot stuff between the sheets, and if a man wanted a bit of excitement, he had to have a woman of rather easier virtue than his wife. If anything, from what Judy had gathered from the always-frank Lennie, her problem was the other way round.

'I rather got the impression that Austin wasn't that interested,' she said.

'Probably didn't have any energy left after his sessions behind the lorries with Mrs Beale,' said Lloyd.

Allison smiled. 'Before this conversation plumbs even greater depths,' he said, 'I'm not really concerned with motive. People get murdered for the most trivial of reasons. I'm assuming we all agree that the murders are connected. I'd like suggestions as to how. Other than by a telephone line.'

'Well, sir,' said Sandwell. 'It occurred to Sergeant Drake and I that as Mrs Beale seems to have been strangled while she was actually making the call, the killer might have known who the call was to, and think that he'd given himself away somehow.'

90

Judy suppressed a smile as Lloyd smothered a correction of the serious Sandwell's grammar.

'It's only ten minutes from those flats to the Austins' flat,' he went on. 'Less, if you put your foot down, and I expect he would. And if he was looking for a likely weapon – he could have picked up one of the ashtrays on his way out.'

Lloyd tipped his chair back on to its back legs as he thought. Then he let it fall forward. 'How did Mrs Austin's wedding ring end up in it?' he asked.

Sandwell looked a little shy.

'Sorry, Bob,' said Lloyd, with a smile. 'I do think that's worth pursuing, myself. We'll find out in the end how Mrs Austin's ring ended up in there, I'm sure. It's just a little puzzle that has to be solved. It may already have been in— ' He broke off. 'Well,' he said. 'We'll work on it, anyway.'

'Pearce was being kicked out,' said Drake. 'He blames Mrs Beale.'

'He'd been drinking,' said Judy. 'Heavily. Enough to pass out. His wife insists he was home by ten fifteen, but I'm not at all sure she isn't covering for him.' She looked at Allison. 'I think Pearce is very frightened,' she said. 'I want to talk to him again.'

Lloyd, she thought to herself, had that look on his face; he had some way-out idea that he wouldn't voice in front of Allison. In fact, she had the uneasy feeling that no one was voicing their ideas. Drake had changed his mind about something that he was going to say; Lloyd clearly had some notion about Lennie, and Jonathan Austin still bothered her. But rather like judging a talent contest, everyone's second choice won. Gordon Pearce.

Allison left, and Bob Sandwell went back to Malworth to see what forensics were making of Lennie's studio and the Beales' flat. Drake went back to the paperwork that so mystified Lloyd.

'If you could give me a moment, Inspector,' said Lloyd, as the other two left the room.

The door closed, and she waited expectantly.

'I thought maybe we could have some lunch,' he said.

She looked at the clock.

'That's what Mr Pearce will be doing, so you might as well,' Lloyd said.

'Well – just something in the canteen,' she said. 'I want to get on, Lloyd.'

91

'The canteen it is.' He frowned. 'You look very tired,' he said.

If one more person told her she looked tired, she would scream. 'Haven't you been home at all?' he asked.

'No, I have not.'

'I got a couple of hours this morning,' he said.

'Oh, good.'

Someone came in then, with a message to the effect that Mrs Austin's car had been discovered where it had been left, at the rear of the garage. Drake was dispatched by Lloyd to find out what he could.

'So Austin lied,' said Judy.

'Not necessarily,' said Lloyd. 'She might have been at the studio, remember. The light was on.'

'Why would she put the car back in the garage?' asked Judy.

'If she was meeting this man, and didn't want her husband to know she'd had the car,' he said, with a shrug.

'That's not like her,' Judy said.

'Well – whatever. I'm not sure that Mrs Austin's car has got much to do with it,' he said.

'Oh, come on, Lloyd,' said Judy. 'Austin says it wasn't there. Either he's lying – in which case, why? – or it wasn't, which is a bit strange. And the wedding ring suggests that the ashtray was in his house while he and his wife were having some sort of row, doesn't it?'

Lloyd nodded. 'All true,' he said. 'And I did find Mr Austin a little too eager for us to find out what his wife was doing. Perhaps he knew only too well.'

Judy frowned. He was still being mysterious, but she knew him well enough by now not to try to press him. 'Let's go to lunch,' she said, with a sigh.

They walked through unfamiliar corridors to the old building, and joined the short queue in the canteen, chose their meals, and sat down.

Lloyd picked up his knife and fork. 'If this is difficult for you, Allison could put someone else on to it,' he said.

'What? Eating my lunch?'

He smiled. 'All right. But I insist that you do not think about any of this until you've finished eating.'

'Then you'd better talk to me.'

'What about?'

92

'Go on with your romantic story of how come your grandmother was French,' she said. She was still none too sure that any of it was true. 'Even if it's just another cock and bull story,' she added, to be on the safe side.

'*Une histoire de le coq et le taureau? Mais, non.*' Lloyd shook his head sadly. 'This shows a distressing lack of trust,' he said.

'*Taureau-merde,*' said Judy.

Lloyd laughed. 'Do you want to hear the story or not?' he asked.

'Yes.' Judy tried to assess the expression on his face, but it was useless. He could make anyone believe or disbelieve anything.

'It's true. Ring my father if you don't believe me. Ask him.'

'Go on, then.'

'Right.' He smiled. 'Granda Pritchard – Ifor Pritchard, to give him his full name – was in France during the First World War. He met my grandmother – who was eighteen . . . '

'I heard a siren,' said Judy.

Lloyd blinked. 'What?'

'I heard a siren. A police siren, when Jonathan Austin was talking to me on the phone.'

'You're supposed to be listening to my story!'

'I *was*. It was when you said war. I always think of sirens when anyone says war. And that reminded me. I think we should check who was on an emergency call up there, don't you?'

'I'll get Drake to check,' he said, wearily. 'That should suit you. He's obsessive, too.'

'I'm not obsessive,' she said. 'But I didn't like that call.'

'No,' said Lloyd. 'I know. I'm not overlooking that, believe me.'

Judy smiled and yawned at the same time. It wasn't easy.

'Why haven't you had any sleep?' Lloyd demanded.

'Freddie had gone home, hadn't he? And he didn't get to the Beales' flat until five o'clock in the morning. Meanwhile, I've got people looking for Beale when all the time he's in my own station. There's efficiency for you. Freddie didn't leave until seven – two hours non-stop graveyard humour – by which time the neighbours were stirring, so I had to talk to them.' She looked at her watch.

'You should go home,' said Lloyd.

'I am going home – to fetch my car. Then I'm going back to talk to Pearce again. And Beale – I want to know what the trouble was about at the Riverside.'

93

'I'd rather like to see Mr Beale,' said Lloyd. 'I'll meet you at Andwell House.'

Beale was her business, she thought. But she didn't say it.

'Fine,' she said, with a short sigh. 'See you later.'

It made no sense. Pauline let soapy water trickle through her fingers, the bath water growing cool as she lay back, and tried to believe what Gordon had told her. Lennie was dead, he had said. Jonathan had rung him. He had rung Pauline first, looking for Gordon; getting a call from him had been the first shock.

He had just said he would ring Gordon at work. Gordon said that Jonathan just hadn't known how to tell her; he always felt more comfortable talking to another man about things he found difficult.

Dead. Lively, talkative, talented Lennie. Dead. She would never see her again. Never feel a little wistful at the ease with which she collected suitors; never feel a little resentful of her hold over Gordon's emotions. Though that seemed to have gone, last night.

She shivered. Because the water was getting cold. She would have to get out of the bath. The news had stunned her; everything she did was something she had to plan for. Stand up, step out of the bath. Remove the plug. Dry yourself.

It *had* gone.

She hadn't discussed it with her doctor, but she had had her own opinion about her lack of desire for Gordon. Perhaps, she had thought, she had simply grown tired of being a substitute. Perhaps, though she had accepted it, she had really objected to Gordon's emotional commitment to another woman. And once he had fulfilled his role as mate, once she was pregnant, she no longer wanted to perform this understudy role. Because she had something else in her life now, and she didn't need to keep offering Gordon something that he only wanted because he couldn't have Lennie. Because she loved Gordon, and she wanted him to love her.

Last night, when he had come in, she had known that that barrier had gone. Lennie's spell, cast unwittingly, had been broken. And Lennie was dead. But Gordon couldn't have known that.

She shivered again, and dressed quickly. Coincidence, she told

94

herself. Nothing but coincidence. Or maybe even, if the attraction was strong enough, a sixth sense, telling Gordon that he was free. She went into the bedroom, and put on a dash of make-up. She would be consulting palmists and tarot cards next, she told herself crossly. It was a coincidence. Gordon didn't know that she was dead, paranormally or otherwise. All that had happened was that seeing him, hurt and angry, needing her more than he needed some idealised fantasy of Lennie, had brought back her normal feelings towards him, that was all it was.

But it still didn't make sense. It was Lennie. It was Lennie. Jonathan, she had thought. It couldn't have been Lennie, because she wasn't *there*. But it had been. She had been there, and she was dead, and none of it made any sense.

But whether or not it made sense to Pauline, the police would be bound to connect the two deaths, and Gordon wasn't strong enough to withstand the sort of intense questioning that that would entail. If only he hadn't woken up.

The entry phone buzzed, making her jump. She touched the switch, and sighed. 'Come in,' she said, pressing the button to admit DI Hill. Gordon wasn't strong enough, but she was.

She unlocked the door, and a few moments later, DI Hill was knocking and coming in.

'Sorry to bother you again, Mrs Pearce. Is Mr Pearce here?'

'Did you know Lennie Austin was dead when you came here this morning?' demanded Pauline, not answering her question. Attack is the best method of defence, she told herself.

'Yes, I did.'

'We were friends of hers!'

'So was I, Mrs Pearce. That's the only reason I knew. I didn't know officially, and I was asked not to make it known to you.'

'Lennie's officially dead, though!'

'Yes.'

She looked at DI Hill. About her own age, well-dressed. Attractive. A little weary-looking now, not surprisingly. Lennie's friends were a complete cross-section of society, from unemployable layabouts to captains of industry. They rarely met one another; on the few occasions they did, they rarely got along. But Pauline could imagine getting along with DI Hill.

'Please sit down,' she said. 'I'm sorry. I've only just heard, and I'm still trying to take it in. What should I call you?' she asked, as she sat down.

'My name's Judy Hill,' she said. 'Judy, Mrs Hill, Inspector – take your pick.'

'So why are you here again?'

'I had hoped to have a word with your husband,' she said, taking out her notebook.

'He's gone into work. There was a fire there.'

'Yes.'

'Why did you want to see Gordon?'

But the inspector chose to ignore her question this time. 'I know you said that you didn't know much about your neighbours,' she said. 'But I wondered if you knew anything about the comings and goings from the Beales' flat. Men, in particular.'

'I never saw Jonathan there, if that's what you want to know,' said Pauline. 'I think he's only been here once, when Gordon brought him to see the flat.'

'So you've heard the rumours?'

'Oh, yes.'

'Do you think they're true?'

'Probably. I can imagine Rosemary Beale might be the kind of woman Jonathan could relax with. Let his hair down a bit.'

'And Mrs Austin wasn't?'

'No. She was too complex. Too much her own woman. She married Jonathan for his money, nothing else.' She saw Judy Hill's face, and smiled. 'I'm not being bitchy,' she said. 'It's just a fact. I liked Lennie. I liked her very much. I've known her a long time. And Jonathan just isn't her kind of man. They were putting on an act for each other. I can believe that Rosemary Beale would offer him a release from that.'

'You seem certain that he was seeing her.'

Pauline raised her eyebrows. 'Gordon found them in the cab of one of the artics,' she said. 'Would you believe they said they were seeing if the design could be improved?'

The inspector smiled a little sadly as she wrote something in her notebook. 'Do you think Mrs Austin knew?' she asked.

'No. Why do you call her Mrs Austin all the time? I thought you were a friend of hers?'

'I was. That's why I call her Mrs Austin.' She looked upset.

Pauline flushed slightly. 'Sorry. I don't understand,' she said. 'What *happened* to Lennie?'

'Someone hit her.'

With the ashtray that was thought to have been used in the commission of another crime, thought Pauline.

'Strictly speaking, my investigation is into Mrs Beale's death. We have to have separate investigations, even if we think there is a connection between the two. Which we do.'

They would. But there couldn't be. It wasn't *possible*. But it was; it had happened.

'Was Mrs Beale involved with any other men, do you know?'

Pauline shook her head. 'I wouldn't know. People who know her better always give you that impression of her.'

'And Mrs Austin?'

'Oh, well – Lennie had men coming out of her ears until she married Jonathan. But she didn't see any of them afterwards, I'm sure of that.'

'There is talk of an old boyfriend turning up,' said Judy. 'And she was seen with a man last night, at about ten past eleven.'

Pauline stiffened. 'Lennie?' she said.

'Mrs Pearce, do you have any idea who that might have been? Had she spoken to you about anyone?'

My God, that had never entered her head. The studio. Was *that* what was going on when she heard the noise? Lennie with *Steve*?

'Mrs Pearce?'

'Pauline. Please call me Pauline.'

'She did mention someone, didn't she?'

She had said she wouldn't dream of having anything to do with him again. He was worthless. Immoral. Unreliable. Protesting too much? And it *still* didn't make sense.

'I thought that wasn't your investigation?'

'I'm not sure where my investigation leaves off and the other one begins,' she said. 'Did she mention someone to you?'

She couldn't tell her about the studio. Not after lying this morning. But she had to tell her what she knew.

'Yes. Someone she used to live with.'

'Live with?'

'Oh, not officially. I mean, I don't think you'll find him on any electoral register or anything. But he was with her at her old flat.'

'Do you know this man?'

'I never met him. She knew I wouldn't approve.'

'Oh?'

'You'll have him on your files, I expect. He went to prison. Drugs. Something to do with drugs.' She got up and went to the window, without thinking. Looking down at the studio. She had been wrong about that. But she couldn't sort it out. 'About a year after that she married Jonathan.'

'You haven't given me his name, Mrs Pearce.'

'Steve,' she said. 'Steve Tasker. He's just got out – about two months ago. He'd seen her a couple of times. Talked to her, chatted her up. She told me she wasn't going to have anything to do with him. He'd messed her life up once, and he wasn't doing it again. She wouldn't do that to Jonathan.'

Now that she was repeating Lennie's words, she realised what an argument Lennie had been having with herself. But she hadn't at the time.

The inspector stood up. 'Thank you, Mrs Pearce,' she said. 'You've been more than helpful.' She turned to go and turned back. 'What *aren't* you telling me, Mrs Pearce?' she asked.

Pauline had stood up to see the inspector to the door; she sank down again. She had pulled that trick this morning. Made it look as though she was going, let the tension drain away, then asked what she really wanted to know.

'Mrs Pearce?' Inspector Hill sat down too, and looked as though she would stay all day, wait all day, for an answer.

Pauline closed her eyes. 'I heard something,' she said. 'A noise – something. Someone . . . ' She tried to hear it again. 'Someone trying the studio door,' she said. 'Or going in there.'

'What time was this?'

She was writing it all down. She had written everything down. Now she would write down a lie. Another lie.

'About quarter of an hour before Gordon came in.'

'So that would be . . . around ten o'clock?'

Pauline looked her straight in the eye. 'Yes,' she said. Greenwich Mean Time, she told herself. It wasn't a lie. Not really.

The inspector closed the notebook. 'Why didn't you tell me that this morning?' she asked.

'Because . . . ' Pauline looked away, now that she was telling

the truth. 'Because until you reminded me about Steve, I thought
– I thought Gordon had been with her.'

Last night, she had thought all sorts of things. Gordon had
been with her, and she had repulsed him. Or she hadn't, and
it hadn't lived up to the fantasy. All sorts of reasons for his no
longer being under her spell.

There was a silence. A terrible, eloquent silence that she was
going to have to fill by explaining to this woman why she thought
Gordon might have been with her.

But Lennie was dead, and it still made no sense.

Steve lay on the bed, thinking about Lennie, and waiting for
Rosemary to ring. But she didn't appear to require his services
today, and Mrs Sweeney didn't run to showers, cold or otherwise,
so he just had to live with the ache. Rosemary would have been
better than nothing. He had realised as dawn had crept into his
room that he couldn't go to Lennie's studio with Rosemary's flat
right above it; he had tried to ring her, but a man had answered,
and he had hung up.

Normally, he'd be glad of a day off from Rosemary. The
job side was boring. Rosemary checked up on Beale's various
enterprises, and those left in charge of them. He would sit outside
the seedy establishments, waiting for her, and watch the doormen
check the customers' club cards, almost openly contemptuous of
them. He would see them come – on foot, always on foot, with
their cars parked anonymously in one of the city centre car parks
– looking round furtively in case someone they knew spotted them.
But if they had seen anyone they knew, he would have been going
about the same shady business, so what the hell?

He smiled. Rosemary had read that someone was trying to
get it legalised. She had had a fit. Legalising it wouldn't make it
acceptable. She preferred things the way they were. Her husband
ran clubs, where the tired businessman could relax to live enter-
tainment, and buy expensive drinks. If people suspected that the
rooms upstairs were probably put to some less visible use, that was
fine. But they mustn't *know*. That way she could keep what she
imagined was her respectability. Massage parlours, health studios,
gymnasia – she was very strong on the Latin plural, was Rosemary
– even a nice detached house in suburbia. Business ventures. Beale
(Brothels) Ltd just wasn't the sort of business venture she wanted

people to know for a fact she was in. She saw it as a social service. They just wanted their ration of whatever sort of thing they went in for, then it would be back on with their business suits and off home to the missus, who presumably did not go in for that sort of thing.

The other side of it, keeping Rosemary amused, was, if anything, becoming even more boring. And last night, with Lennie, he had discovered his self-respect. He was no better than the girls Beale employed to revive the tired businessmen; it wasn't even his prowess that qualified him for the job. It was simply his proximity, and the trust that Beale had mistakenly placed in him.

He thumbed through a girlie magazine as he lay there, waiting for the phone to ring, but the combination of thoughts of Lennie and the girlie magazine weren't doing him any good; he pulled a car magazine over the table and looked through it instead.

Now, he could imagine driving one of them. Unlike one of Rosemary's newly acquired lorries. He'd got an HGV licence; he had mistakenly told her that, and he was being targeted. She would make sure he got the job.

Thanks a lot, Rosemary. Driving through every kind of weather condition imaginable from foggy motorways to desert roads, harried by customs officials and police, never getting any sleep. Trying to communicate with excitable foreigners who couldn't speak English. Rolling on and off ferries, getting stuck in jams at the docks. Getting caught in some outlandish country and hanged.

Still it paid well. Very well. He might even be able to afford one of these jobs. Right now, he couldn't afford a fifteen-year-old van. He'd looked at it the other day; almost bought it. But he'd have had to have got the money from Rosemary, so he didn't. Was that the beginning of his self-respect asserting itself?

He wished he had bought it now. If he'd had a van last night, Lennie would have been in it with him, no danger.

He looked up as a shadow fell across the window, blocking the bright sunlight, and heard the doorbell ring. He didn't pay much attention, until Mrs Sweeney knocked on his door.

'Mr Tasker,' she said, disapproval in every line of her face, 'there are two gentlemen to see you.'

* * *

100

The problem was, as ever, producing enough evidence to give the lie to what had been said. On his way to Malworth, Lloyd perceived that one possibility was to arrange for a reconstruction of Mrs Beale's walk home from the Riverside Inn. He stopped at the traffic lights just before the bridge, waiting to turn left along the river bank, and looked at the terrain.

There would have been some traffic and people on the main road which crossed the river; the pub had been about to close. But her walk alongside the river would have been lonely. A children's play park on one side, closed shops and studios on the other. Someone sitting unnecessarily at the traffic lights, with nothing to do but wait for them to change, may have seen something: a car, another pedestrian, someone hanging about by the river, or in the phone-box. A reconstruction, a woman walking home alone late in the evening, might just jog someone's memory.

He pulled into the parking area, and pressed the pad beneath Beale's name.

'Yes?'

'DCI Lloyd, Stansfield, Mr Beale.' Lloyd looked into the eye of the camera. 'I'm enquiring into the death of Mrs Leonora Austin.'

'What's that got to do with me?'

'Nothing, sir. But we think she may have been in this area last night.'

'*My* wife was killed last night!'

Lloyd nodded. 'I know, sir. I'm very sorry. We think the two deaths may be connected.'

It was odd, talking to a camera and having a wall answer. Lloyd rather wished he had been around in the days of hansom cabs and Sherlock Holmes. He could have called the Great Detective in, and gone to the south of France with Judy while he sorted it all out.

'Come up,' said Beale, and the door buzzed, and clicked. The Great Detective would have had his work cut out getting into the bloody building, never mind sorting out what had gone on there.

Lloyd saw what Judy meant about the reception area. She was sitting amid the potted plants, smoking.

'I've been listening to some interesting stuff,' she said.

Lloyd listened to a potted version of her talk with Mrs Pearce. 'Shouldn't be too hard to trace Tasker,' he said. 'It wasn't just hash if he's only just got out of prison.'

'I've put the wheels in motion,' she said. 'But I don't have a description – it might not have been him that Mickey saw.'

'Surely Mrs Pearce knows what he looks like?'

'She says she never met him. I think she's quite strait-laced – she said Mrs Austin knew that she wouldn't have approved. She stopped seeing her altogether after Tasker was arrested, because every time she went round there there was a police car outside, and she didn't want to get involved in that sort of thing.' She smiled tiredly. 'She's involved with us now whether she likes it or not,' she said.

'So she disapproved of Mrs Austin's lifestyle,' said Lloyd thoughtfully. 'But her husband fancied her?'

'So she says. He'd known her practically all her life – Pauline thinks he only married her because Jonathan Austin got the first prize.'

Lloyd sat down. 'That doesn't sound too healthy,' he said.

'No. And I'm not keen on Tasker, despite his pedigree.'

'Why not? Drake's had him down for it all along. If it was him he saw, which seems more than likely.'

'She had a lot of ex-boyfriends,' warned Judy.

'Did you ever meet any of them?'

'No,' said Judy. 'She was just about to marry Austin when I met her.' She paused. 'I'm not happy about him, Lloyd.'

'I know. But why would he tell us he'd gone for the car if he hadn't?'

'Because he didn't want us to know where he had been, and that was the first thing that came into his head. He said it wasn't there because he had to explain why he hadn't got it.'

He looked at her. 'You *are* getting like him,' he said.

'Who?'

'Drake. He's an obsessive. He's at the station now, going through piles of paperwork instead of going home.'

'I'm *not* obsessed! Neither is he – he's just trying to make up for showing himself up last night. And he likes his desk to be as clear as possible. You're the only one who likes it piled to the sky with rubbish.'

'He might not be obsessive, but you are. Don't keep trying

to prove it was Austin, Judy. It may have been, but it may not. You'll blind yourself to all the other possibilities.'

'Jonathan Austin is deadly serious, Lloyd. He intends to be prime minister one day, believe me he does. Anything that endangers that could make him angry enough – frightened enough – to kill without even thinking of the consequences.'

Lloyd stood up. 'Speculation isn't a very good idea,' he said, seeing the irritation sweeping over Judy's face as he spoke. 'Let's go and talk to Beale.'

Frank Beale was waiting at the door; Lloyd apologised for the delay.

'Do you feel up to a few questions?' Judy asked.

'I don't see how I can help you,' he said. 'I was in the police station all night.'

'Yes, I know, Mr Beale,' said Judy. 'I'd like to know about the trouble at the Riverside Inn.'

His mouth opened. 'My wife gets murdered, and you want to ask me about a bit of a fight in a pub?' he said.

'No, Mr Beale. I want to know if your wife was involved in that in any way.'

He subsided. 'Oh, I see. Yes – well, not involved in the fight, you understand. But someone insulted her.'

'The man who was taken into custody with you?'

'Yes.'

'What did he say?'

'Something about her playing a home match. Meaning she was in the habit of playing away from home,' said Beale.

'Was she?'

Beale's face grew dark. 'No,' he said.

'And what did your wife do when you made a fuss?'

'She said she was going home. Legged it.'

'What time was this?'

'Just after the police arrived, I think. Once she knew they were involved, anyway.'

He hardly seemed to have noticed that she had been strangled; Lloyd took the same hard line.

'We've heard rumours, Mr Beale,' he said. 'About your wife and Jonathan Austin.'

Beale began to cry. There was something much worse about someone like him giving in to his emotions; someone who was always in control, someone who regarded violence as a way of life, a means to an end, or just retribution. But the violence that had taken his wife wasn't the same. It was more bewildering, more horrifying than it would have been to someone else, and Lloyd wanted to shoot himself. Judy, he rather gathered from the look he got, would have cheerfully saved him the trouble.

When he had got himself under control, he wiped the tears. 'My wife was not having an affair,' he said defiantly, and blew his nose.

Too defiantly; Judy didn't want Malworth to become too exciting, Lloyd was sure. If Beale suspected someone, they had better find out who that was.

'Mr Beale,' said Judy. 'When I came here last night, the front door was open. It looked closed, but it just opened when I touched it. Would you know why it was like that?'

He nodded. 'Rosemary took my keys,' he said. 'Quick as a flash, as soon as the cops were called.' He smiled. 'Just as well she didn't go in for picking pockets,' he said. 'I didn't know what she was doing, but I realised later when your colleagues tried to have me breathalysed.'

So, thought Lloyd, Rosemary Beale had foiled the police once again in a last act of defiance. That would give Beale some quiet satisfaction, once the shock had worn off.

'She didn't know what time they'd let me go, and my door key is on the same ring. So she would leave the door on the latch. But these doors only close if you lock them.' Tears were back in his eyes. 'She'd be going to go to bed,' he said. 'She was annoyed with me for starting trouble. She'd think she was safe,' he said, his voice anguished. 'This bloody place – you pay the earth for all the security, and then someone can just walk in and— ' He stood up, and turned away from them.

The security certainly didn't seem to have helped. They had looked at the videos automatically made when the cameras switched on; the visitors to the flats had been few, and were accounted for. The cameras came on when the door phone was answered, so residents using their cards were not on video. The conclusion was that someone with a card had murdered Rosemary Beale, or that she had brought someone home with her, which seemed unlikely, in the circumstances.

'Why didn't she take the car?' asked Judy.

'She doesn't drive. I got her a driver to take her round the clubs.'

Judy tried not to look irritated as Lloyd interrupted her. 'Could I have the driver's name, Mr Beale?'

Beale frowned. 'What for?'

'We need to know of anyone who had contact with your wife.'

'He just drove her around. Tasker. Steve Tasker.'

Lloyd and Judy manfully avoided looking at one another; it took Lloyd a moment to ask his next question.

'Do you have an address?'

'Not on me,' said Beale. 'It's at the office.'

It was clearly untrue; Lloyd just had to hope that they had got to Tasker first.

'Mr Beale,' said Lloyd, 'you gave Mrs Austin a lift home yesterday evening.'

Beale turned. 'Yeah.' He sighed. 'I was downstairs in her studio. She had to get home in a hurry. I said I'd run her there.'

'And you drove the car yourself?'

'Yes.' Beale frowned. 'Tasker only drove my wife,' he said. 'If that's what you're getting at.'

'What time did you and Mrs Beale go out last night?' asked Judy.

He shrugged. 'Late. Half nine, something like that.'

'Would you have noticed if there had been someone in Mrs Austin's studio?'

'The light was on. I just thought she had left it on, though, earlier. I remember her putting it on just before we left. It got dark because of the rain. There didn't seem to be anyone in there.'

'You didn't see anyone . . . hanging round, maybe?'

He shook his head.

'And you didn't try the studio door, did you?'

'No.'

They took their leave of Mr Beale, and neither of them spoke until the lift doors were firmly closed.

'Well,' Lloyd said. 'The outsider's coming up on the rails.'

'Fast,' said Judy. 'Tasker. Does the name mean anything to you?'

'No,' said Lloyd. 'But the court case was probably just before I came back to Stansfield. Jack'll know.' He sighed. 'Let's hope we've traced him – I'd rather we got to him before Beale does.'

Outside, he surveyed the car park. 'Where's your car?' he asked.

'Parked halfway down the road,' she said. 'Some woman went on at me about it being in her husband's space and he'd be home from work soon.'

'Leave it there,' he said. 'You shouldn't be driving. You're too tired.'

She didn't argue; she just got in to his car like a lamb. She must be tired.

'So what now?' she asked.

'I'm taking you home.'

'What about Tasker?'

Lloyd sighed deeply. 'Judy, there are a great many more people working on this besides you and me.'

'Shouldn't that be you and I?'

'No, it should not. And you have got them looking for Tasker. They will have traced him, and spoken to him.'

'They won't have arrested him,' she said. 'And Beale's after him.'

'You couldn't arrest him either. All we know is that he works for Beale and he may or may not be the man Drake saw.'

'If he is,' Judy said slowly, 'then he couldn't have had anything to do with Mrs Beale's murder. He was in Stansfield at ten past eleven.'

Lloyd raised his eyebrows. 'True,' he said. 'Curiouser and curiouser. And another good reason for your not arresting him.'

'He's not the one I want to arrest.'

Lloyd sighed again, more deeply, more loudly.

'Mrs Austin probably wasn't at the studio at all,' said Judy.

'Drake's wife left him,' Lloyd said, conversationally.

'What?'

'Drake's wife left him,' he repeated. 'Because when he decided to knuckle down and get on with it, she never saw him. She left him. He became obsessed.'

Judy nodded. 'And you're going to leave me, are you?'

'If you don't take time off.' He smiled.

'And if she wasn't in the studio, then Austin *is* lying about the car.'

Lloyd shook his head. 'Totally illogical,' he said. 'Not like you at all. Now – I'm banning work as a topic. Shall I tell you more about my French grandmother?'

106

'What was her name?' asked Judy suddenly, clearly determined to catch him out if he was making it up.

'Françoise,' he said immediately.

Judy's eyebrows rose slightly.

Lloyd lifted his shoulders in a Gallic shrug as he turned on to the Stansfield Road. 'That was her name,' he said. 'I'm sorry her parents couldn't be more imaginative.'

'I almost believe you,' said Judy. 'You would have been more imaginative.'

He smiled again. 'Ifor met Françoise. He was twenty-two, she was eighteen, and they fell in love.'

'Mm,' she said, leaning back in the seat, getting herself more comfortable.

'No emotions stirring there? Beautiful young girl in the devastated battlefield that had once been the peaceful countryside surrounding her home . . .'

The evening sun flickered through the branches of the trees, dazzling him; he pulled down the visor.

'Lonely, frightened young man hurtled into trench warfare by English generals who had apparently thought that a good cavalry charge would sort the Hun out by Christmas? Meeting fleetingly in a brief, uncomfortable respite from the fighting . . .'

He glanced at her, and smiled. She was sound asleep.

Five

His landlady had thought it was the police. He had thought it was the police, until he had seen them, and then it had been too late. The police, he could have coped with. But the two gentlemen were anything but; if the police were sometimes less than gentle, that was nothing compared to Beale's heavies. Not that they'd done anything yet except bundle him into Beale's Rolls and drive him to the middle of nowhere, but that was quite enough to be going on with. They hadn't spoken, not even to indicate who had sent them. Steve hardly needed telling. They just sat there, large, brainless, young and fit, one either side of him, in the back of Beale's Rolls, hidden from view behind a derelict barn. Twenty, thirty years younger than him.

The man who had driven them was just as silent and still, but looked as though he had more brain than brawn. He was older, but Steve was still giving him fifteen years at least. Beale wouldn't entrust the driving of the Rolls to just anyone. Not even Steve had been allowed behind the wheel. And Steve had been a trusted employee; a good enough driver to have Rosemary's safety in his hands, and sharp enough to be given the job of spotting any irregularities in her behaviour.

Had been a trusted employee. He swallowed nervously. He hadn't expected retribution to be this swift. Or this savage, come to that. He had only told Lennie, for God's sake. But she must have used the weapon he had given her, and it was now being pointed at him.

Despite the warmth of the day, Steve was cold. Tell me, he had shouted, tell me what's happening. But one of them told him to shut up, and he had thought it best to do as he was told.

He had never been convinced that it would work, though Rosemary had been. But only with Austin's co-operation, of course. And thanks to Steve's sudden rush of self-respect to the blood, that co-operation had presumably been withdrawn now that Lennie knew. But there was nothing Austin could *do* to Rosemary. He'd never go to the police.

So why, he thought, as they sat in the silent, invisible car, why was he here? He had thought at worst that he was risking his favoured position with Rosemary – something that his irritating self-respect had decided wasn't worth hanging on to anyway. He wouldn't be sharing the fortune, other than as a well-paid lorry driver and a diversion for Rosemary. The Beales would be the ones with the villa in Spain; he'd be the one running the risks. That was what he had thought he was giving up, if Lennie said anything. He had thought that Rosemary would keep him out of it as far as her husband was concerned.

But she hadn't, evidently, or he wouldn't be here. If he had thought for one moment that he was risking life and limb, then his self-respect would have taken a back seat, and Lennie's would have been nowhere. Austin could have gone on using her, Rosemary could have gone on using him. Everyone would have been happy.

And he wouldn't be sitting in a Rolls-Royce full of hired muscle just itching to bring him to book.

'What?' said Beale.

'I want to let Gordon Pearce have his pick of them,' said Jonathan. 'But I thought you might want to have the rest.'

Beale looked round at the canvases adorning the walls of the studio, his mouth slightly open.

'There are more in the back,' said Jonathan. 'And some watercolours. She did them for a while. And old sketches, that sort of thing. I thought you might be interested in them.'

Beale turned back to him, frowning. 'I thought *I* was a business-man,' he said.

Jonathan wasn't really listening; he was searching his pockets for his lighter, the unlit cigarette between his lips. 'Sorry?' he said, finding it.

'That's why you asked me down here?' Beale shook his head. 'You don't let the grass grow, do you? Maybe you should hang on to them,' he added sarcastically. 'They'll be worth more in a couple of years.'

Jonathan took the cigarette from his mouth. 'Oh, no,' he said. 'I'm not selling them. I just want you to have them.' He lit the cigarette. 'After Gordon's taken what he wants,' he said.

'You're *giving* them away?'

'Yes.'

'To *me*?'

Jonathan expelled smoke.

'You shouldn't really do that in here,' said Beale.

'Oh.' Jonathan looked at the cigarette. No, no, he shouldn't. Leonora had always said . . .

'One won't matter,' Beale said.

Beale's disapproval at Jonathan's apparent cashing in on his wife's death was having to adjust to sheer astonishment; he had covered his confusion with the diversion. Jonathan had known he would get this reaction; it hadn't occurred to him that anyone would assume he was selling the work.

'Why?' Beale asked.

'You like them.'

Beale smiled, still bewildered. 'Sure,' he said.

'You understand art.'

'Yes,' he said, with a slightly bitter laugh. 'Frankie Beale, wide boy. I'm not supposed to know a Degas from a day centre, right? But I do.' He smiled again. 'Art galleries were the only places you could go for nothing,' he said. 'When I was a kid, I spent hours . . . ' He stopped, slightly embarrassed.

'So I want you to have them,' said Jonathan.

'I think,' said Beale, 'that we should discuss this in my flat. Don't you?'

No. No, Jonathan didn't want to do anything of the sort. But he nodded, and the two men left the studio, and went round to the flat entrance.

Jonathan still had his cigarette as they waited for the lift; he looked round for somewhere to put it, and found himself staring at an ashtray exactly like the one Sergeant Drake had described.

'Where did that come from?' he demanded.

'Eh?' Beale turned and looked round the foyer. 'What?' he said.

'That! That ashtray.'

Beale frowned. 'Oh – yes. Pearce put it there. People were putting ash in the potted plants.'

Jonathan let his cigarette slip into it, and stepped into the lift. His mind was barely aware of what Beale was saying as he followed him in to the flat.

'Can I offer you a drink, Mr Austin?' said Beale. 'I've got whisky, gin, vodka, brandy . . . '

'Vodka and tonic, if that's . . . ' He needed a drink.

'One VAT.'

He poured Jonathan's vodka and a gin and tonic for himself. 'My wife,' he said, handing Jonathan his drink and indicating the leather sofa, 'wanted respectability, Mr Austin.'

Jonathan didn't know what to say to that; he sipped his drink.

'You,' he said. 'You were respectability.'

Was he? Jonathan felt that she could have chosen a better role model.

'I said, "Rosemary, what the hell do you know about engineering?" "Nothing," she says. "I don't need to know about engineering. I know about business." She wanted to work, see, Mr Austin. Me – I'm semi-retired. I'm coming up for my pension. But she was just in her mid-forties. She wanted to keep busy. That's why I got her to go round the clubs, keep an eye on things. She was sharp, Rosemary. Clever. But she didn't really want to do that.' He shook his head. 'I don't understand why she chose your outfit, though.'

Jonathan thought saying nothing had to be the wisest course. She had told him Beale didn't know, and thank God, she had been speaking the truth.

'The police say it's because she was having an affair with you. It would explain things.'

Jonathan shook his head, still not speaking.

'It doesn't surprise you, though?'

'No,' he said. 'I've been made aware of the rumours.'

Beale sat down. 'And there's no truth in them?'

'None,' said Jonathan.

Beale drank, then stared into his glass. 'How do rumours like that start?' he asked.

'Who knows?' Jonathan sighed. 'She was taking a more active role in the business – we were working together a great deal. And your wife was very . . . ' Obvious was the word that came to mind. Jonathan searched for another one. ' . . . glamorous,' he said, after a moment. 'I've got a reputation as a bit of a

111

stick-in-the-mud,' he said. 'I think it appealed to them to think that there might be something going on.'

Beale nodded slowly. 'But there wasn't,' he said.

'No, I assure you, there wasn't.'

'Were you happily married, Mr Austin?'

The question took Jonathan by surprise. 'We had our ups and downs,' he said.

'Yeah. So did we. Rosemary and me. She . . . she has been known to . . . stray, now and then. But I loved her.'

'Mr Beale – my relationship with your wife was purely a business one,' he said. If he said it often enough, he might believe him.

'So why the paintings?'

'I don't understand them. I shouldn't have them. You encouraged her, you bought a lot of her work – you were going to commission work. I want you to have them. That's all.'

Beale looked back into his drink. 'Look,' he said, 'you don't want the paintings because they remind you of your wife, and all that. But you and I – we're in a peculiar position. I mean, I don't know why in God's name it's happened, but we've both lost . . . ' He cleared his throat. 'We've both lost our wives. Without any warning, without any reason that I can see – so I know how you're feeling.'

Jonathan nodded briefly. He had known this would be difficult. He just hoped it wasn't going to be impossible. Big, flash Frank Beale had gone; this man was devastated. Frank Beale didn't know, couldn't know how he felt. No one knew. All he could do was try to hold himself together, knowing that his only aim was to survive it all, maybe even realise his ambition . . . no. His dream. His dream of being in a position to make the world a different place because of his existence in it.

Once, it had been a worthy ambition. But it had become tarnished over the years of seeking nomination, of finding success there only to fail at the polls, because no one wanted to risk him in a reasonably safe seat. Stansfield were prepared to, but only after he had told them that he would be marrying Leonora. One hypocrisy. Taking that flat was another. Show the voters of Stansfield that you are just like them. You understand their problems. Their problems are your problems. Bullshit. He had never known money worries; his father had made money, and

112

Jonathan had gone on making it. Once his voters had safely elected him, he would move to the country house he had already earmarked, for which he had already had interior designs roughed out, which was already landscaped on paper, on which he had already paid out thirty thousand pounds to the old lady to make sure he got it.

He could see his dream now for what it was, now that it might be snatched from him. But it didn't stop him wanting to survive it all. And here was Beale, who cocked a snook at the very laws that he wanted to frame, giving him a lesson in morality.

'You see,' Beale said, 'your wife was good. I mean – people were sitting up and taking notice. I mean – you don't get headlines in the *Sun* for it, but . . . well, I think her work will get quite valuable. It's unusual for a woman to be that highly thought of . . . I'm not talking Van Gogh, you understand, but you still don't want to give it away.'

Jonathan swallowed, and took a deep draw on the cigarette. 'I have money, Mr Beale,' he said. 'I don't need her paintings to make money for me.' He looked up for the first time. 'And neither do you,' he said. 'I don't mean you shouldn't sell them – they're yours. But you'll enjoy them. I can't.'

Beale half shrugged. 'Well,' he said. 'I'll give you a cooling-off period. How's that? You can change your mind.'

Jonathan shook his head.

'Have another drink,' said Beale, taking his still half-full glass.

The CID room was empty, which was how Mickey Drake liked it. Not that he didn't get on with his colleagues; he did. But on this nice, sunny evening the air in the room was fresh, and he could hear the birds call to one another as they settled for the night. If his colleagues were all here, the room would be smoky and stale in no time. He smiled at himself. He was a reformed smoker at heart, but he tried not to behave like one.

He had found Tasker's digs, but his landlady said he had gone out. Mickey had left a car there waiting for his return, and had rung Lloyd to let him know. Tasker, Lloyd informed him, had been chauffeuring Mrs Beale about. Mickey hadn't known that; he would have to give it some thought.

He read the fire officer's report on Austin-Pearce; entry had been effected through a window in a gents' lavatory. The fire had been started under the wooden cabinet; no traces of inflammable spirit being used. Just combustible materials. The cabinet had resisted the flames; it was the plastic floor-covering which had given off smoke and fumes and set the sprinklers off. Hence the limited damage. Forensic were going over Mrs Beale's office. He thought about Pearce, and about what Inspector Hill had said about his wife, and the more he thought, the more likely it seemed. He ought to talk to Lloyd first, though, so there wasn't much more he could do there, and he might as well try to catch up on his other work.

The chief inspector had said that an incident room was being set up, and that the routine stuff would still be there when they got back to normal duties, but Mickey couldn't really relax knowing that there was a backlog. So, he thought, if he got rid of as much of it as he could, he would feel more able to address himself to the puzzle of the fire.

DI Hill seemed to favour Austin himself, but Mickey wasn't so sure. And he had considerable doubt about Austin's supposed affair with Rosemary Beale, however much evidence there was to support the rumours. He didn't know what sort of reception he'd get from the chief inspector if he voiced his beliefs about Austin, but he would have to tell him. He had made a fool of himself in front of Lloyd, and he didn't want to do it again; he just hoped he was right. He glanced at the door of Lloyd's office, and tried to imagine himself in that position. He wasn't all that far off it: inspector next year, providing Lloyd gave him a good report. A year's probation as inspector, and if he made the grade, the rank would be confirmed, and he would aim for chief inspector next. Two, three years at the most. And yet, for the moment, there seemed a world of difference. Sergeants were other ranks.

It was good in Stansfield, though. A good atmosphere. He hadn't wanted to come back, and he hadn't really wanted to be at Divisional HQ; he had thought it would be likely to stifle personal initiative. But Lloyd left you to get on with whatever you were doing; it was teamwork, of course – Mickey didn't want to be a maverick, anyway – but he felt reasonably confident that Lloyd would notice if his contribution made a difference.

But for the moment, he was trying to clear his desk. He sighed, and picked up the file he had begun on the improbable

114

crack factory at the Mitchell Estate flats. No point in carrying on with that. He would tell Lloyd he had been spotted.

'Stephen Arthur Tasker,' boomed a voice, and Mickey leapt to his feet as the chief inspector came into the room, a file in one hand, and a plastic holder with machine cups of coffee in it in the other.

'Sorry,' he said. 'Didn't mean to make you jump.'

Not much. Mickey sat down again.

'One sugar, no milk – that's right, isn't it?' Lloyd removed a cup from the plastic holder and put it on the desk.

'Yes, sir,' said Mickey, putting it on to the drip mat. 'Thank you.'

Lloyd removed his own coffee from the holder, and perched on the edge of Mickey's desk. 'Stephen Arthur Tasker, age forty-nine.' He frowned. 'I was expecting him to be a younger man,' he said. 'Anyway,' he said, blowing away the steam that rose in waves from the cup, and taking a sip, 'what can you tell me about him?'

Mickey felt flustered. He had been expecting this ever since he'd been given Tasker's name by Judy, but it didn't make it any easier. 'Not much more than it says in there,' he said, indicating the file in Lloyd's hand.

Lloyd drank some more coffee.

Mickey looked at him, fascinated by how he could possibly be drinking the boiling liquid in his cup. He felt a little like a rabbit with a snake.

'You were the arresting officer,' Lloyd said.

Oh, God. This man would think he was a congenital idiot, and no wonder. Mickey opened the file, and nodded. 'Yes, sir,' he said. 'I got the credit,' he said. 'But only because he ran and I played rugby.'

'You caught him before he could ditch the stuff,' said Lloyd.

Mickey smiled. They had been watching the place all night before they had raided it; he had been determined to make it worth while. 'Got him with a flying tackle,' he said. 'But there were dozens of us on the raid – I didn't really think of it as my arrest.' He was talking to delay the inevitable, but it didn't delay it long.

'Was that who you saw with Mrs Austin?'

Mickey sighed, resigned to the fact that Lloyd would now be

considering having him assigned to directing traffic. 'It must have been, sir,' he said. 'The description tallies. But it never crossed my mind. I thought he was still inside. He got three years plus he had to serve two years of a suspended sentence. I didn't think he would be out yet.'

'Well he is. And he isn't at his digs.'

'Do you think he's done a runner, sir?'

Lloyd shrugged. 'Either that or Beale got to him before we did,' he said.

Mickey's heart landed fairly and squarely somewhere in his stomach. 'Oh, God,' he said. 'Sorry, sir. Do you think he's our man?'

Lloyd shrugged. 'Not unless he had transport, and as far as we know, he didn't. So if you did see him with Mrs Austin, he didn't kill Mrs Beale. I'm banking on Beale realising that. He'd be no good to us in a coma.'

'No, sir.'

'What else do you remember?' asked Lloyd.

'About the raid? It was a studio flat in Queens Estate – it was rented by the girl he was living with.'

'Do you remember her name?'

'No, sir,' said Mickey. 'I don't know if I ever knew it. I was a probationer – I had nothing to do with the planning. I was just muscle.'

'Hovak,' said Lloyd. 'Leonora Hovak.'

Mickey wanted to die.

Lloyd got up, and pulled a chair across, sitting down, leaning his arms on the desk. 'Look,' he said. 'No one could deny that you work hard.' He glanced at the clock. 'It's late, you were on duty half the night, you had a very traumatic experience, and you're still here, working. Your paperwork's always bang up to date – you do all your follow-up calls, you're prepared to go out on a limb if you think it's worth it – like your intelligence on the crack factory.'

Christ. He couldn't tell him about that, not now. Not yet. Perhaps he could redeem himself somehow first.

'But CID work is about more than that,' said Lloyd. He smiled. 'You have the opposite problem to most people,' he said. 'I usually have to tell detectives that it isn't any more glamorous than being a bobby. It's a damn sight more boring, most of the

116

time. Hours spent on the phone. Days spent watching nothing happen. Months of work going down the drain in two minutes because you can't prove what you know. Writing endless reports and statements. But that's the bit you're good at. It's the one per cent inspiration that you're missing out on – and you needn't.'

Mickey couldn't look at him as he listened to the lecture. He kept his eyes on the desk, on the Mitchell Estate file that he wished he could just tear up.

'Everything you learn about a villain is worth knowing. Who his women are, who his contacts are – which addresses he can use if he's in a jam. I keep a lot of it in my head – Inspector Hill writes it all down. Connections. You have to be able to make connections. This woman's called Leonora – that woman was called Leonora. It's not a very usual name . . . then, Tasker would have crossed your mind. You'd have checked, discovered that he'd been released from prison two months ago . . . and *we*'d have him, not Beale.'

'Sir,' muttered Mickey.

Lloyd sat back. 'Tell me something,' he said.

Mickey lifted his eyes.

'I've been looking at your file,' said Lloyd. 'You started off eager and keen – you were always in the thick of it, you were being noticed by the top brass – well, your flying tackle on Tasker is a case in point. Then after that you . . . well – you'd have been kicked out if it hadn't been for your previous record. You missed more than one court appearance, you were persistently late on duty, you were worse than useless. What happened?'

Mickey sighed. 'I gave up smoking, sir,' he said, with a hint of hostility.

Lloyd looked angry for a second, then relaxed a little. 'It had that bad an effect on you?' he asked.

'I gave up because someone asked me to,' said Mickey, with a reluctant little sigh. This was always going to happen. Getting the man's back up wasn't sensible; besides which, he was trying to understand. He lifted his head. 'I got involved with a woman,' he said defiantly. 'My marriage broke up. It didn't officially break up until a couple of years ago, but that's when it really happened. I couldn't keep my mind on work.'

Lloyd nodded. And understood. Mickey had heard bits and

pieces about Lloyd and Judy Hill; their story wasn't dissimilar, and Lloyd wasn't pretending that it was.

'You're not the first that that's happened to,' he said sympathetically. 'You were married then? How old were you? Twenty-one?'

'Yes. I'd been married two years by then, sir. I was . . . well, just going through the motions at work.'

'Not even that on occasion,' said Lloyd. 'And it's cost us valuable time now, hasn't it? And what I have to know is – are you about to go walkabout again? Because if you are, you're no good to me.'

'No, sir,' said Mickey vehemently. 'There's no one. Not now. Nothing. I just want to do my job.'

Lloyd nodded briefly. 'Then I suggest you start doing it,' he said.

Mickey had no option; if he didn't give Lloyd some reason to respect his ability now, then he was done for. He could be wrong; but he couldn't let that bother him. Judy said he had a sharp tongue, but he gave credit where it was due. He just had to keep his fingers crossed that he was right, and that some credit would come his way before the man gave up on him altogether.

'Sir,' he said.

'Yes, Sergeant.'

'Mrs Beale's office,' he said. 'Someone had helped themselves to her whisky. She doesn't use the office much, and the other bottles were unopened.'

Lloyd nodded.

'I think we can discount vandals,' said Mickey. 'Whoever it was used a glass.'

'I'll have you know we've got very cultured vandals in Stansfield,' said Lloyd, just as though the previous conversation hadn't taken place. 'Wouldn't dream of drinking out of the bottle.'

Mickey smiled. Lloyd confused him, but it was a joke, so he would smile. 'Thing is, sir – if whoever it was had a drink beforehand – Dutch courage, or whatever – the natural thing to do would be to use the drinks cupboard to stand the bottle on. And it would just have got left there when he tried to set it alight.' He could feel Lloyd listening to his every word, and suddenly it didn't seem so intriguing. It seemed of monumental unimportance. He took a deep breath. 'But it wasn't there,' he said. 'It had been dropped, by the look of it. Near the door. Bottle and glass.'

118

Lloyd looked a little uncertain, and Mickey licked his lips nervously.

'I think he was drinking *after* he'd started the fire, sir,' he said. 'I think he was in there, and dropped the bottle and the glass when the smoke got to him.'

Lloyd frowned a little. 'He?'

'The fumes, sir. They'd make him seem drunk – especially if he had had some alcohol. But he'd be functioning quite clearly. He might well be able to drive home, and pass out for a few minutes when he stopped being active. I – I asked the fire officer. He says it's quite possible. He'd be a bit light-headed for a few hours, he said. Those were Pearce's symptoms, sir.'

'And memory loss?'

'I asked if it could result in memory problems, and he said it had never done that to any of his firemen. Sir.'

Lloyd raised an eyebrow.

'You see, sir, I can't see *when* Pearce got drunk. Austin says he had two at his house, and his wife says he came straight home. Inspector Hill didn't believe her, and I think he was . . . '

He tailed off.

'I think I'll have a word with Mr Pearce,' said Lloyd. And smiled.

Mickey could only hope that this bit of inspiration wasn't misplaced.

'Jonathan?'

Pauline was startled to find Jonathan Austin at her door. In these security-conscious flats, only neighbours could call unannounced.

'I was in Frank Beale's flat,' he said, by way of explanation. 'I thought I should— '

'Come in,' she said, belatedly remembering her manners. She didn't know what to say to him. 'How are you?' she asked.

'Oh, you know.' He sat down. 'Frank Beale's taking it very hard.'

'Is he?' Rosemary had seen him, once or twice. He didn't seem much different. Still going about his dubious business, as far as she could see. A couple of unpleasant-looking characters had called on him in the afternoon.

119

'Yes,' said Jonathan. 'He tries to look as though nothing's happened, but it's hurt him.'

Pauline raised a disbelieving eyebrow. 'I wouldn't put it past him to have done it himself,' she said.

Jonathan looked up at her. 'Are the police saying that?' he asked.

'How should I know?' She sat down. 'All I know is that they think Lennie died because she heard what was happening to Rosemary Beale.' Too late, she remembered that she was speaking to Lennie's husband. It was strange; she had never really been able to think of Jonathan like that. 'Sorry,' she said.

'It's all right,' he said. 'She is dead; not talking about it won't alter it.' He sighed. 'They've told me their theory too,' he said.

Pauline caught the nuance. 'You don't think that's what happened?' she asked.

'I don't know. I've told them about an ex-boyfriend of hers that turned up. She was frightened of him, I know she was.'

Pauline hadn't got that impression, not at all.

'Do they have any . . . theories about Mrs Beale?' he asked, getting her back on to what he regarded as safer ground, presumably. But that rather depended on where you were standing, and it didn't seem like safer ground to Pauline.

'They seem to be suspicious of Gordon,' she said icily.

'They asked me what our meeting had been about. I had to tell them.'

'And did you tell them about you and Rosemary Beale?' she asked.

'That isn't true! Gordon's wrong about that.'

'It isn't just Gordon.'

'Then everyone's wrong. And they asked me about it, if you must know. Pauline, I didn't come in here for a row – is Gordon here?'

'He's asleep.'

'This early?'

In Jonathan's world, you did everything at properly arranged times. You ate, you slept, you worked, you – She remembered with a stab of conscience what she had heard that night. Was Lennie working? Was she with this man? She had lied about when it was.

'He's hardly had any sleep,' she said.

He wasn't asleep. He was lying, fully clothed, on the bed, staring at the ceiling. He wouldn't talk to her, wouldn't come out.

'I just wanted to tell him that he can forget about that agreement,' said Jonathan. 'The board won't be making any changes now.'

Pauline frowned a little. 'You've spoken to them?' she asked.

He shook his head. 'I don't have to. It was Mrs Beale who wanted the changes made, and that doesn't apply any more.'

Pauline felt her legs grow suddenly weak. 'Did Gordon know that?' she asked.

'He guessed that Mrs Beale was the moving light,' said Jonathan. 'The other thing is just Leonora's paintings. I want him to have whatever he'd like. I'm giving the others away. Tell Gordon I'll . . . I'll talk to him later,' he said.

He showed himself out.

Slowly, Pauline got up. Her legs shook as she made her way out of the room, into the bedroom, where Gordon still lay, staring at the ceiling.

'We have to be very certain of what we are going to tell the police,' she said. 'They'll be back, I know they will.'

He looked at her, then got off the bed. 'I'm going to the pub,' he said. 'Tell them what you like.'

Lloyd was right.

Judy put her hand over her eyes to block out the daylight that still streamed through the closed curtains, and tried to sleep, but the image of Lennie's body stayed in her mind, as it had all day. She shouldn't have gone. Lloyd was right; Lloyd was always right. It must be boring.

But she had had to go. After that call, what else could she do? She had been so sure that he was lying, that something terrible had happened. A hollowness in his tone, a falseness; she had heard it hundreds of times in a career which consisted for the most part of talking to liars. She had heard it then. She had heard lies, and something else. Something worse.

And then the call about Lennie. How could she have stayed at home? So, she told herself sternly, if you felt you had to see for yourself, then stop trying to forget what you saw. Face it.

Think about it. If you think about it, you won't keep dreaming about it.

The flat, the door standing open. Looking into the room first; seeing Lennie lying there. Then making herself go in. Lennie, lying in amongst upturned furniture. Broken, smashed chairs. A bookcase with splintered shelves. All around, the destruction which had terrified the neighbour. One blow had killed her; one blow to the temple, apparently from behind. She would have turned away from the inevitable, Freddie had said. But perhaps she didn't even see it. Perhaps he had hit her from behind. One blow, and she was dead.

Then what? Why would he ring her, of all people? If he'd just killed his wife, perhaps his powers of reasoning were at a low ebb. He'd killed her, and he wanted to get away with it. Ring a convenient police officer and say she isn't home and he's worried. But no . . . the phone wouldn't work.

But she had heard a police siren. And he could have phoned on his way back to the house, from the telephone-box at the post office. But then, he would have had to ring *before* he killed her, and the desperate reason didn't apply. Then it would have been premeditated, thought out, if only for a few moments. He wouldn't have been ringing her in the after-shock of having committed murder. And why make it sound as though he was at home, when that would be the last place . . .

She opened her eyes. What? What was she thinking about? She had lost the place somehow. Jonathan Austin. That's what she was thinking about. Austin, and his phoney call. A phoney-call. From a phoney-box at the post office.

She opened her eyes again. Phoney. Who's a phoney? Austin. Austin is a phoney, living in a flat that Lloyd could afford, when he was rolling in it. Rolling. Rolling in it.

Judy, he's rolling in it.

She opened her eyes. Who said that? Lennie. Lennie said it. She'd met her just before she got married. And she wasn't like a bride-to-be, and didn't pretend to be. *Judy, he's rolling in it*. Not a figure of speech; not just by comparison to someone trying to live on the proceeds of her art. Really rolling in it. Chief Superintendent Allison said so. Rolling in it . . . rolling in money. Lying on the floor, banknotes scattered round like so many tissues, killed by a single . . .

She opened her eyes. No, not Jonathan. Jonathan wasn't killed. He was rolling in it, but Lennie was killed. He wasn't the victim – what made her think he was the victim? He was a phoney. A rich phoney. Lennie was the victim. Lennie, killed by a single blow. She shouldn't have gone in. She shouldn't have gone to see for herself. She shouldn't . . . Lloyd was right.

She closed her eyes; sleep finally came, but it was fitful and troubled, and her racing, confused thoughts were overtaken by the dreams that she had tried and failed to chase away.

'Mind if I join you?'

Gordon looked up to see one of the policemen who had been at the Beales' flat that morning.

'Your wife said I'd find you here.'

Gordon sighed, and looked out at the river, sparkling this evening in the setting summer sun. 'I had hoped to have a quiet pint,' he said.

'Oh, I'm very quiet. Lloyd – DCI, Stansfield Division.' He held out his hand; reluctantly, Gordon shook it.

Just let me do the talking. So why send the chief inspector to the pub? How was she going to do the talking at the pub? Tell them what you like, he had said. So, she had told them he was at the pub. Fair enough. He didn't know how long he could go on with it.

It was your idea, Gordon, old son. You said you were drunk. Couldn't remember a thing. Long before Pauline did her Joan Crawford bit.

It wasn't Joan Crawford, it was Barbara Stanwyck. I remember now. And that was when I thought it was my problem. She made it hers, and I don't know how she knows . . .

'You were very unhappy when you left Mr Austin last night, weren't you, Mr Pearce?'

'I know,' Gordon said carefully, 'what Austin's told you. I know how it must sound. But I wasn't angry with her – I didn't *mean* those things. I know, I know . . . ' He let out a long sigh. 'I know how it must sound. I . . . I blamed her for what was happening.'

He looked out at the sunshine; people strolled along the river bank, families out on the fine evening, enjoying the weather. He and Pauline could have had that. Late. Late parents. He'd thought that might be a good thing, might keep them young. But now that might not be possible.

'Who are we talking about, Mr Pearce?'

'Mrs Austin,' he said. 'I loved her, Mr Lloyd. I've known her all her life, and I loved her. I trusted her, and it seemed to me that my trust had been betrayed. But it hadn't. She wasn't to know he would take up with a woman like that.'

Lloyd took another apparently unconcerned sip of beer. 'Austin didn't tell us any of that,' he said, removing a fleck of foam from the corner of his mouth.

Oh. That hadn't occurred to him.

'Were you with Mrs Austin last night?'

'Only until she went out.'

'When was that?'

Gordon shrugged a little. 'Nine – something like that.'

'And you didn't see her again?'

Gordon shook his head.

Nice one, Gordon. Pauline got you into this.

No, she didn't. I got myself into it.

She's the one insisting you got home at quarter past ten, Gordon, old son.

Lloyd finished his drink. 'Shall we take a walk by the river?' he asked, as the pub began to fill.

The sun hung low in an impossibly blue sky; pink-tinged children who would be crying when the sheets touched the tender skin still laughed, and chased the ducks along the bank. An old man in a white linen jacket and a panama hat took a stroll. People wore bright colours and extravagant clothing; next week, they might be switching on their central heating and taking their dark suits back out of the wardrobe.

'We believe that Mrs Austin was a witness. She heard what happened to Mrs Beale. Oh, it wouldn't have meant anything at the time, but we think the killer believed she would be able to identify him once she knew.' He looked over the river to the flats on the other side. 'And what Mr Austin did tell us was that you were very resentful of Mrs Beale.'

Gordon closed his eyes. 'Yes,' he said.

'You were asked to come in to let us have your fingerprints for elimination – have you done that yet, Mr Pearce?'

Gordon shook his head.

'Why not?'

He didn't speak.

'Is it because we'll find your prints on the bottle in Mrs Beale's office?'

Gordon sat down on a bench, and stared at the river.

'You did set fire to her office, didn't you, Mr Pearce? You were affected by the smoke when your wife saw you.'

'Yes.'

Lloyd sat down beside him. 'Why?' he asked.

Gordon looked at him. 'I tried to set fire to the whole place,' he said. 'I wanted it to go up in flames, with me in it. But then I couldn't breathe, and I wanted to breathe. I didn't want to die. So I ran. I left the way I had got in, and came home. Pauline thought I was drunk, and I let her think that.'

'When did you go to the factory?'

Oh God, trying to remember all the lies was almost impossible. 'When I left Austin.'

'So you got there just after ten?'

Gordon nodded, his eyes closed.

'Your wife says you were home by ten fifteen.'

He shook his head. 'About an hour later,' he said.

'Did you see anything, or hear anything when you got home?'

He shook his head again. 'I wasn't taking any notice of anything. I could hardly see. And I thought I had burned the place down,' he said. 'Pauline smelt burning – I thought that that was the factory ablaze. But it was just me. My clothes. I couldn't believe it when the factory manager rang me and said would I be coming in because there had been a bit of a fire.' He looked at Lloyd, and smiled. 'A bit of a fire. That's about my range,' he said. 'A bit of a fire. Pauline lied for me.' He swallowed. 'Will I go to prison?'

'Not up to me,' said Lloyd. 'But I doubt it.' He got up. 'We will want to talk to your wife again,' he said. 'She did hear something, Mr Pearce. About twenty minutes before you came in, she said. Only she led us to believe that that made it ten o'clock – I presume that we're an hour out.'

Gordon covered his face with his hands. 'Please don't blame Pauline,' he said.

'I'm a bit stuck for anyone else to blame,' Lloyd said sharply. 'I'm sorry to have spoiled your quiet pint.'

125

And he walked quickly away, down the path, across to the
pub. In the fading light, Gordon could see him get into his car,
and drive out on to the main road.

He walked slowly back to the bridge. Over, turn right, past
Lennie's studio.

He told Pauline.

'Did you tell him anything else?' she demanded.

*No, you didn't tell him anything else, did you, Gordon? No
mention of Pauline being out in the middle of the night.*

'No. He doesn't think anything terrible will happen to me.'
He held Pauline close to him. 'He's angry with you,' he said.

'Good,' she said, and kissed him. And went on kissing him.

*You'd think she was never going to see you again, Gordon, old
son. What does she mean, good? What's good about a policeman
on the warpath?*

'We'll be all right,' she said. 'You'll see. You've still got
your business – you've still got me. It'll be all right – we'll
be all right.' Kissing him, unbuttoning his shirt, wanting him.
They were making love, and still all she said was that it would
be all right.

It wouldn't. He couldn't let her do this to herself, to the baby.

*You know what you have to do, don't you, Gordon? Old
son. You know what you have to do.*

They hadn't found Tasker. Beale had declared himself quite
unable to account for his disappearance, and allowed the officers
the run of the flat, eager to help. Beale's Rolls had gone from the
Riverside Inn car park; Beale had sent someone to fetch it from
the Riverside Inn – you couldn't trust anyone these days. Taken
it for a spin, more than likely.

Lloyd had given vent to his feelings on Drake when Jack
Woodford had come to tell him.

'I think you're being a bit hard on the lad,' Jack had said.

'Why? He should have recognised him, Jack. And we'd have
had him. Now Beale's got him holed up somewhere, and God
knows why.'

Jack had raised an eyebrow. 'It was a long time ago, Lloyd,'
he said. 'He tackled him in the dark, over three years ago. Are
you so sure you would have recognised him?'

Lloyd had refused to give in that easily. 'He gave evidence in court, didn't he?' he had said. 'Or was that one of the times he didn't turn up?'

Jack had smiled at that. 'No,' he had said patiently, 'he gave evidence. Go home, Lloyd. You're tired and irritable. Your mum would be putting you to bed.'

Lloyd had started to feel uncomfortable. Jack Woodford could get away with making him feel like a petulant schoolboy, because he knew him so well. But Tasker had disappeared, all the same, and he still hadn't given up.

'Leonora,' he had said. 'How many women do you know called Leonora?'

'Be fair,' Jack had said. 'I was here then too, and I didn't make the connection.'

'You weren't involved in the arrest.'

'Neither was she! She had nothing to do with it – we knew that all along. We weren't bothered about her. She was in bed with him when the lads went in, or her name wouldn't even be on the file.'

Lloyd had grunted. He had gone off at half-cock again, and he had been told off again, in Jack's inimitable style. But Judy would never have missed the connection, he had thought, as he had packed up his briefcase, and wished he was still working with her.

'And he was right about Pearce,' Jack had added, as Lloyd had left the station.

Yes, thought Lloyd as he drove home, he had been. He ought to tell him it was good work.

He let himself into the flat, being as quiet as he could; he couldn't be bothered cooking, and made himself a sand-wich, going into the sitting-room, putting on the TV. He kept the sound low, though there was usually no need; Judy could sleep through anything. There was a film on that he wanted to see . . . well, wanted was pitching it a bit strongly. He doubted very much that he would enjoy it, but watch it he would, because if he didn't they might stop showing anything but *Superman* and old Bond movies.

And they were showing it in letterbox format – another good reason to watch. Prove to them that the nation doesn't really switch off in droves if the screen is blank top and bottom, or the image is black and white, or there are subtitles or four-letter words. What the viewer doesn't like, he said, in the letter that he was eternally composing to various TV magazines, is a camera endlessly panning and scanning, or seeing half of a two-shot, and hearing the other half. What it doesn't like is bad dubbing by bad actors, all the major characters apparently having severe speech defects, and some minor characters disappearing altogether. Not to mention key scenes in the plot, on occasion. That, sir, is what the viewer doesn't like. Yours faithfully . . .

He had always had a problem with letters. He couldn't sign formal letters 'Lloyd', as though he was a peer of the realm. He had to use his initial, and he didn't like even doing that. D. It looked so innocuous, but he knew what it stood for.

That, however, wasn't the reason that he had never actually written his letter about films on television. No – the reason he had never actually written was that he was on the side of the angels, and everyone knew that it was only the people who did apparently like see-sawing through edited Technicolor films dubbed into inoffensive English who wrote and complained every time they saw anything other than that.

The result was that no one knew that he was sitting here watching a small strip of screen on which a film that he wasn't enjoying was playing, so it was all a waste of time, really.

It was just after nine thirty when the bedroom door opened, and Judy appeared, blinking a little, her hair tousled.

'Hello, love. I thought you'd sleep right through.'

'I keep having dreams,' she said, joining him on the sofa as he put his arm round her.

'It'll pass,' he said, kissing her on the top of her head.

'I don't think she was in her studio,' said Judy.

Lloyd groaned. 'Judy – this way lies a nervous breakdown,' he said gently.

'Beale said he thinks she just left the light on when she closed up.'

He sighed. 'Austin thought she was in the studio,' he said. 'Pauline Pearce *heard* someone at the studio door. Her car was gone from the garage . . . that adds up to her being in the studio, Judy.'

'Why would she put the car back in the garage?'

'To cover her tracks with Tasker,' he said. He was sure that was why, wherever she went with him. He didn't think the car had anything to do with it. The wedding ring, though . . .

'She didn't. Austin's lying. He's a fraud – look what Allison said about this house he's going to buy once he's safely elected.'

'Judy,' he said sternly, 'you have no proof that he's lying. You don't like the man – all right, I probably wouldn't care for him either. But that doesn't mean he . . . ' He shook his head. 'He doesn't strike me as someone who has murdered his wife,' he said.

'Well, that's all right. Not guilty because he doesn't strike Chief Inspector Lloyd as someone who has murdered his wife.'

'I'm not the jury! I'm the investigating officer. And the investigating officer doesn't usually have to live with a friend of the victim, who received a phone-call that bothered her just before the victim died!' He realised what he was doing as soon as the words were spoken and he saw Judy's reaction. 'I'm sorry,' he said, hugging her. 'I'm sorry. But it isn't easy, Judy. So far, we have no proof that Austin did anything other than what he says he did, and I can't do anything until we have.'

'I know. I'm sorry.' She squeezed his hand. 'Maybe it's time to take my mind off it again.'

He knew that that was just what he should be doing, but he broke his own rule. 'What did bother you about Austin's call?' he asked her.

Judy thought for a moment. 'The fact that he called at all, for one thing,' she said. 'We just didn't have that sort of friendship. It was a couples thing, really. I mean, I met her in the first place, but in a way, it was Michael and Jonathan who were friends. They had quite a lot in common.'

Lloyd smiled at the implicit criticism.

'And I'm sure he was lying.'

Lloyd nodded. 'But that could have been for a dozen reasons,' he said. 'He didn't want to admit they'd had a row, or he really thought she was with Tasker, and didn't want you to know that – any number of reasons.'

'And there was something about the way he spoke that just seemed . . . ' She looked him straight in the eye. 'It gave me the willies,' she said.

It had. He knew that. But . . . He smiled. 'Guilty,' he said. 'By reason of giving Detective Inspector Hill the willies.'

'I'm sorry,' she said, and smiled a little. 'And I'm spoiling your film.'

Lloyd looked at the screen. 'No,' he said. 'No, the director spoiled it. You're not spoiling anything.'

She sniffed a little, and wiped what might have been a tear. 'Why are you watching it?' she asked.

'It's one of those films you're supposed to have seen,' said Lloyd. 'I avoided it when it was in the cinema, but I've got no excuse now.'

She smiled. 'There isn't a law,' she said.

'Oh, yes there is. It's a natural law. Like having to finish a book once you've started it. You have to see any film which is described as a milestone, a classic, a departure, a *tour de force*, or seminal.'

'Which is this?'

'Seminal.'

'What does that mean?'

'It's the seed from which a hundred other films just like it spring up.'

'Do you have to see the hundred other films?'

'Yes. Because some of them may be merely derivative.'

She laughed. 'You're mad,' she said. 'You can put it off. I won't tell anyone.'

He felt quite guilty as he picked up the remote control, and pushed the little red button to remove the band of light from the screen. And quite relieved. It had another hour and a half to go, and he wasn't going to have to sit through it after all.

'Gordon Pearce is into old films,' she said. 'He's got loads of videos.'

Lloyd smiled. Funny. People with whom you might have become friends turned into suspects. Not people any more.

She looked up at him, her eyes dark and worried. 'I think . . . ' she began, then looked down again. 'I think I just want it to be Jonathan who killed her,' she said.

Lloyd frowned. 'What do you mean?'

'You know I saw her yesterday,' she said. 'She was really going places, Lloyd. People were getting very interested – she was getting commissions. Not just Frank Beale – other people. People who didn't live upstairs from her, she said.' Judy smiled a little. 'Someone was coming from one of the Sundays to interview

130

her. She was excited, and — ' She pursed her lips together. 'And someone just wiped all that out.'

There wasn't much Lloyd could say. He held her tighter.

'And why?' she went on. 'Because they thought she could *identify* them? I'd much rather it was Jonathan. I'd much rather it was anger, or jealousy, or hate, even. I – I don't want her to have died because someone found it inconvenient for her to go on living.'

Lloyd sighed. There were no words of comfort. The best thing he could do for the people Mrs Austin had left behind was to prove who had killed her, and soon.

And his best hope of a witness was at Frank Beale's mercy, or he was a Dutchman.

Six

He was in Beale's flat, the heavies either side of him, Beale in front of him.

'Forgive the cloak and dagger stuff,' said Beale. 'But I couldn't accommodate you until now. The police are taking a great deal of interest in the area. In this flat in particular.' He sipped a cup of coffee.

Oh, God. What had Austin told them? Still – he couldn't prove any of it. Not unless Rosemary had done something stupid, and she had never done anything stupid in her life.

'You know what happened last night, Stevie?'

Stevie was bad.

'My wife was murdered. Here, in this flat.'

Jesus Christ. Steve couldn't take it in. 'Rosemary?' he said, after a moment.

'Rosemary.'

'Dead?' Steve still couldn't believe what he was hearing.

'That is the usual result of murder,' said Beale.

'My God.'

Beale nodded. 'The police say my wife was playing around.'

Steve shook his head.

'I employed you to keep an eye on her, Stevie.'

'I did. She wasn't, Frankie.'

Beale looked at his men again, and again they moved almost imperceptibly closer.

'The police say it was Austin.'

Under other circumstances, Steve might have found that amusing. 'No,' he said. 'No one. There was no one. I'd have told you.'

'Maybe.' But Beale hadn't yet given whatever invisible signal it was for his minders to stand easy. He walked away, his back to

132

Steve. 'Did my wife pay you to keep quiet about it?' he asked.
'No!'

Beale turned. 'That's a very expensive watch, Stevie,' he
said. 'You didn't buy that on what I pay you.'

Steve looked at the watch. 'I nicked it,' he lied.

'Has Austin paid you to keep your mouth shut?'

'No! He hasn't, Frank, I swear it. Nothing was going on with
her and Austin!' His position was very slightly better than he had
thought it would be. His protests had the merit of being true.

Beale came close to him. 'If you're lying . . . ' he said, and
there was no need to finish the sentence.

'I'm not,' said Steve, desperately. 'She wasn't seeing Austin,
I swear.'

'Why would the police say she was?'

'They're just trying to rattle you, you know that!' Steve said.
'They'll think you— ' He broke off. 'They always go for the
husband, don't they?' he said.

'Not in this case,' said Beale. 'They know where I was, Stevie.
But they are very interested in you,' he added.

Steve's mind raced. 'I had nothing to do with it!' he shouted.

'Then you'll be able to tell me where you were last night,'
said Beale. 'At eleven o'clock.'

Steve glanced nervously at the two men, who had moved
simultaneously very slightly closer to him. 'I was in Stansfield,'
he said.

'Witnesses?' asked Beale.

'Yes. You know her. Lennie Austin – she has the studio
downstairs from here.'

Beale stepped back, his eyes widening very slightly; the two men
on either side of Steve tensed up. Beale wasn't happy, and they
knew that. You'd swear they were almost human, thought Steve.

'You know Mrs Austin, do you, Stevie?'

'Yes,' he said, and looked nervously at the two men, to
see if that offended them. It didn't seem to.

'When did you see her last?'

'Last night,' said Steve, a touch desperately. 'That's what
I'm telling you. I was with her last night – and if you think
I had anything to do with killing Rosemary, just ask her.'

Beale shook his head very slowly. 'You don't know, do you?'
he said. 'You really don't know.'

'Know what? What the hell's going on?' Panic, bewilderment, a strange sense of unreality all served to make Steve forget, just for a moment, his unhappy position. 'You drag me here, no one tells me why – you're saying the cops are after . . . '

But Beale was nodding to the men, and Steve's voice trailed away.

But they left. They just nodded back, and left the room. At last, Steve relaxed. Relaxed was what he told himself he had done. The truth was that he had almost fainted with sheer relief.

'You were with Mrs Austin,' Beale said. 'Last night.'

'Yes.'

'Then I have some bad news for you, Stevie.'

Jonathan let the phone ring. Someone had to answer it. And, eventually, someone did.

'Gordon Pearce.'

There had to be an explanation. Jonathan looked at the painting on the hotel wall, at the blue and green swirls of colour. It looked as though the colours had met and mingled on the canvas by their own free will; they hadn't. Leonora had painted that effect.

'It's Jonathan.'

'Oh – hello. Is everything all right?'

Not really, Gordon, he thought. Not really.

'Sorry, I'm being . . . ' Gordon foundered. 'You know what I mean.'

'I called to see you, but you were asleep,' said Jonathan.

'Yes. Pauline told me about the paintings. Thank you.'

'Tell me about the ashtray, Gordon,' Jonathan said, his voice sounding desperate despite his efforts to control it. He looked at the painting again.

'Ashtray?' Gordon's voice sounded uncomprehending.

'The ashtray you put in the entrance at your flats.'

There was a silence. Then: 'Oh, that. What about it?'

What about it. Perhaps he shouldn't be doing this.

'Was there another one?'

'What?'

Oh, please Gordon, please. 'Were there two?'

Another silence.

'Gordon, were there originally two ashtrays?'

134

'Yes. Why do you want to know?'

'That's . . . what he used,' he said.

'What?'

Jonathan took the receiver from his ear, and closed his eyes. For God's sake, Gordon, take some time off from being obtuse, please. He addressed himself to the phone once more. 'To *kill* her,' he said through his teeth.

The silence went on so long that he thought Gordon had just gone off and left the phone. When he did speak, it was as though he had been pre-programmed.

'They were both there on Monday,' he said.

'Right,' he said, and hung up.

They still hadn't found this man she had been with. He tried to remember everything she had said. They had to find him. They had to.

'He's been here a couple of times. I thought you ought to know.'

'I'd rather your ex-boyfriends didn't make waves, Leonora. Try to make him understand.'

'I have, Jonathan. And I've told him I know his boss. He'll be in trouble if he comes here again – he knows that. I just don't think he'll care.'

Jonathan sat down on the bed, and lit a cigarette as he thought. That was what she had said. It didn't narrow the field as much as it might; he and Leonora knew a lot of Stansfield's employers. But every little helped.

God, it was the middle of the night. No wonder Gordon had taken so long answering the phone. Day and night had merged into one in Jonathan's life; nothing seemed real, nothing seemed logical.

He lay back, and looked at the painting. The sergeant was right. It was restful. He'd tell the police in the morning.

Pale light could just be seen behind the curtains as Judy opened her eyes. Sunrise. A new day, and she was happy. She often woke, these days, to that knowledge. It was a bit like thinking you were late for work and remembering it was your day off.

She turned to look at Lloyd, and found him looking at her. 'I thought you were asleep,' she said, and moved closer to him.

He kissed her on the temple.

135

'I wish I had run away with you when I was twenty,' she said. 'Instead of wasting all that time.'

Lloyd shook his head. 'Time's never wasted,' he said. 'It shapes us. Makes us who we are.'

She had to have had the years of nothingness first, or she wouldn't have been able to appreciate the happiness. He was probably right. Lloyd was always right. Annoying, but right.

'Funny thing,' he said. 'I was lecturing young Drake, and asking him why he had nearly got himself thrown out – and he said he'd got involved with another woman. Broke up his marriage. Not then and there, he said. But that was what did it.'

She smiled. 'Not an obsession about work, then,' she said.

Lloyd laughed. 'No. A woman – what else? But it took the wind out of my sails a bit. It struck a little too close to home.'

'Are you mixing metaphors?' she asked sternly.

'Yes. I mix a mean metaphor. Do you want one?'

She turned so that she could see him properly. 'Did I break up your marriage?' She said the words quickly before she could change her mind. She had done everything she could think of not to break up his marriage. She had married Michael, for God's sake. She had moved away.

Lloyd touched her hair. 'Oh, love – that wasn't what I meant,' he said. 'No. But . . . the situation did, I suppose. But we had started having problems before I ever met you.' He sighed. 'If you'd been a different person, we might have had an affair, and that would have been that. But you weren't, and we didn't, and it wasn't. I fell in love with you. I knew what I wanted, and I knew I hadn't got it.'

'So I did break up your marriage.'

'It fell apart, Judy. Or if someone did break it, then it was me. It certainly wasn't you.' He smiled suddenly. 'Do you remember Sergeant Compton's leaving do?' he asked.

Judy nodded, smiling too.

'I've never tried so hard to get someone into bed with me,' he said. 'Before or since.'

'I'm sorry,' she said, kissing him. 'I should have said yes. Broken up your marriage the easy way, and saved everyone a lot of bother.'

'No,' he said. 'That wouldn't have been you. I fell in love with someone who kept saying, "No, Lloyd, it's wrong." '

136

She lay back. The sun, peeping through the crack in the curtains, had started to travel along the wall. 'But I don't think that's why I said no,' she told him honestly. 'I think I was just scared to start something I couldn't control.'

He sat up a little, and looked down at her. 'But that is you,' he said. 'That's what I mean.'

She smiled up at him. 'When you're not being a male chauvinist pig,' she said, 'or unbearably patronising, or absolutely infuriating, sometimes I think you're the nicest man in the world.' She kissed him. 'And sometimes I know you are,' she added.

'Oh, you'll make me blush.'

'Fat chance.' She pushed him down on to the pillow. 'I fell asleep on your last round of cock and bull,' she said. 'I promise to stay awake this time.'

'It's five o'clock in the morning.'

'I'm not sleepy. Go on – tell me lies. I like it.'

He sighed. 'It's true,' he said. 'My grandfather was injured, and was taken to a field hospital which had been set up in the grounds of a château. She lived there. That's how they met.'

Judy was seeing this in black and white. The wounded soldiers, stretched out under makeshift tents in the grounds. The young girl whose home had been transformed by war into a military hospital. She had seen it. In dozens of the old films that Lloyd was so fond of.

'It's all true,' he repeated, in response to the look she gave him.

'How come she met him? Out of all the soldiers that were there?'

'She met a lot of them. She was helping out where she could. But then she met him, and . . . they fell in love.' He smiled. 'I like to think there's a lot of my granda in me,' he said.

'Mm.' Judy tried to sound dubious, but she didn't find it difficult to believe that Françoise had fallen in love with Lloyd's grandfather.

'OK,' she conceded. 'Carry on.'

She lay back, listening to Lloyd's voice as he produced snippets of information, or disinformation, about his grandfather, and his brief but touching romance with his supposedly French grandmother. She loved to listen to him; that was why she was putting up with being told all this nonsense. He'd surely have mentioned it before now, if it was true, she reasoned. She'd just have to catch him out.

'He recovered, and was sent back to the front. They wrote to one another . . . '

'Which language?'

'English. He could speak French, but he could never write it.'

'And you can produce these letters as evidence?'

He shook his head. 'He lost the letters, and his right leg – when a shell got him.'

Trust Lloyd to make her feel guilty.

It's morning, Gordon.

Gordon looked at Pauline, sleeping soundly beside him, her breathing deep and regular. She had turned into someone else, someone he didn't know. Someone he was a little frightened of.

Get up, Gordon, old son. You have something to do today. You know you have.

He had been asleep too, until the phone had rung. Eventually it had penetrated, at first as a dream in which he couldn't make the alarm clock stop ringing, even when he took it to pieces, and then as dim reality. It hadn't wakened Pauline.

No, well – it's tiring, all this lying, isn't it? You got a few minutes off when you told the chief inspector the truth about the fire. She didn't. Look at her, poor thing. She's exhausted.

And when he'd taken the call, he had stayed in the sitting-room, crying like a child.

Much good that did, Gordon. Look at her. Go on, look. She's expecting a baby, Gordon. Your baby.

All right, all right! I know. But I wasn't to know that she was going to turn into Barbara Stanwyck, was I?

He didn't like being in a *film noir*. No one had told him his lines, for one thing.

He slid out of bed, and walked naked into the bathroom. People killed themselves like that, he thought, as he ran water into the bath. He was found naked in the bathroom, having cut his wrists.

No thanks. No, he would be found naked in the bathroom having a bath. Then having a shave. Then he would be found fully clothed going to the police station to let them have his fingerprints, because they needed them for elimination, and to arrange their case against him for arson, presumably.

And then?

You don't have any option, Gordon. Pauline did it because of

138

you – she's got the police on her back because of you. If it wasn't for you, old son, she would be nice, dependable, truthful Pauline, not some fugitive from a forties American movie. You don't have any option, and you know it.

But he hadn't wanted her to –

What you want and what you get are two different things, as you of all people should know, Gordon. What you wanted was someone who didn't give a toss about you. What you got was someone who loves you, whether you want her to or not. But you were too busy feeling sorry for yourself, weren't you, Gordon, old son, to notice? All along, poor Gordon. Poor Gordon couldn't have Lennie, so he settled for Pauline. Poor Gordon.

He cut himself shaving. He was found naked in the bathroom, with a piece of toilet roll stuck to his chin.

'Where are you going?'

'Work,' he said.

Lying got easier.

'Is my boss here?' said a voice.

Mickey turned to see the tall figure of Bob Sandwell. 'In there,' he said, inclining his head towards Lloyd's door. 'With the chief inspector and the chief super.'

'I think we've got another meeting,' said Sandwell. 'Either that or her car's broken down again.'

Mickey smiled. 'How do you like having a woman for a boss?' he asked.

'Judy's OK.'

Mickey heard the defensive tone, and held up his hands. 'I think she's all right too,' he said. 'I worked here with her for a few weeks. She was acting inspector until Barstow arrived.'

Sandwell smiled. 'I'm getting as bad as her,' he said. 'Hearing sexist remarks when they're not intended.'

'I just wondered if it bothered you. It bothers some.'

'Most of them are at Malworth,' said Sandwell. 'I'll tell you something – if they don't give up soon, I'll be a raging feminist before the year's out.'

Mickey got to his feet as Chief Superintendent Allison came out of Lloyd's office, and nodded acknowledgement to the two sergeants. Lloyd beckoned them into his office, where Judy Hill sat, looking even more attractive than usual. Lloyd was a lucky sod, thought Mickey. He had always blamed his red-haired hot temper for his inability to sustain a permanent relationship, but the chief inspector had a temper too; Mickey had heard him. Sheer luck, he decided.

Lloyd invited them to sit. 'Right,' he said. 'The chief super wants to see some movement on this. We've had confirmation that the prints found on the Austins' phone are those of Stephen Arthur Tasker. Allison is not happy that we haven't found him yet.' He sighed. 'And if Tasker was responsible for Mrs Austin's death, then our theory is blown away,' he said, and smiled briefly. 'Our revered pathologist is always pointing out that theories come to grief,' he said.

'I'd like to speak to Austin,' Judy said. 'Question him a little more closely about what he was doing.'

The chief superintendent didn't sigh; he just looked as though he was going to. 'I know Mr Allison said that he wasn't too concerned with motive, but Austin doesn't strike me as the type who would lose control too readily,' he said.

'Why did he lie about going to fetch the car?' she said. 'If Pauline Pearce was lying about when her husband got home – and she was – then she was probably lying about when she heard someone going into the studio. And if that was eleven o'clock, it wasn't Mrs Austin.'

'He may not have lied about fetching the car,' said Lloyd.

'And I'd like to know why Mrs Beale was so keen to ring the Austins,' said Judy, almost to herself. 'She'd hardly want them to know that Frank had been arrested, would she? So what was she ringing them about?'

'Ringing Austin,' said Lloyd. 'Sweet nothings.'

'I . . . I don't know if it's relevant,' said Mickey, taking the bull by the horns. 'But I'm not so sure he was having an affair with Rosemary Beale.'

'Oh?' Lloyd looked at him, eyebrows raised, waiting.

'When I went to see him at the hotel,' said Mickey, 'I – well – I got the feeling that *I* was more his type, sir.'

They all looked at him. Lloyd sat down again, smiling, but interested. 'Do go on,' he said. 'Did he make a pass at you?'

'No, sir,' said Mickey. 'But he . . . ' Damn it, he knew when he was being appraised. It was just that it was more usually women who did it.

'Fancied you,' supplied Lloyd.

'Not exactly, sir, but—'

Lloyd relented. 'All right,' he said. 'You were aware of his interest.'

'Yes, sir. And he was almost forty when he got married,' Mickey went on. 'And he only did that because he was told he stood more chance as a married man. And Inspector Hill said that he wasn't all that interested in his wife . . . '

Lloyd tipped back his chair, and stared into the middle distance. 'Does it alter things?' he asked, after a while. 'If it is the case? I suppose it could explain why he lied about going for his wife's car.'

'You agree that he lied, then?' said Judy.

'Perhaps,' said Lloyd. 'But I still don't discount Mrs Austin's picking it up herself. And I don't think we can go on the assumption that Austin is homosexual from the impression he gave to one officer.'

Mickey looked at Judy, who was definitely giving Lloyd an old-fashioned look. 'Oh – I checked into the siren thing,' he told her. 'No police vehicle used its siren round the Mitchell Estate at eleven twenty on Thursday night.' He shrugged. 'Sorry,' he said. 'I checked the other emergency services, but it's no go. Maybe it was a car alarm.'

'I do know the difference!' she snapped.

'Sorry.'

'All right, all right,' said Lloyd. 'It could have been the TV, for all we know.'

Mickey couldn't really imagine Austin watching a cops and robbers show. It was odd, about the siren. And Austin reckoning he couldn't find her car. And phoning Judy Hill. And his story about going out again to look for his wife was pathetic. The whole thing was odd. Perhaps it did have something to do with his sexual preferences, because he was right about that; he was sure he was.

'As to Pearce,' said Lloyd, 'now that he's admitted trying to burn down – with quite startling ineptitude – the Austin-Pearce factory, does that make him more or less likely as a candidate?'

'The murderer wasn't inept,' said Sandwell. 'Or we'd have him by now.'

141

'No, he wasn't, as you'll see from this.' Lloyd gave out copies of the forensic report on the Beales' flat.

Mickey read the report, which was basically only of negative use. Everything had been wiped. The phone, the wire, the table, the door. Everything, except the outside of the front door, on which there were a number of prints, and it would take time to sort out any that couldn't be accounted for.

'The fire didn't work. He says he didn't know that, but perhaps he did. And perhaps he was still angry. He told me he went directly to the factory, but he didn't – he waited outside Austin's flat for some time before he left. Altering the time could be a clumsy attempt at an alibi.'

'You don't think he planned it all, do you, sir?' asked Sandwell. 'And the fire was meant not to work?'

Lloyd shook his head. 'He'd have had to have had advanced knowledge of the wiring system, which is unlikely,' he said. 'And this was almost an opportunist murder, if you ask me. There she was, alone, her back to him, using the phone with its nice strong cable . . . ' He rubbed his eyes. 'At last, the murderer thought, this is my chance. So who would be most likely to catch her at just the right moment? Pearce.' He looked at Judy. 'I take it you're going to have another go at Mrs Pearce?'

'Yes,' she said. 'I'll just give her time to think I'm not going to.' Mickey smiled.

'The incident room is being set up at Malworth,' said Lloyd. 'We've got access to a computer, which Sergeant Sandwell is welcome to play with.'

He got up, and looked out of the window, speaking with his back to them. 'And we're still evidence-gathering on the Austin murder, of course. We've got a house-to-house being conducted in the streets near the Mitchell flats, and I'm hoping that that might tell us if Austin's car really did remain unused all evening. It may even turn up a witness.'

He turned. 'And the reconstruction of Mrs Beale's walk home will go ahead tonight. Someone may have seen something useful – perhaps someone saw her being followed, or possibly even saw *Mrs* Austin's car.' He smiled at Judy. 'If it was away from the garage,' he said, 'can Austin finally take a back seat, and we concentrate on what *she* was doing rather than what he was doing?'

She smiled back, her good humour restored. 'Done,' she said.

142

* * *

'You might as well move in.'

Inspector Hill smiled friendlily enough at Pauline's greeting, but Pauline didn't suppose she would enjoy her visit.

'Do you have a moment, Mrs Pearce?'

Pauline nodded, stepping aside to let the inspector through. 'I know why you're here,' she said.

They went into the sitting-room. 'Am I allowed to offer you coffee?' she asked. 'Or would that be fraternising?'

Inspector Hill looked at her for a moment, then smiled. 'I'd love a cup of coffee,' she said.

She followed Pauline into the kitchen, which Pauline could have done without. Worse than that; she didn't speak. She didn't demand explanations, or truthful answers. At least Gordon was at work. 'What's going to happen to Gordon?' she asked, as she took two mugs off the tree.

'The factory is in Stansfield,' she replied. 'Nothing to do with me.'

'You must know!' Pauline banged down the mugs.

'I imagine they'll prepare a case for the CPS,' she said.

Initials. Everyone talked in initials these days. She looked at the inspector, eyebrows raised in a query.

'The Crown Prosecution Service.'

Pauline closed her eyes briefly. The kettle began to murmur, the birds were singing outside. At night, when it was quiet, you could hear the river flow. Her kitchen looked out on to old Malworth, her sitting-room overlooked the river and the park. Gordon had got her that. 'Arson's very serious, isn't it?'

'Of course. You know it is.'

The kettle became slightly hysterical, as it did just before it boiled.

'What'll happen to him?'

'I honestly don't know, Mrs Pearce.'

'What do you *think* will happen to him?' She had opened her eyes, but it was the kettle she watched; she still hadn't looked at the inspector.

'I really don't know. But he's never done anything like that before. He was under a considerable strain, he didn't do it for insurance or anything. No one's life was endangered – he didn't use petrol or paraffin – I'd say he's not in too bad a position.'

143

Pauline smiled a little, and turned. 'Maybe you should defend him,' she said.

'Mrs Pearce – I'd say there was an even more serious crime to be considered.'

The kettle stopped complaining, and steam burst from the spout as it clicked off. 'Gordon hasn't committed an even more serious crime,' said Pauline.

'Did you know that he had tried to set fire to the factory when you lied to me about when he came home on Monday night?'

'Yes.' Another lie. Pauline spooned coffee into the mugs, and poured the water carefully, stirring as she did so. 'Milk and sugar?'

'Please. So that's why you lied?'

'Yes. How much sugar?'

'One, please. You told me that you heard someone in the studio – you thought it was your husband and Mrs Austin. Was that true?'

'Yes.'

'When was that?'

'About quarter of an hour before Gordon came in.'

'Which would make it eleven, not ten o'clock.'

Pauline picked up the mugs and went back through to the sitting-room, putting them down on the coffee table. 'Yes,' she said.

'In which case,' said the inspector, sitting down, 'it wasn't Mrs Austin that you heard.'

Pauline almost laughed at the simplicity of it all. Her brain hadn't been able to sort it out. She had just kept telling herself that Lennie couldn't be dead, because Lennie wasn't home. It was simple. It wasn't Lennie in the studio.

'Did you hear someone actually go in to the studio?'

Pauline thought hard, listened in her head to the sound. 'No,' she said. 'It was like someone trying the door. Rattling it. But when I looked there was no one there, and the light was on. So I thought— '

The inspector put down her mug and walked over to the window. 'You can't actually see the shop fronts,' she said. 'The ledge cuts it off.'

'No. So when I looked out, and saw the light . . . I just

thought she had gone in there. I watched almost until Gordon came in, but I didn't see her.'

'Did you see Mrs Beale?'

Pauline shook her head, but the inspector was still looking out of the window herself.

'Did you see Mrs Beale?' she asked again, turning. 'She was walking home from the Riverside at about that time.'

'No.'

'Did you see your husband?'

Pauline went cold. 'No!' she shouted.

'He came home quarter of an hour later?'

Don't let her fluster you. You knew this was going to happen. You knew all along that this was going to happen if you left Gordon alone with them. You sent that other policeman to the pub, you knew Gordon would tell them about the fire, you knew. You wanted to tell them the truth about when you heard someone at the studio.

'Yes. Don't forget your coffee.'

She smiled. 'Thank you,' she said, sitting down again. Then her attitude changed; something had obviously occurred to her. 'Could someone have been leaving the studio, rather than entering?'

Pauline shook her head. 'I'd have seen her,' she said. 'Unless she was coming up to the flats.' She realised what she was saying, and her eyes widened. 'You don't think *Lennie* . . . ' Her hand pointed vaguely next door.

Inspector Hill didn't react at all. She finished her coffee, and stood up.

Pauline was ready for her this time. For whatever casual question she threw over her shoulder on her way out.

'You and your husband were both here at eleven fifteen,' she said, her voice stern and uncompromising.

'Yes.'

'Is that the truth this time, Mrs Pearce?'

'Yes!'

'Then who do you think killed Mrs Austin?' she asked.

Pauline stared at her. 'What? How should I know?' she asked. 'Isn't that your job?' She stood up. 'You think it was Gordon,' she said. 'You think I'm lying.'

'Why would I think you were doing anything else?'

'He was here, with me, at quarter past eleven. He was ill

from the fumes – I thought he was drunk, but it was the smoke from the fire. He was at the factory, then he was here – Gordon didn't kill anyone!'

'So who killed Mrs Austin? Tasker?'

Pauline, Pauline. You're letting her rattle you. 'No!' she shouted. 'She wasn't afraid of him – Jonathan Austin's told you she was afraid of him, but she wasn't!'

'You told me that she wanted nothing to do with him,' the inspector reminded her.

'She didn't want to get involved with him again, but she wasn't afraid of him!'

'You think Jonathan Austin killed his wife?'

Pauline didn't know what to think any more. But that much she knew, now that she was being made to think about it. 'Yes,' she said. 'I think he did.'

She was gone. Pauline went over the conversation again in her head. She hadn't been in control of it, not at any point. But she hadn't let anything slip. She'd have to ring Gordon; tell him. She had said that she knew about the fire. He would have to know she'd said that.

It took her frightened mind long moments to remember the new number; it rang out.

'Austin-Pearce.'

'Mr Pearce, please.'

'I'm sorry, Mr Pearce isn't in today. Can someone else help you?'

Pauline hung up.

'Between eleven o'clock and midnight,' said Freddie. 'But then, you told me that.'

Lloyd grunted, standing as far away as possible from what Freddie was doing.

Drake, just like Judy, had found something very important that he had to do at just the same time as the post-mortem. Lloyd hadn't pressed him; he was in a rather mellower frame of mind today.

'Nothing to add to what I already told you, really. I told Judy at the time – I can't really say whether she turned away from the blow, or was actually hit from behind. I'd think the former – she saw it coming, turned her head, and . . . ' He demonstrated on

146

Kathy, who acted her part with the same dispassionate ease as Freddie. He couldn't have found himself a better disciple. Judy said that she and Sandwell were very serious now; Lloyd thought he preferred the squeamish approach to pathology himself. Kathy was a nice girl, but he'd feel much happier about her if dead bodies made her sick.

'. . . and it would catch her there,' said Freddie, describing a circle on Kathy's head, just above the right temple.

'Could a woman have done it?'

'A shot-putter, maybe,' said Freddie. 'The average woman wouldn't have anything like enough strength.'

'What about if she was out of her mind with . . . I don't know – rage, jealousy?'

Freddie shook his head. 'I'm talking about a shot-putter who is out of her mind,' said Freddie. 'There were six ferocious blows,' he said. 'To the walls, the furniture – and finally to the victim.'

Lloyd raised his eyebrows. 'We know that, do we? The damage to the furniture happened first?'

'Yes. There's no trace of blood or— '

Lloyd held up his hand. 'Fine,' he said. 'Yes. Of course.'

'And it *was* the murder weapon that caused the damage to the furniture,' said Freddie. 'So that was first. It was the sixth and final blow that killed her. A man,' he said decidedly. 'I won't wear a woman unless she's got biceps like a boxer.' He smiled. 'I thought the lady next door heard a man's voice?'

'She heard someone screaming, and someone hysterically shouting one word,' said Lloyd. 'I just wanted to be sure.'

The next-door neighbour hadn't heard raised voices before the commotion that had so alarmed her, which didn't suggest a row that had got out of hand. But then, some people didn't shout. Lloyd could never imagine not shouting when he was angry. Maybe that's what stopped him picking things up and attacking people with them. But she had heard the one word shouted, over and over again. Whore. Lloyd sighed. Sex had a lot to answer for.

There seemed to be an element of premeditation, despite the ferocity of the attack; no row, and prints removed from the ashtray. But not from the phone.

'The swabs are negative,' said Freddie.

'No assignation with Tasker in the back of her car, then,' said Lloyd.

147

'I didn't say that,' said Freddie. 'They could have taken precautions. But there's nothing which suggests intercourse. And she was fully dressed, her underwear was all present and correct – no forcible removal or hurried dressing. Apart from the blouse being unbuttoned, that is. But that just suggests a goodnight kiss and a cuddle, really. Her wedding ring wasn't removed forcibly, either. I think she chose to take it off.'

'They've done tests,' said Lloyd. 'The ring could have been in the ashtray all along – wielding it with that amount of force would keep it in there, rather than shake it out.'

'I smell a theory,' said Freddie. He looked up from the body, rather crestfallen, Lloyd thought. 'She was a normal, healthy woman of thirty,' he said. 'Nothing odd or unusual about her at all. Oh – she had been drinking,' he said. 'Gin. But not to excess.'

'You're just waiting for the day when you can tell me that someone died of arsenic poisoning, aren't you?' Lloyd said.

'Ah, those were the days. Spilsbury didn't know he was born. Now it's all brute force and ignorance. Murderers in those days had a bit of style, don't you think?'

'I'll settle for ignorance, thank you,' said Lloyd. 'I don't think I could bear working with you on a stylish murder.'

Freddie laughed. 'I'm doing the other one after lunch,' he said. Lloyd skipped lunch.

Back in his office, he read the forensic reports again. The balcony doors had been opened, not forced. They could only be opened from the inside, even when unlocked. The prints on the handle were smudged, and the ones they could decipher were those of Jonathan Austin, whose prints they had managed to obtain, unlike Pearce's. Mrs Austin's prints were on the phone, as were Tasker's. Austin's prints were everywhere, not unnaturally. And his story sounded weak, but perhaps it was true.

He couldn't tell Judy what he had in mind about that.

The knock was perfunctory, and she walked into his office. 'You think Mrs Austin killed Rosemary Beale,' she said, sitting down.

Oh, well. She was a good detective. 'Yes,' he admitted, but he didn't get the look. He raised an eyebrow. 'You don't want to demolish the theory?'

'Not yet. I want to talk it through.' She sat back. 'Did Mrs Beale die in Malworth, or didn't she?'

148

'I didn't want to advance the theory until I had a bit more to go on,' he said.

'That's never stopped you before. You didn't tell me because you thought I would be biased in Mrs Austin's favour!'

'No!' he said. 'I thought it might upset you.'

Judy relaxed a little. 'I'm sorry,' she said. 'I just wish that—' She didn't finish the sentence.

'You wish that your first case didn't involve me and Stansfield,' he said.

'Yes. And I wish my divisional DCI wasn't on holiday. I don't even know who I'm supposed to be reporting to, you or Allison.'

Lloyd knew something about that, but she would be even angrier if he told her, so he didn't. 'Allison,' he said. 'You're liaising with me. You're reporting to Allison.'

'All right,' she said. 'So let's liaise. I don't really see how the times work.'

Lloyd sat back. 'The fight in the Riverside started at about twenty to eleven,' he said. 'If she left as it started, she would have passed Mrs Austin's studio before eleven.'

'Beale says she left when the police came.'

Lloyd nodded. 'Or maybe when they were called,' he said. 'He wasn't sure.'

Judy nodded.

'Let's say she was in there, with Tasker. And this woman who, according to rumour, is already threatening her security, sees her. She goes up to talk to her, but Mrs Beale is already on the phone to Austin to tell him what she's seen – which answers your question about why she was so eager to ring Austin – and Mrs Austin flies into a rage, and strangles her.'

'How did she get in without being on the video?'

'She just followed her in – that door takes an age to close.'

'Yes,' said Judy, frowning a little. 'It does.'

'She goes back down, knowing Austin knows, throws her ring into one of the ashtrays, and picks up Tasker. Tasker is going to take the car back to the garage for her.'

'Does he know?' she asked.

'I don't know. Maybe he thinks he's just covering up their having met. They part company at the post office, and that's where Drake sees them. The car's parked out of sight.'

'All this by ten past eleven?' Judy looked dubious. 'She's a quick worker,' she said.

Lloyd shrugged. 'Between ten and quarter past. It's just possible. And she and Tasker didn't part company, of course – he was in the flat. We have to find him.'

'So who killed her? Tasker?' asked Judy. 'And did she bring the ashtray with her to make it easy for him?'

He smiled at the enormous flaw in his theory, but he felt a little unhappy. It was Tasker she was querying, not Mrs Austin, because she was so convinced that Austin killed his wife. He wished she didn't have such tunnel vision where Austin was concerned. It seemed to him that Mrs Austin seemed capable of inspiring passion in everyone but her husband.

'What was Mrs Austin like?' he asked.

'She was very attractive,' said Judy. 'To both sexes. But she had . . . I don't know. Sex appeal isn't quite what I mean. Men chatted her up,' she said. 'All the time. I heard them myself. People she didn't know from Adam. Postmen. Delivery men. They'd come in off the street, and they'd be asking her if she fancied coming out for a drink.'

She looked at him, the way she did when she was working out whether or not he would take her seriously. She evidently decided that he would, and went on.

'I've worked in a male-oriented environment for nearly seventeen years,' she said. 'And I've met all the chauvinist remarks going. You should be at home bringing up babies, what use would you be in a fight, I wouldn't let my wife do this job, and so on. And I've been chatted up from time to time. But I have never been sexually harassed. No one has ever suggested that sleeping with him will get me promotion, or whatever. But she would have met with it, I'm sure. Men wanted her.'

'So this man wanted her,' said Lloyd. 'And wouldn't take no for an answer – Austin says she was afraid of him. The ashtray is a teensy-weensy problem which I had spotted myself.' He grinned. 'But perhaps there's an explanation,' he said.

'I don't know,' said Judy. 'Pauline Pearce says she wasn't afraid of Tasker – she says Austin's lying.'

Lloyd sat back. 'I see,' he said. 'You've found an ally.'

'Drake couldn't be sure what was going on,' she said.

'If she was shilly-shallying – that's all some people need to lose control. Especially if they've been in prison for three years.'

'I don't suppose he was waiting for Mrs Austin to come across,' she said. 'He'd been out for two months. I think he was just chancing his arm. Why would he kill her?'

'And why is Austin so keen for us to believe she was frightened of him?'

'Quite.'

Oh, well. Their liaison – could that possibly be the right word? – hadn't got them very far. They were just as much in the dark as they were before.

'Why is my theory about Mrs Beale's murder not being laughed to scorn?' he asked. 'Even if you discount the ashtray part, it's totally unlikely, virtually unworkable, and I have no reason at all to think that that's what happened. And you're just sitting there.'

She smiled. 'Because there's a lot of good stuff in there,' she said. 'As usual.'

A knock on the door was followed by the duty sergeant. 'Sir?'

'Yes, Joe.'

'Sir, Mr Pearce is here. To let us have his fingerprints.'

'Good,' said Lloyd, a little puzzled as to why he was being informed.

'Thing is, sir,' said the sergeant, 'he says he wants to make a statement.'

Lloyd and Judy looked at one another.

'To what effect?' asked Lloyd.

The sergeant's face was quite impassive. 'To the effect that he murdered both Mrs Beale and Mrs Austin, sir,' he said.

Seven

Gordon looked up as the door opened and both Chief Inspector Lloyd and Inspector Hill came in.

'You know Inspector Hill, Malworth CID, I believe?' said Lloyd briskly.

'Yes,' said Gordon, half rising from the chair.

He watched as the uniformed man set up a cassette recorder, obviously unused to its intricacies.

Lloyd sighed. 'Let me do it,' he said, impatiently, and efficiently got it into operation. He picked up the microphone, and rattled off the date and all the other details of the interview about to take place.

'We now record all interviews, Mr Pearce, as you can see. Now – the sergeant tells me that you want to confess to two murders.'

He pulled two chairs from the wall and set them at the table, but only Inspector Hill sat down. Lloyd walked about the room, looking with interest at everything but Gordon.

'So go ahead,' he said. 'The constable here will write down what you say. You have been cautioned, I understand.'

Gordon looked at the constable. 'Er . . . yes,' he said.

'He will read it back to you, and then you can sign it as a true account, or alter it as you wish. Or, of course, you can write it out yourself. The inspector will almost certainly write it all down too, so we should have a very accurate record by the time we've finished, shouldn't we?'

'Yes,' said Gordon.

'Right.' Lloyd wandered to the window, and stood on tiptoe to look down at something outside. 'Off you go, Mr Pearce.'

Gordon wasn't sure what he had expected. Not this, at any rate. Questions. Questions that he had to answer. 'I thought you were going to interview me,' he said.

152

Lloyd whirled round from the window. 'It's not a chat show, Mr Pearce. I thought you were going to make a statement about murdering two women.'

'Yes, but— '

'Oh, do get on with it, Mr Pearce,' he said, looking at his watch. 'The inspector has a post-mortem to go to.'

Gordon swallowed. 'I don't know where to start,' he said.

'How about with the first one? Who did you murder first, Mr Pearce?'

Gordon's eyes widened. The inspector sat with a thick note-book open at a clean page. The constable had a statement form, pen poised above it. The chief inspector was now standing behind his empty chair, his fingers lightly tapping the back, waiting for an answer.

'I've asked you a question,' he said. 'That was what you wanted me to do, wasn't it?'

'Rosemary Beale,' said Gordon firmly.

'Ah – not mine, then,' said Lloyd. And left the room.

Gordon twisted round to watch the door close, and slowly turned back to Inspector Hill.

'When?' she asked.

'What?' Gordon could feel his palms grow sweaty.

'When did you kill Mrs Beale?'

'When I went home,' he said. 'I killed her, and then I went back to the Austins, and . . . ' He couldn't say it.

Inspector Hill frowned. 'What time was that, Mr Pearce?'

'After I'd been to the factory,' he said.

'So you went to the factory, started the fire, left, killed Mrs Beale, then left there and killed Mrs Austin?'

Gordon nodded.

She wrote it all down. 'What time did you get home, after all that?' she asked, still writing.

'Quarter to twelve,' he said, without hesitation.

She looked up. 'Your wife says you came home at eleven fifteen.' She raised an eyebrow. 'At least, that's her latest esti-mate,' she added. 'Is she still lying, Mr Pearce?'

'Only to protect me.'

The door opened and Lloyd reappeared with four paper cups in a holder. He didn't offer them round; he put them down in a line on the window-sill. 'They have to cool,' he said.

'You left Mr Austin at ten o'clock,' the inspector said pleasantly. 'And by quarter to midnight you had tried to burn down the factory and murdered two women?'

'Yes.'

'Quite impressive,' she said. 'What time did you arrive at the factory?'

'About five past ten,' said Gordon.

'And leave?'

'Twenty to eleven.'

He saw the tiny glance that passed between the inspector and the chief inspector.

The inspector looked at her notes, leafing back through the book. 'And you told your wife what you had done, did you?' she asked.

Gordon shook his head.

'So why did she lie?'

'She . . . she guessed. About the fire.'

Lloyd looked startled. 'Guessed?'

'Yes,' said Gordon.

'She said, "Good evening, Gordon, I'll bet you've been setting fire to the factory, haven't you?" Is that right?'

Gordon looked away.

'Guessed, Mr Pearce?' said the inspector with a look that reminded Gordon of his mother when he was little.

'Yes! Not like that, but she— ' He broke off. 'Why don't you believe me?' he asked.

'Coffee,' said Lloyd, and the constable went and fetched the cups.

'I got them all without sugar,' said Lloyd, leaning back dangerously on his chair and sweeping packets of sugar off the window sill. 'Filched these from the canteen,' he said, letting them fall on to the table.

'All right,' said Inspector Hill. 'Let's get down to the important part, Mr Pearce. How did you kill Mrs Beale?'

Gordon almost sighed with relief. That was more like it. That was what he'd rehearsed for hours in the library, under the guise of reading the papers. 'I strangled her,' he said. 'With the telephone cord.'

'Why was she ringing the Austins?'

Oh, God. 'What?' Gordon asked dully.

154

'She was on the phone to the Austins. Why?'

'I don't know! I wasn't there when she made the call.'

The inspector wrote that down. He could read it, upside down. *Wasn't there when she made the call.*

'She was already on the phone when you got there?'

'Yes.' Gordon waited for her to speak, but she didn't, so he expanded. 'She let me in, and went back to the phone,' he said.

'Ah.' She wrote that down too. 'And you strangled her.'

'Yes.' Gordon bit his lip, watching her pen move.

'Why?'

'I was upset.'

She looked up. 'Do you always strangle people when you're upset?' she asked.

He didn't reply.

'Did you go with the intention of strangling her?'

Gordon ran a hand over his hair. 'No,' he said. 'But I did.'

But I did, she wrote. 'What was your intention?'

'To talk to her. But I . . . I didn't.'

'No. Then what did you do?'

'I went back to the Austins'.'

'No – I mean, before you left Mrs Beale.'

Gordon looked at the constable, who was also labouring over his version of this statement. He couldn't read it; it was too far away. 'Nothing,' he said.

'You just left her there.'

'Yes.'

She drew a line under what she had written, and looked at the chief inspector.

He smiled at Gordon. 'My turn, now, Mr Pearce,' he said. 'This might be more difficult.'

Gordon frowned slightly.

'How did you kill Mrs Austin?' Lloyd asked.

'I hit her.'

'With what?' asked Lloyd.

He had to be right. He had to be. The papers hadn't said. They just said a heavy implement. It had to be, though, or why would the inspector have asked about them? And why would Jonathan? And why would Pauline have lied? He had repeated that lie to Jonathan, but he had decided in the library that the truth would

155

be better. Take a leaf out of Pauline's book. As much of the truth as possible.

'Well, Mr Pearce?'

He looked into frankly disbelieving blue eyes. 'The ashtray,' he said.

'What ashtray?'

'The ashtray I took with me.'

The inspector looked up from her notes then. 'Where from?' she asked.

Now. Decision time. Go along with Pauline's lie? No. The truth. Tell them the truth. His mouth was dry; he could hardly breathe. He had to make a decision.

'Not from anywhere,' he said. 'I had it with me all along. I bought them in an auction.'

Lloyd sat forward, almost as though he was going to tell him a secret. 'How many times did you hit her, Mr Pearce?' he asked.

He didn't want to think about that. Bludgeoned, the papers had said. Oh, dear God. Lennie. It was all his fault. He couldn't think about it.

'Once? More than once? Over and over again?'

Gordon stared at him. 'I . . . I don't *know*!' he said.

'We do,' said Lloyd.

Bludgeoned. 'I just kept hitting her,' Gordon muttered.

Lloyd sat back again, and regarded him. 'Mr Pearce,' he said, 'why don't we stop this nonsense?'

'Please,' said Gordon. 'I did it. I – I . . . ' He looked away. 'Sorry,' he said. 'I've wasted your time.'

'Not necessarily,' said Lloyd. 'Not if you tell me what you do know. Tell me about the ashtray, Mr Pearce.'

'It – it was a joke,' Gordon said, helplessly.

They looked at one another again then, but neither of them spoke. They just waited for an explanation.

'Pauline and I got them at an auction,' he said. 'We go to auctions – just for fun, really. Local ones. You know. And I saw this big ashtray – I thought we should get it for the lobby. People smoke, you see. And they . . . well, I bid for it, and I got it. But when I went to collect it, the lot was two ashtrays. I hadn't realised.'

The inspector was writing it down. His stupid joke.

156

'I said to Pauline I'd give one to Jonathan. It was a joke – it was so big, and he smokes such a lot. Everyone was always trying to get him to stop, especially— ' Oh, God. Poor Lennie. He swallowed. 'Well anyway, I left it in the car to give to him, and I took it in with me when I went to see him on Monday.'

'You gave it to him?' Lloyd asked.

'No. I just left it in the hallway, for him to find. It was so big, you see – it was for him to put his cigarettes in before he went into the sitting-room, so that he wouldn't get into trouble for smoking. It was a joke, it was just— ' He broke off, and gathered himself together again. 'Then he told me I was out – the board wanted me out. That – that woman . . . '

They didn't help him out; they just waited.

'I left. And I saw it in the hallway, and I picked it up – I didn't want . . . I didn't want him to have it. But then I was outside his door with this bloody thing in my hand, I felt silly. So I just put it down again.'

'Outside his front door?'

Gordon nodded. 'It was a joke, it was just a stupid joke!' he repeated, his voice breaking on the final word. He could hardly speak for the tears. 'If I hadn't taken it, she wouldn't be dead,' he said.

'No, Mr Pearce,' said Lloyd, his voice quiet, and angry. 'She would still have been dead. He wanted her dead. By whatever means.'

Gordon looked up slowly. 'He?'

Lloyd nodded.

'Who? Austin?'

'We don't know that yet, Mr Pearce.' He thought for a moment. 'The ashtray was inside the house when Mrs Austin left?'

Gordon nodded again.

'She was irritated by Mr Austin's attitude, I believe.'

Gordon smiled, involuntarily. 'She was livid,' he said. 'I hadn't seen her that angry since she was about five.'

'Angry enough to take off her ring and throw it into the ashtray?'

Gordon frowned. 'Yes,' he said. 'That would be just the sort of thing she would do.'

'And then you picked it up again, and left it just outside the door?'

Gordon sighed his confirmation.

'Where?' asked the inspector.

Gordon shook his head. 'I just put it down,' he said. 'By the wall. I didn't want anyone tripping over it.' Tripping over it. My God. He'd thought it might be dangerous.

'So someone leaving the flat might not have noticed it?'

Gordon thought. He had put it down carefully. Quietly. He had felt so foolish about the whole thing. 'They wouldn't,' he said. 'They'd see it when they came in, but not leaving.'

'Thank you, Mr Pearce,' she said.

'Sneakers.'

Mickey frowned. 'In Stansfield?' he said. 'I thought I knew all the pubs in Stansfield.'

'It used to be the Red Lion. They've done it up.'

'Oh, in the old village.' Ah well, it had been three years. They were always rubbing Stansfield out and starting again. 'And you're certain it was Mrs Austin?'

'Oh, yes. There was a crowd of us. We all saw her.'

'And you all work at Austin-Pearce?'

'Yes.' She smiled. 'I saw you there after the fire,' she said.

Mickey smiled back. 'This man she was with – can you give me a description?' he asked.

'He was a lot older than her,' she said. 'But he wore jeans – you know the sort.' Her gaze was fixed on the corner of the ceiling, which seemed to help her powers of recall. 'Dark,' was all she came up with, however.

'Tall, short, fat, thin?'

'Taller than her – and she was quite tall, wasn't she? Not fat, but not thin either.'

'Average build? Bigger, smaller?'

Between them they arrived at a description, which fitted Tasker.

'Do you think you would recognise him if you saw him again?' he asked.

She nodded. 'Everyone would,' she said. 'We were all having a laugh about it. You should have seen them. They didn't care.'

He did see them. 'Did she seem . . . alarmed, at all, by him?' he asked. 'Was she trying to get away from him? Was he annoying her?'

'No! Just the opposite.'

She signed her statement; Mickey was showing her out when the girl at the desk spoke to him.

'Mr Austin to see you, Mickey,' she said, nodding across at the waiting area.

Mickey nodded. At least they wouldn't be in an hotel room, he thought. He almost asked her to be present, then decided that he couldn't stand the laughter. Anyway, even if he was right, that didn't mean that that was why he was here. He wanted a cigarette. Three years since he'd given up, and he wanted a cigarette.

'Yes, Mr Austin,' he said as he showed him into an interview room, trying to copy Lloyd's bright and breezy manner. It didn't really suit him, he decided. 'What can I do for you?' he asked.

'I . . . er . . . I've been trying to do what you said,' said Austin.

Mickey racked his brains, but nothing fell into place. He sat down. 'Sorry about the smell of paint,' he said. 'Sorry, Mr Austin – trying to do what, exactly?'

'Remember what Leonora told me about this man,' said Austin.

'Oh – yes. We think we know who he is,' said Mickey. 'We should have him quite soon now.'

'Well, perhaps I shouldn't have . . . '

'Oh, no – not at all, that's fine. We need all the information we can get. What have you remembered?'

'She said that she had told him she would tell his boss if he didn't stop bothering her,' said Austin. 'I don't know if that helps at all.'

Mickey thought about that. Did it help? Yes, it did. If Tasker said he hadn't been bothering her, which he would. It fitted. She knew Beale, and Beale employed Tasker; he certainly wouldn't have taken kindly to Tasker upsetting her. He smiled. 'Everything helps, Mr Austin,' he said.

Austin clearly hadn't finished. Mickey began to feel uneasy again. No, sorry, Mr Austin, I'm washing my hair. God – did women feel like this all the time?

'I think you might have the wrong idea.'

Mickey frowned a little. 'The wrong idea about what, Mr Austin?' he asked.

'About . . . ' Austin searched his pockets, and took out cigarettes, automatically pushing the packet across to Mickey. 'About . . . about Mrs Beale's murder and my wife's murder being linked.'

159

Mickey sat back a little. Now he knew what Judy meant. He could hear it too. A disconcerting air of certainty, of knowing what had happened. 'You don't think they are?' he asked cautiously.

'I . . . ' Austin shook his head. 'No,' he said.

'Why not? She was on the phone to your number when she died.'

'I know. I just don't think that . . . ' Austin looked haunted.

'Was she ringing you, Mr Austin?'

He shook his head. 'Or – if she was, I wasn't there,' he said.

'Why would she ring you at that time of night?'

'I've no idea.' Austin rose. 'But my wife was killed by someone who . . . who went mad. You're looking for someone who wanted Mrs Beale dead, and you're wrong. You think someone had a reason to kill Leonora. But he had no reason. He had lost his reason. He didn't reason! He just hacked away at everything until he got her. Over and over and over, until he got her. Look what he did! Go to my flat and look at what he *did*!'

Lloyd had said that Austin had given Judy the willies; she wasn't the only one. There was such certainty.

'Were you *there*, Mr Austin?' he asked quietly.

The chilling question hung in the air, and Austin blinked at him. 'What?' he whispered, then shook his head. 'No,' he said. 'No. You think I . . . I didn't have to be there to know,' he said.

'All right, Mr Austin,' Mickey said, relieved. 'Don't worry. We're sure he's still in Stansfield. We will get him.'

Austin wiped perspiration from his upper lip. 'I don't want anyone else to die like that,' he said.

Mickey stood up. 'No one else will, Mr Austin,' he said, extending his hand.

Austin shook it. 'It's the one that went to prison,' he said. 'Isn't it? They say she was with him at some pub.'

She was, thought Mickey. Which means that she wasn't at her studio at all, and Austin's claim that his wife's car wasn't at the garage seemed doubtful again. It was all very odd.

'That's who we're looking for,' he said.

Austin nodded slowly, and left.

His cigarette packet still lay on the table. Mickey looked at it, then picked it up, and closed it with determination.

'Mr Austin,' he called.

* * *

'Lloyd, Stansfield CID. This is WPC Alexander.'

Pauline had thought it might be Gordon. But it was Lloyd, Stansfield CID, and WPC Alexander. 'Come in,' she said, pushing the button, and waiting at the door.

The lift arrived after a moment, and he got out, with a uniformed policewoman. For an instant, Pauline thought they had come to arrest her.

'Mrs Pearce,' Lloyd said as they followed her into the sitting-room, 'your husband is at Stansfield police station, answering questions.'

She stopped walking, her back to them. 'Why?' she asked.

'Because he has confessed to the murders of Mrs Beale and Mrs Austin.'

She turned. 'Lennie?' she said. 'But – but that's ridiculous! Gordon would no more harm Lennie than – anyway, he was *here*! He was with me!'

Lloyd looked totally impassive; the policewoman looked motherly and sympathetic. Pauline didn't suppose she would be.

'He says you are lying to protect him.'

Pauline couldn't believe this was happening. Not this, not the one thing she was sure of. 'He was *here*,' she said again. 'He came home at quarter past eleven, and he passed out on that chair!' She pointed to it, as though its presence somehow proved what she was saying. 'She was alive at ten past and dead by half past – Gordon couldn't possibly have killed her!'

'How do you know what time she died, Mrs Pearce?' he asked.

Her energy, her will seemed to drain out. She could feel it flow from her body, and she sank down in the chair. 'I was there,' she said.

Lloyd sat down. He didn't speak.

'I heard someone at the studio door,' she said, her voice flat, unemotional. 'And about fifteen minutes later, I heard a car leave. Then Gordon came in. I knew he'd done something wrong. I knew he felt betrayed by her. I thought he'd been in her studio, and I could smell burning. I could smell it on his clothes. I thought he'd set fire to her studio, burnt her paintings. When he passed out, I went down there. But the studio was all right.'

She looked at him. Clear blue eyes watched her as she spoke.

'Then I thought she must have been in there, and that I had heard Gordon going in. And that he'd done something

161

– maybe even tried to rape her or something.' She closed her eyes. 'I knew he'd done *something*. So I drove over to Stansfield to ask Lennie what was going on. And – there were police cars, and an ambulance, and no sign of Lennie. Her car wasn't there – I didn't know where she'd got to, but I thought then that he'd done something awful to Jonathan.' She looked at him again. 'Because I thought Lennie wasn't *there*,' she said. 'I thought she had left the studio just minutes before me.'

'You heard a car drive away,' Lloyd said. 'You didn't see it?'

'No.'

'Had there been a car parked in the street?'

Pauline frowned a little as she thought. 'No,' she said. 'No, there wasn't. I actually remember that there wasn't, because I was looking for something to account for the noise.'

Lloyd nodded. 'Anyway,' he said. 'You went over to the Austins', saw that the police were there, and you came back here, thinking that your husband had killed Jonathan Austin?'

She nodded. 'Or that he'd hurt him, at any rate. Then I found out it was Lennie who was dead. And I didn't even consider Gordon – he couldn't possibly have done that to her. Then Inspector Hill told me that she'd been seen with Steve Tasker – and that was when Gordon was here with me. So I *knew* he didn't have anything to do with it.'

It was almost easy to forget Rosemary Beale, she thought, enjoying the sheer luxury of telling the truth. She didn't hold out any hope that the chief inspector had forgotten her, but she very nearly had.

'Why would he say that he killed her?' asked Lloyd.

Pauline sighed. 'I can only think of one reason,' she said. 'He knew I'd been out. He must have thought I'd done it.'

Lloyd agreed. 'I have a pathologist who could have told him that that was out of the question,' he said. 'It would have saved a lot of heartache.'

'You do believe me, then? That Gordon was here?'

'I don't have to believe you, Mrs Pearce. Your husband hadn't the faintest idea what had gone on in the Austin flat.'

Pauline felt scared. 'What did happen to her?' she asked.

Lloyd thought for a moment before he spoke. 'She was hit on the head with the ashtray that your husband left outside the Austins' door,' he said. 'But that isn't the whole story.'

162

It was all she was going to be told. All she wanted to be told.

'That leaves us with Mrs Beale,' said Lloyd.

Pauline said nothing.

'Did you know Mrs Beale was dead when Inspector Hill came to see her that night?'

'No,' said Pauline.

The short holiday from lying was over.

It was Wednesday afternoon.

Jonathan looked out of the hotel window at the people who hurried past, hot and bothered and busy. Once, Wednesday had been early closing; people didn't believe in that any more.

He was hot – the hotel didn't run to air-conditioning. But he wasn't busy – he wasn't expected to go to work, so he had nothing to do. And he was bothered. Not like these women with their bulging plastic carrier bags, who somehow manhandled them, a pushchair and a toddler through the town; they were another species. His future constituents, he hoped, still, despite everything. He just had to get through. He'd come through this far.

They had come, offering their condolences, from the party. It was hard enough under normal circumstances to know what to say to the suddenly bereaved; they were completely out of their depth with murder. An intruder, they seemed to have decided, amongst themselves. He could almost imagine the sub-committee, formed to discuss the best approach to the husband of a murder victim. Ignore the fact that the spouse is always automatically under suspicion; ignore the rumours that she had been out on the town with some man who was just out of prison. Offer condolences, and refer vaguely to an intruder.

But Leonora's murder shouldn't affect his chances. The public had a short memory, and anyway, he would be cleared of any suspicion once they picked this person up.

Until then, there was nothing he could do, except worry about what was going to happen. All the people that he had regarded as his friends, were, now he came to think of it, Leonora's friends, and they were giving him a wide berth. The police had offered to take him to friends; that was when it had come home to him that he really didn't have any.

But it was Wednesday, and the prospect of unquestioning human companionship beckoned. Not friendship, not by any stretch of the imagination. Not even the ill-at-ease sympathy of his party acquaintances would be offered, and that was, in a strange way, the attraction. People who didn't know who he was, or care. People who had no interest whatever in what was happening to him, and did not feel obliged to pretend any.

A couple of hours off, that was all it was. All it ever had been. It wasn't so much to ask. He hadn't been going to go, but he would. He deserved some time off, because his mind, despite his efforts to stop it, kept reviewing what had happened, what Leonora had been frightened might happen.

But they had to find this man; even though Sergeant Drake had seen her, and she seemed to have been at the pub with him – he wouldn't be cleared of suspicion until they actually had him. His boss. Leonora had threatened to tell his boss. Jonathan frowned. In what circumstances would telling his boss have any effect on his behaviour? He had merely been making a nuisance of himself. Hanging about, trying to talk to her. His boss could hardly be expected to do anything about that. He hadn't been paying much attention when Leonora told him.

And maybe that wasn't who she was with at all; they said it was this ex-convict, and it seemed unlikely that he would have a boss at all. If he wasn't the one who had been hanging around, that would leave it all up in the air again.

He needed some time off.

'No surprises,' said Freddie, when he'd finished. 'She died of asphyxiation. I can't narrow the time down any more than you already know, I'm afraid. Between eleven and one, give or take.'

Judy nodded.

'No struggle. She tried to pull the restriction away, but she doesn't seem to have got hold of her attacker at all. Taken entirely by surprise, I'd say. No other assault of any sort.' He washed his hands, and ushered her out of the room.

'I don't suppose there's any evidence that the same person attacked both of them?' Judy said.

'No,' said Freddie. 'I'm told there are some fibres on Mrs Beale's clothes that should be able to be matched up once you've got a suspect, but nothing that ties in with Mrs Austin.' He walked with her to the door, opening it for her. 'And there's no similarity in the type of attack, or the amount of strength required – a woman could have killed Mrs Beale, but not Mrs Austin.' He cleared his throat a little. 'I was sorry to hear that she was a friend of yours,' he said.

It almost took Judy by surprise to hear Freddie being serious. She gave a short sigh, and nodded.

'Can't be easy for you,' he said. 'I hope it's over soon.'

Yes. Judy went out into the late afternoon, and walked to her car, which had been sitting in the sun for two hours before the clouds had rolled in, making the sky dark and depressing. She spent some moments, her mind on other things, trying to get into the car with Lloyd's key. She found her own, and opened the door to heat that she was quite certain would have happily cooked a small chicken. In winter, the cold would have kept the same chicken fresh for days.

She joined the shoppers and commuters on their way back from Barton to Stansfield, getting stopped at every red light. The open windows made it a noisy, smelly journey out of the city; the oppressive, dark heat was depressing her as she sat waiting at an unexplained hold-up.

A water-main had been ruptured by telephone workers; Judy glared at the orange-jacketed constable who waved her right, on to a diversion through Barton's seedier back-streets. In unfamiliar territory, she slowed the car down as she negotiated tiny cobbled one-way streets barely wide enough for the car. Frank Beale would have been risking scraping the Rolls on the walls of the buildings; he needed two spaces to park at Andwell House.

Another hold-up, waiting to join the side-street which took traffic back to the main road. Escape from this hot stuffy city was almost in sight, but the main stream of traffic would not give way; perspiration trickled down her neck from her hairline, and Judy pulled on the hand-brake, resigned to her fate.

A tall, fair man walked briskly past the line of traffic; Judy watched as he made his way along the litter-strewn pavement, past a cinema the attraction of whose bill eluded her, and in through the door of something called the Apollo Gymnasium.

Judy looked ahead, counting the cars between her and freedom; the traffic on the main road, having escaped whatever dire diversion it had had to endure, was not about to let anyone in. She pulled the car over, driving its nearside wheels on to the pavement, and got out, walking quickly towards the door.

'Sorry, love – men only.' The large, suntanned tattooed figure had appeared as if by magic, as soon as she had touched the door.

'I thought that was against the law these days,' she said.

'Yeah, well – you take us to court, darling.'

She produced her identification. 'Do your members sign in?' she asked.

'Have you got a warrant?'

'No,' she said, and smiled. 'I just want a look at the book,' she said. 'That's all.'

She had not, it would appear, pulled the car over far enough. The traffic ahead of her car was moving, and horns started to sound.

'I'm going to get lynched,' she said. 'Go on – just one look, that's all.'

'What for?'

'Nothing to do with the club,' she said. 'Look – I'm not vice squad – I'm not even Barton. Not my problem. Someone who attacks women is – and I'm told he was in here today. I just want a quick look at your book to see if his name's there.' It was stretching the truth wafer-thin, but sex offenders weren't protected by the honour amongst thieves code, and it might work.

It was beginning to sound like Paris on a bad day. She glanced back, and her heart sank as she saw a yellow-banded cap make its sinister way along the double yellow-lined road. 'One look,' she pleaded.

He reached into the void behind him, and produced the book, open at the appropriate page. 'He won't use his right name,' he said.

Judy looked at the last signature, and smiled again. 'You're a toff,' she said.

The dreaded ticket was being placed under her windscreen wiper by a traffic warden who was enjoying unheard-of popularity as a cheer went up.

'Sorry, sorry!' Judy grabbed the polythene package, and thanked God that the threatening downpour had had the decency to stay off, or the car wouldn't have started.

Once on the dual carriageway, everything on the road was determined to pass her with a growl of its engine and a rush of air that made the car shudder; all the people she had kept

166

waiting outside the Apollo, she reckoned. Lloyd would be telling her to get a new car. One that was less likely to fall apart if a lorry passed it. One that could possibly pass other vehicles.

The traffic slowed to a crawl, and stopped. Judy didn't believe it. Defeated by the nameless, darting hedgerow insects and the dirty exhaust of the van in front of her, she closed the windows, and baked as the line inched its way towards temporary traffic lights erected for roadworks that no one seemed to be working on. A new car wouldn't have prevented this, she told herself. No, but a new car would have a fan which would distribute cold air. And hot air, when the occasion arose. Unlike hers, which hadn't worked for years, and confirmed the car in its belief that it was actually a piece of kitchen equipment.

Her thoughts strayed to Mrs Austin's car. The lab said that only the mechanic's prints were on the ignition key under the seat; he would hardly have taken it for a joyride, not knowing when it was likely to be picked up. Anyone else using it would either have destroyed his prints or left their own. The rest of it was clean; that could be accounted for by the fact that it had just been valeted. Therefore, it had never moved from the spot, and Jonathan Austin was lying. And now she knew that Drake was right – well, she'd check with him. He'd know Barton's dives. She wasn't sure where it got her, but she felt as though something had clicked into place. She wasn't sure what; she'd have to go over her notes.

She drove through Stansfield, thanking God for its traffic-light-free streets, making for Malworth, now very late for Lloyd, with whom she was supposed to be eating before they started organising the reconstruction, and arrived at the station hot, crumpled, sweaty and bad-tempered. It did nothing for her morale to discover Detective Chief Superintendent Allison passing the time of day with the desk sergeant.

'Ah, Mrs Hill,' he said. 'May I take up some more of your valuable time?'

Freddie being serious and Allison being positively gallant; Lloyd would be putting it down to body snatchers. Well, she thought, as they went through the usual impossibility of who went through doors first, if this is my first taste of sexual harassment, it won't last long, the state I'm in.

'This is what you might call baptism by fire,' he said.

You might, she thought. If you talked in clichés. Oh, my God, she was getting just like Lloyd. She'd be correcting the man's grammar next. Not that she could. 'Yes, sir,' she said.

'Your divisional chief inspector is in Marbella or somewhere, and his deputy, I am reliably informed, has just managed to break his leg.'

'Yes, sir. Painting his window-frames.'

Allison nodded. 'The problem is,' he said, 'that on-the-spot decisions do have to be made, and Chief Inspector Lloyd is making them at the moment.'

Judy was puzzled. Had she said something this morning that had made Allison think she wasn't showing Lloyd due deference? He was only one rank above her, after all. Did she have to behave as though he was the Chief Constable to prove that they weren't going to start having domestic differences at work? They weren't even having them at home yet.

Anyway – he'd just said himself that the circumstances were quite exceptional. Under normal circumstances, she would be taking her orders from her own DCI, and they would not be investigating a crime which happened to be in telephonic communication with another one in another division. It was hardly her fault that despite transferring out of the division she was finding herself working with him still. And quite apart from all that, Allison had never even hinted that he knew about their private lives, so why start complaining now that she had transferred?

'But DCI Lloyd is Stansfield division, and one of the murders occurred in this division. The incident room will be here, and some decisions which may have to be made on a purely local basis can only be made at chief inspector level or above. If neither Mr Lloyd or myself is available, this could cause problems. Your divisional superintendent is very heavily committed with a major enquiry, and can't really leave divisional headquarters.'

Oh, that's what it was. So we're sending in someone from another division to take local charge, Mrs Hill, and we all know that as a rabid feminist you are extremely touchy about women not being regarded as capable, so I've come here to pacify you by going on about your valuable time, instead of just getting on with it.

'It is therefore felt that you should – for the duration of this investigation, or until the return of your divisional chief inspector – take the temporary rank of Acting DCI.'

And she hadn't even had to wink at him.

'Yes, sir,' she said. Not 'Who, me?' which was what she was actually thinking.

He smiled. 'It's an unusual step to take, I know, so soon after your promotion. But it's an unusual situation. The chief is sure that his confidence will not be misplaced.' He smiled. 'Good afternoon, Mrs Hill,' he said.

She felt almost light-headed as she went out, to find Lloyd waiting impatiently for her. Allison waved as his car wafted him away back to Barton. His car wouldn't be hot and stuffy, she thought. He didn't even have to drive it. She watched as it went off, wondering a little how it must feel.

She told Lloyd; he seemed pleased. But then Lloyd could seem anything he liked. He should have been on the stage. And she couldn't be sure how he really felt.

'It doesn't mean anything,' she said, as they ordered spaghetti in Malworth's pride and joy, a yuppie Italian wine bar and restaurant which charged too much, but had a good chef. 'It's only because we're so undermanned they can't spare a real one.'

Lloyd smiled. 'Oh, I think they could if they thought it necessary,' he said.

'They'd have thought it necessary if it wasn't all mixed up with your case,' she said. 'They think you'll babysit me.'

'Possibly,' he said. 'But I doubt it.' He patted her hand. 'I told you when they offered you the job – they're seeing how you handle command.'

Their meals came; Lloyd issued a stern warning about eating and working.

'He'd lost his leg,' she said.

'Oh, yes.' Lloyd twirled spaghetti expertly round his fork as he spoke. 'He woke up to find himself this side of the Channel, invalided out. He wrote to her, but he never got a reply.'

Judy's fork didn't twirl. It would get halfway round, then slip back, and ship its cargo. 'What did he do?' she asked, trying again. Some Italians must starve to death.

'When the war was over, he went back. The family had left the château, and the people there didn't know where they'd gone.'

She watched him for a moment, and tried hard to do what he did. This time she got it round her fork, all right, but she doubted very much if she could actually get it in her mouth.

'You should take two or three strands,' he said helpfully. 'It builds up. Anyway, he did odd jobs to keep himself going while he asked everyone for miles until he found someone who knew them. Then he followed the trail until he found her.'

All with just the one leg, she thought, but she couldn't speak. It was like parking, she thought. He made it look so easy, but it never worked for her. He wouldn't have held up an entire streetful of traffic; his car would have slid exactly the correct distance on to the pavement. And he wouldn't have got a parking ticket, she thought sourly, determinedly getting through her mammoth mouthful. 'What did he do once he'd found her?' she asked.

'He brought her back to Wales, and they got married in the chapel.'

Wales. Judy had been there with Lloyd, very briefly. Even in the eighties they had regarded her, a Londoner, with deep suspicion. What would they have thought of a French girl, seventy years ago?

'What sort of reception did she get?' she asked.

'Oh, the usual, I think. In the front parlour. The Co-op Hall wasn't built until the thirties.' He smiled. 'Now – hurry up and finish your coffee. We've got work to do.'

You can't give me orders, she thought. But she didn't say it out loud.

Back at Andwell House, people milled around, getting things organised for the reconstruction. Lloyd went off to talk to Allison, and Judy spied Drake.

'Mickey! Just the man I want.'

'That's nice to know,' he said.

'The Apollo Gymnasium, in Barton,' she said. 'What is it?'

'Caxton Lane?'

'That's it. Above a cinema.'

'It's a gym,' he said, his eyes widely innocent, the accent American. 'Where we macho men can go pump iron.'

'And?'

'And meet a lot of like-minded people, some of whom are quite definitely juveniles,' he said, his face grim.

Judy nodded. 'You don't approve?'

170

'No, I don't. I don't care what anyone's sexual preferences are, but I don't approve of kids being exploited, and I don't approve of the drug culture that the whole business encourages, and if that makes me a prude, that's too bad.'

She smiled. 'It can't make you a prude,' she said. 'Because I agree with you. I'm broad-minded, you're conservative, and he's a prude.'

Drake laughed.

'Not mine, needless to say. Lloyd's.'

'We tried to raid it once, but it was no go,' said Drake. 'Rosemary's too clever for that. Was too clever.' He brightened a little. 'Maybe we'll get Beale now that she's not there to keep him in line,' he said. 'What's your interest?'

'Austin,' she said. 'You were right, Mickey.'

He smiled. 'I think he's gone off me, now,' he said.

'He signs himself in as David Morris, would you believe?'

'Morris as in Austin?'

'And David as in Jonathan. He's got less imagination than me,' she said.

Drake walked with her along the river bank as the lowering sky grew dark for real. 'Do you think he was just doing something he'd rather no one knew about when he says he was going for his wife's car?' he asked.

'I'm sure he was,' she said. 'I didn't like that call.'

'No,' said Drake. 'I know what you mean. I felt as if he knew a lot more about this than he's saying.' He stopped, and looked down into the river. 'We let Pearce go,' he said. 'There didn't seem much point in passing him on to you. He hasn't murdered anyone.'

'No. I don't know what Mr Pearce's problem is, but I never fancied him for a murderer.'

'No.' Drake looked at her. 'Do you think a woman could have killed Mrs Beale?' he asked.

Judy nodded. Freddie said it was possible.

'The chief inspector wants to see if Mrs Austin's car was here,' said Drake. 'He's got a theory.'

'Mm. I know.' Judy was about to point out that the car hadn't been anywhere, when she knew what had clicked into place. 'Do we still have it?' she asked.

'What?' Drake looked lost.

'Mrs Austin's car – is it still at the police lab?'

'Yes, as far as I know.'

'Would you do me a favour, Mickey?'

Steve had been given accommodation, he had been fed, he had been looked after better than Beale's mother would have been. He just hadn't been able to leave. Not that Beale had actually said so, or locked him in or anything. It was just made clear that any attempt to leave would be met with resistance from the heavies, who had reappeared about the time he was thinking of leaving, of course. He wasn't afraid of them now; he had got used to their looming presence in his life, and if he didn't touch them they would do him no harm, like little pussy. The nursery rhyme made him five again, for a moment. He wondered what his mother would say if she could see him now.

Beale was introducing him to his solicitor, a thinly handsome fortyish West Indian in an expensive grey suit. Steve frowned. 'I don't get it,' he said.

Beale sighed. 'Steve, if I had let you go last night just after I'd told you about Mrs Austin, what would you have done?'

'Run,' said Steve, with feeling.

'Run. And how far do you think you would have got?'

Steve shrugged.

'I'll tell you. You'd have run right back into prison.' He shook his head. 'No wonder people like you spend half your lives there,' he said. 'You've got to use your brain sometimes.'

Steve used to think he had one, of sorts. Now he wasn't so sure.

'You're going to go to the police of your own accord,' said the solicitor.

'What?' Steve twisted round to Beale. 'I was in her *flat*, Frank! They'll have my prints – they'll do me for it!'

Beale was shaking his head again. 'See?' he said. 'You were seen with her. You went home with her. Your prints are there. So what were you going to do when they caught up with you, which they would have done before you got to the end of the street?' He sat down, and looked at the solicitor, raising his eyes to heaven. Then he turned back to Steve. 'Denied it,' he said. 'Right?'

Steve thought. No . . . no, he wouldn't have been stupid enough to try to *deny* it, but— He sighed.

172

'You are going to go to the police,' said the solicitor. 'I will accompany you. You will say you believe they want to talk to you, and you will tell them what happened.'

Steve gasped. 'What happened is that I took her home, and left her there and now she's dead and they're looking for me!' he shouted. 'What use will you be?'

'Did you kill Mrs Austin?' he asked.

'No, but they won't believe that – and neither do you.' He looked suspiciously at Beale. 'What is this?' he asked. 'Why's he here? Not because you believe me – not because you want to help.'

Beale leant across the solicitor and looked closely at Steve. 'I think he might be using his brain at last,' he said. 'I don't know what you did, Steve. But someone killed Rosemary, and I want the cops to find out who. No – I don't want to help you. But you are going to help them.'

'But – didn't you say they were questioning someone?'

'Yes. But I know who it is, and I know he hasn't got the guts to kill anyone.'

'But if they think they've got him – where does that leave me?'

Beale beckoned him to the window, and he looked down to see police everywhere. He went pale. 'Are they waiting for me?' he asked.

'No, they don't know you're here. They think they know you're not – it'll take them a while to come and check again. You're safe for the moment. No, Steve, what they're doing is getting ready for a reconstruction of my wife's last few minutes on this earth. Which means that they don't believe they've got him. And they think the two crimes are linked,' he said.

Steve felt his legs go again, and walked shakily away from the window.

'I don't know enough about what went on in the Austin place to make my own investigation,' said Beale. 'But they do. And I have faith in that young woman,' he added. 'She's no one's fool. She knows Pearce didn't do it – he's home already. I saw him. But, if she fails – and even the best fail sometimes – Mr Mervyn will have learned a whole lot more about what went on than we know at present, and I can make my own investigation then.'

Steve sat down with a bump. So he was Frank's key to inside information. Carrying out his own investigation might have been how he put it to Mervyn, but what he really wanted was a way of getting information early enough to exact his own revenge before the police could stop him.

'I look after my employees, Steve.' He bent down towards him. 'Mr Mervyn is the best. You listen to what he says, and do what he says. Co-operate with the police, Steve. And if they find out who killed Rosemary as a result of your co-operation, you're on a fat bonus.'

Steve swallowed. 'What if I'm doing life?' he asked.

Beale shrugged. 'That won't really concern me too much,' he said. 'I'll have got the information I need.'

Steve knew when he was beaten.

The solicitor let loose a long, long sigh. 'Right,' he said. 'I want to know what you did from the moment – the *moment* you saw Mrs Austin that evening, until the moment you left her. And I mean everything.' He sat down. 'We may decide that the police don't need to know everything,' he said. 'But I do.'

Oh well. Things could be worse. They could have brought back hanging.

Lloyd hadn't seen the riverside development at night before; he watched as Drake and Judy walked along a pathway lit by fake Victorian lamp standards. They feigned gas-lighting, creating small splashes of weak light at regular intervals, dimly reflected in the water. He wondered if the reconstruction would produce anything. It would be hard to see anyone walking along here, if you weren't deliberately looking; harder still to spot anyone following.

They parted company; Judy walked back down to her car, parked close to the Riverside Inn, and Drake joined Lloyd. He was impressed by Judy's temporary promotion; Lloyd needed a little time to think about how he felt.

Only the day before yesterday, it had been something that might happen one day, and Jack Woodford had taken him by surprise by pointing that out to him; now, it was something that was obviously going to happen much sooner than later. A chief constable with an eye to current preoccupations, and a late flowering of ambition in a more than able female officer made for speedy promotion, or a shrug of the shoulders over missed opportunities. The chief constable had clearly opted for the former, and Lloyd had to think about that. He had been thinking about it longer than Judy had: Allison had told him what they had decided.

But all that would have to wait, and be examined at three o'clock in the morning, when he would be awake with a book and Judy would be asleep. Right now, he had work to do. He was parked opposite Andwell House; it was late twentieth-century twee, with its craft shops and dwelling units faced with coloured stone, the paintwork picked out in primary colours. Spaces had been cut into the building every so often, and greenery sprouted. They knew that greenery was important, these days. It never occurred to them that they were directly opposite natural parkland. He glanced over at it. On which they had put unnatural objects for children to amuse themselves with, he added to himself. What was wrong with climbing trees, for God's sake?

'Horrible, isn't it?' said Drake.

Lloyd smiled. 'I suppose it's an improvement on Mitchell Engineering effluent fouling the river,' he said. 'Judy pointed that out to me. She likes it.'

'If they would just clean up the rivers and leave it at that,' said Drake. 'Why do they have to build toytowns everywhere half decent?'

'Don't ask me,' said Lloyd. 'It used to be an empty warehouse. I suppose it's more useful now.'

'That factory's worse,' said Drake. 'Pity Pearce didn't burn it down.'

'Oh – I meant to congratulate you about that,' said Lloyd. 'You were spot on. Wanted to go up with it, apparently.' He glanced up at the flat. 'I shouldn't think he's too far off suicide now,' he added.

Drake grunted.

'That's why he made the false confessions, if you ask me. He wants to be punished for something, does our Mr Pearce.' He laughed at himself. 'You'll have to get used to half-baked psychology,' he said, and looked at Drake, who seemed less than cheerful. 'What's up?' he asked.

'We're investigating two murders, sir. I come up with a failed arson attempt,' said Drake.

'It was a little puzzle, and it's been solved. Ask Acting Chief Inspector Hill – in my experience, if you solve the little puzzles, the big one stops being just as puzzling as you thought it was. Like the wedding ring. Another little puzzle that needed sorting out.'

Drake smiled. 'And which little puzzle would you like me to turn my hand to next, sir?' he asked.

'Mrs Hill's siren,' said Lloyd, and wound down his window as the police officer impersonating Mrs Beale came into view.

'I thought you thought it was just the TV, sir.'

Lloyd watched as the cars were waved down at the temporarily disabled traffic lights, and their occupants questioned. 'I don't think,' he said, his mind only half on Drake's question, 'that Mr Austin will watch that sort of television.'

'That's what I thought, sir,' said Drake. 'I didn't like to say.'

Lloyd grinned at him. 'Mickey,' he said, 'you can tell me I'm wrong any time you like. I'll soon pull rank when it suits me. And unless the circumstances are highly inappropriate, for God's sake call me Lloyd, like everyone else.'

They did it for over an hour, the policewoman walking six times from the pub to the flats from eleven until after midnight, walking through the pools of light, more slowly probably than Mrs Beale would have done. Not perhaps as nervous as Mrs Beale might have been on the final, lonely stretch. She knew she was surrounded by police; Mrs Beale had no such back-up. But then, Mrs Beale had had a long apprenticeship walking the streets at night, and Lloyd doubted if any aspect of human nature could have surprised her. But the psychologists said that people lost that essential wariness when they were within sight of home. Even Mrs Beale.

Drake rubbed his eyes as she made her final journey, with the traffic now virtually non-existent, and yawned. 'She looks just like Rosemary Beale,' he said. 'I hope Beale's not watching.'

There was a rumble of thunder, and large, heavy drops of rain sliced across the windscreen.

'Mrs Hill's asked me to tell the lab to hang on to Lennie Austin's car,' said Drake. 'And I've to ask Austin to collect it himself, and watch him doing it.'

Lloyd looked at him. 'And has she been so good as to indicate why you have to do all this?' he said. He leant out of the car. 'Thank you, Anne,' he called. 'I'll bet you're glad this stayed off until you'd finished! Let's all go home.'

'I've to tell her what happens,' he said. 'But she didn't say why.'

'Did she by any chance strongly resemble a gun-dog at the time?'

Drake laughed. 'She did a bit,' he said.

176

'Then do it,' said Lloyd.

Drake smiled. 'I will,' he said, getting out.

Lloyd watched him go to his own car, and drive off, reaching the junction just as the lights were switched on again, at red. He smiled. Drake was signalling right as he waited, but as the lights changed he pulled his car into the left lane, and on to the bridge.

Lloyd started his car, and followed suit, curious to know what had made Drake change his mind about going home. From the crown of the bridge, he could see Drake's car heading for the Riverside Inn, where he turned into the car park, pulling up beside Judy's car. Lloyd drove down and parked in the street outside, watching him.

Drake bent down, talking to Judy through the window as the rain grew heavier; then he got in with her just before the heavens opened.

Lloyd waited, his fingers drumming on the steering wheel, but they seemed to be there for the night. His windscreen wipers whipped back and forth, sending showers of rain off at either side; it grew even harder, bouncing off the pavements, and he glared at it as he waited for it to ease off. It did, after a fashion, but Drake didn't take the opportunity to leave Judy's car, and Lloyd switched off his engine. After a few moments, he sounded his horn twice but they took no notice. Swearing to himself, he got out and strode towards them, standing by the still open window.

'But there aren't any in Stansfield,' Judy said gloomily.

'No. It's a non-starter, really. But it seemed like a good idea at the time.' Drake sat back a little. 'I'll tell you what puzzles me,' he said. 'If Rosemary didn't sleep her way on to Austin-Pearce's board, how the hell did she get there?'

Judy nodded. 'What puzzles me even more,' she said, 'is why she wanted to be there at all.'

'Right,' said Lloyd. 'Ring Obsessives Anonymous if you need someone to talk to, but I want to go home, and I can't because the chances are that this bloody car won't start. I'm not staying here all night. Go home, Mickey.'

Drake looked up, startled. 'I was just trying to work out what this siren could have been,' he said.

'It's nearly one o'clock in the morning. You have to be back at work at nine o'clock, and you are entitled to eight hours away from the station. Take it. That's an order.'

'Sorry, s— ' Drake bit off the automatic mode of address. 'Sorry,' he said to Judy, and scrambled out of the car. 'Goodnight.'

'Night, Mickey,' said Judy, smiling a little at his confusion.

'Home,' said Lloyd, opening the car door.

'I'll try it first,' she said.

'Don't bother,' said Lloyd.

'It might be all right – the rain's only just come on.'

Lloyd slammed her door, and ran back to his own car in a crash of thunder that would have done Hollywood proud. He got in, getting angrier by the minute. They had to go through the ritual. He started the engine, and waited. He knew what was going to happen – she knew what was going to happen. But they had to pretend they didn't. Her car coughed and wheezed and shuddered, but it did not start. Eventually, she got out and ran to his car. He opened the door, and looked at her as she got in beside him.

'Listen, Acting Chief Inspector Hill,' he said. 'That car does not enhance your image.'

She shook rain from her hair, showering him. 'I like it,' she said obstinately.

'Now? You like it right now?'

'It's friendly,' she said.

'Friendly?' He drove into the car park, sweeping round to turn, and made his way through the teeming rain to the exit. 'Nothing works on it. And every time it rains, it gives up the ghost. And speaking of friendly – a new car would run on lead-free petrol.'

'So would that one,' she said.

'If you got it converted, which you haven't.'

He was stopped at the bloody lights now.

'I can't afford a new car.'

'Well, it doesn't look as though it'll be too long before you can,' he said.

There was a silence.

He pulled away on amber and turned on to the bridge, at last pointing in the right direction to get home, and away from here.

'Is that what's put you in a bad mood?' she asked, after a moment.

'I'm not in a bad mood.' A fork of lightning split the dark sky, and he peered through the rain at the tree-lined road. He wanted to be home. He wanted to be wrapped round a large whisky, and possibly Judy, if she was still speaking to him. He did not want to talk to Judy about her temporary promotion, and that was what he knew he was going to do.

'You could have fooled me. It bothers you, doesn't it?'

'Don't be ridiculous.'

He was supposed to be thinking about this rationally. Not arguing about it while he was trying to drive through a thunderstorm.

The car made its way along the Stansfield Road for some minutes before she spoke again.

'If I wasn't working on the same case, would it still bother you?' she asked.

'I can't very well answer that, since it doesn't bother me in the first place!'

'Pull in at that lay-by,' she said.

'What?' Automatically, he was signalling. Maybe she'd seen something going on. He pulled the car to a halt, and looked out at the empty road. 'Why?' he said. 'What's wrong?'

'Us,' she said. 'And I want to talk about it.'

He turned to her. 'We can talk about it at home, for God's sake!' he said.

'No, we can't. As far as I'm concerned, when we are at home we don't have ranks, and we're not going to discuss them there. We're going to sort this out here and now, once and for all.'

Right. That was clear enough. He switched off the engine, and listened to the rain battering the roof.

'So what's the problem?' she said.

He looked at the streaks of light through the streaming windscreen, and tried to think of the right words, but he couldn't. He hadn't been expecting it, that was the main problem. 'I saw you watching Allison when he left today,' he said. 'You fancy that, don't you? Senior management. It appeals to you.'

'Yes,' she said, defensively. 'What's wrong with that?'

'Nothing.' He wound down the window pointedly as she reached into her bag for a cigarette. Lightning lit the road, the woods; a train passed alongside them, silenced by the crack of thunder. This

179

was crazy. Sitting here with a thunderstorm raging over their heads instead of being at home.

She hadn't spoken. She did that; she used her interviewing technique when they were having a row. He used words. She used silence.

'I just don't know when it happened,' he said. 'My God, it took you ten years to take your sergeant's exam – now all of a sudden you want to be chief constable.'

'For one thing,' she said, after a moment, 'I joined a force that thought that women were for making the tea and looking after lost children. They were forced to call them women police officers rather than policewomen, and give them the same pay, but they didn't have to give them any opportunities. Or encouragement.' She paused. 'For another, I was married to someone who thought that my job was expendable, and his was the only one that mattered.'

'And it took you ten years to discover yourself, did it?'

'Yes.'

'And another three to get up the courage to apply for a sergeant's post,' he muttered.

She didn't say anything, but it wasn't technique this time. He'd hurt her. He was very good at hurting her.

'I know what I'm like,' she said quietly, after a few moments. 'But they offered me this job. And the temporary rank. I am getting more confident – it gives you confidence if people believe in you. It's because you believe in me that I've got this far, however belatedly.'

He sighed. 'I know,' he said. And she was good enough, and confident enough to go on. He knew that too. He also knew that he was ten years older than her, and even if his chance hadn't gone, he had neither the energy nor the ambition to keep one step ahead of her.

'I've got another fifteen, twenty years to go,' she said. 'Why shouldn't I try to go as far as I can?'

'No reason.'

'Lloyd, if this rape squad gets set up, it'll be headed by a DCI, and I'm going to apply,' she said.

He nodded. And get it. Clearly. She was practically being ordered to apply for it.

'Are you saying I shouldn't?'

180

'Of course not.'

The scene was bathed in white light again, and it sounded as though the sky was falling in. Perhaps it was.

'Would you resent it?'

Smoke drifted past his face, out into the pounding rain. He looked at her. 'No,' he said. 'I'd find it . . . difficult. I'm used to being senior to you,' he said, ashamed of himself even as he said it.

She looked baffled. 'I don't understand you,' she said. 'You don't think a woman's place is in the home – you don't think there are men's jobs and women's jobs – why does this matter?'

'The three-quarters Welsh,' he said. 'Men must work and women must weep.' He took her hand. 'If you catch up with me, the next step is overtaking me.'

'But you encouraged me to get promotion!'

He nodded. 'I just didn't realise you'd want to go further,' he said. 'I don't mean I wouldn't have encouraged you. I just never thought about it.'

'I don't know what I want, Lloyd. Sometimes I wish I was back on the beat. Being visible – being there when people need help. There's much more job satisfaction.' She was holding tight to his hand as she spoke. 'That or higher up,' she said. 'At this level, you're not one thing or the other. You're not on the front line, and you're not influencing policy. So if I want to move, the only way is up.'

Lloyd listened. 'I told you you'd end up as my chief super,' he said. 'You laughed.'

'Anyone listening to us would have hysterics,' she said. 'I've only just been promoted to inspector.'

Lloyd smiled, despite himself. Little drops of water, deflected by the open window, splashed his face.

'You and I are more important than any promotion,' she said.

He turned to her. 'You're not saying you'd hold back just because I don't like the idea,' he said, illogically appalled by that.

'No,' she said. 'Not with something like the rape squad. But if it was going to affect our lives, I wouldn't do it if you weren't happy with it. Neither would you. I wouldn't expect you to drag me off to West Yorkshire if I didn't want to go, and I've no intention of putting you in that position either.'

'No,' he said. He hadn't thought she would.

She still held on to his hand as though he might run away if she didn't. 'And if I really thought I might lose you,' she said, 'then I wouldn't do anything at all.'

'I said I'd find it difficult.' He smiled. 'Not impossible.'

'Right,' she said, releasing his hand. 'You can go home now.'

He started the engine, which he thought for one stricken moment had done a Judy on him, but it fired at the second attempt, and he moved off.

'What's this you're up to with Mrs Austin's car?' he asked.

'I just want to know what he does,' she said.

'But you're not telling anyone why?'

'I'm tired of being told I'm obsessed.'

'And you're going to prove that he's lying?' said Lloyd, quite unable to work out how.

'No,' she said. 'But Mrs Austin's car is really quite important, I think.'

He indicated left. 'You always call her that, don't you?' he said.

'Yes,' she said. 'It just . . . distances me from it a little, that's all.'

They didn't speak for the rest of the journey home; it was an unnatural silence, and it made the time pass slowly. He pulled in behind the flats, and they ran through the thunder and lightning to the door, getting soaked.

Judy went to have a bath, and he poured himself the drink he had been looking forward to. His usual practice was to read a book, or watch something on the video, but tonight, he pulled his briefcase on to his knee, and took out copies of the statements. He read them all, such as they were. Pearce's withdrawn nonsense, Austin's dubious declaration of his movements, Pauline Pearce's several different versions, the next-door neighbour's, written in Mary Alexander's neat, sloping hand, and police officerese.

I made the 999 call to the police while the sounds were still going on. My telephone is positioned by the window, and I was looking out when the noise ceased, and remained there until the police car arrived. I saw no one entering or leaving the flats during this time. I could hear a woman screaming, and someone shouting the word 'whore' repeatedly. I did not recognise the voice. I believe it was a man's voice.

Useless. Saw nothing, knows nothing. It was always the same.

Whatever Judy had in mind about Jonathan Austin, she was going about it the wrong way, he was sure of that. She had set him up as the villain from the start, and now she was trying to prove it. But that wasn't how it was done – she knew that usually. Facts, she would tell him. Look at the facts, and see them in a different light. She insisted that she wasn't letting her emotional involvement get in the way of her judgement, but calling her Mrs Austin like that was proof that she was, and she was forgetting her own advice.

Her newly kindled ambition did bother his male chauvinist soul; he knew that, and was honest enough with himself to admit it. But their relationship could survive a bit of male ego bashing. That wasn't what had put him in a bad mood.

It was his case, not Judy's, and he had to find the evidence he needed. He had to find Tasker, for one thing, but he felt that that would not be likely to get him any further forward. He had got all he was going to get; he simply had to look at what he'd got in a new light.

And he had to do it without Judy's help.

Eight

Lloyd. Mickey Drake didn't think he could ever call him Lloyd. It seemed all wrong, calling a senior officer by his surname. But it was true that everyone else did. He'd heard Jack Woodford call him Lloyd – even Judy did. He had some sort of hang-up about his first name. Anyway, you never knew where you were with the man. All pals one minute, and ordering you home like a stray dog the next. Still, he seemed all right. And he had warned him that he pulled rank when it suited him.

He pulled the phone across the desk, and dialled Malworth.

'DCI Hill, please,' he said.

'Judy Hill.'

'I've just come back from the lab,' he said.

'Oh, good. What happened?'

Mickey didn't know what she had been expecting to happen. 'He picked up the car,' he said.

'What did he do?' she asked.

Mickey gave a short sigh out of earshot of the phone. 'He got in and drove it away, ma'am.'

'Don't you start,' she warned him.

'Call me Judy,' had been the first order she had given him, when they had worked together. That had proved to be a whole lot easier than calling the chief inspector Lloyd. He smiled. 'Sorry, but I don't know what else you want me to say. He just drove it away.'

'But it was locked, wasn't it?'

Mickey ran a hand over his face. 'Yes,' he said. 'Sorry. He *unlocked* it, got in and drove it away. Ma'am.'

'What with?'

Mickey frowned. A key. What did people usually unlock cars with? His mouth opened slightly. A *key*. He closed his eyes.

'Does the dead silence mean you've stopped being sarcastic?' she asked.

'He had a key to it,' said Mickey. 'On his key-ring.'

'And she didn't. The garage had her key – that's the one under the seat, that Mr Austin didn't need to use, because he's got one on his ring. I've got Lloyd's on my ring – he's got mine, though God knows why. He'd sooner crawl through broken glass than use my car. But most people with two cars do.'

'Do you think he actually used her car, then?'

'Oh, I'm sure he used it,' said Judy.

There was a minor hubbub outside the office, and Mickey half rose, craning his neck to see through the glass partition to the desk. 'Good God,' he said.

'What?'

'Tasker's just walked in with Mervyn the Mouthpiece.'

'Who?'

'Beale's solicitor. He's reasonably straight, though. But he's good. And very, very expensive, so Tasker must be in good with Beale.'

'Whatever you have to do, Mickey, keep Tasker there until I get there,' she said.

'That shouldn't be too difficult,' said Mickey. 'I think Mr Tasker's going to be with us for some time.'

Lloyd had now joined Tasker and Mervyn, looking heartily relieved to see Tasker all in one piece. As they were being taken into an interview room, Mickey relayed Judy's message, and her belief about Mrs Austin's car.

He didn't seem even to be listening. 'Right. I'll go in first – you come in after about quarter of an hour, and ask anything you think is relevant. I'm assuming that the high-powered legal advice means that we'll have plenty to discuss with Mr Tasker.'

Lloyd went off, and Mickey twiddled his thumbs for fifteen minutes, whiling away the time rehearsing informal conversations that began 'Lloyd, I've been thinking . . . ' He still couldn't imagine it. He'd have to settle for not calling him anything. When the time was up, he knocked on the door, and joined the grim-looking tableau.

Mervyn was being smooth and conciliatory. 'My client was alarmed, Chief Inspector. That's why he . . . went to ground. He has explained that he was worried that he would be implicated in this crime.'

'He is implicated in it,' Lloyd said.

'Look,' said Tasker, leaning over the table towards him. 'I haven't killed anyone. Why would I want to kill her? We'd arranged to meet the next day. At her studio – she was . . . she was going to see me again.'

'Her studio?' queried Lloyd.

'Yes.'

'You didn't go there,' he said. 'We were there all day, Mr Tasker.'

Tasker looked a touch desperate. 'No,' he mumbled.

'Why not? Because you knew there was no point?'

'No!' He saw Mickey for the first time, and sighed. 'Oh, it's you,' he said.

Mickey smiled, and sat down. 'Yes,' he said. 'It's me.'

'This is Detective Sergeant Drake,' said Lloyd to Mervyn.

Mervyn stood up and shook hands. 'How do you do, Sergeant Drake.' he said, smiling, and sat down again.

'Detective sergeant?' said Tasker. 'You've done all right for yourself.'

Mickey still smiled. 'You haven't answered the chief inspector's question,' he said. 'Why didn't you go to the studio?'

'I was busy.'

'Doing what?'

'None of your business,' said Tasker.

Mervyn fixed him with a stare, and Mickey watched interestedly as Tasker wilted under it.

'I just changed my mind,' said Tasker. 'It didn't seem such a good idea next day.'

Lloyd sat back, tipping the chair back, rocking gently on its back legs. 'Why are your fingerprints on the Austins' phone?' he asked.

Tasker glanced at Mervyn before he spoke. 'The phone was ringing when we got to the door,' he said. 'She went in to answer it, and I followed her in. I – I stopped her picking it up.'

Lloyd let the chair fall forward with a thump. 'You certainly did,' he said.

'No! I just stopped her . . . I wanted to say goodnight.'

Lloyd raised an eyebrow. 'A very permanent goodnight,' he observed.

'I never touched her!'

'Oh – you just said goodnight. Hardly worth stopping her answering the phone, was it?'

Mervyn was watching Tasker like a cat; Mickey got the odd feeling that Tasker was on his own in here. Mervyn was on their side.

'I don't mean that,' Tasker said miserably. 'I mean I didn't hurt her.'

Constable Merriwether was writing, and Tasker looked over at him. 'I just kissed her goodnight,' he said. 'You make sure that's what you put down!'

'When did she remove her wedding ring?' Mickey asked.

He shrugged. 'Before I saw her,' he said.

'Why?'

'I don't know! She said she was angry with herself.'

Lloyd rocked gently back and forth. Mickey hoped the chair legs held out. 'Someone else was angry with her too,' he said. 'Who, do you suppose?'

Tasker looked at Mervyn again.

'My client really doesn't have any knowledge of that,' said Mervyn.

'But he must have thought about it,' Lloyd said. 'If he didn't kill her. She died minutes after you left her, Tasker. The place was practically demolished – you disappeared off the face of the earth.'

Mickey saw Tasker begin to understand what he was getting at. Mervyn, who had understood all along, was tense, still watching Tasker as though he could pull his strings. Lloyd's chair waited in suspended animation, and Mickey held his breath.

'You think I saw someone,' said Tasker. He shook his head. 'I didn't. I'd have killed *him*, believe me.'

Mickey did. Lloyd relaxed, and resumed the rocking.

'I reckon her old man was in there all the time,' Tasker said. 'Watching us.' He looked down at the table. 'She was surprised the flat was in darkness. She thought he'd be in. I think he was.'

Lloyd tipped the chair way, way back, as he thought. It was all for show, as though this was a wholly new concept, and not one that Judy Hill had been putting forward for some time.

'It was a bit dangerous, wasn't it?' he asked, after a moment.

187

'Getting close enough to see the flat, if she thought her husband was home?'

Mickey smiled inwardly at the sudden Welshness, normally only just apparent.

'I made her let me walk up with her,' said Tasker.

Mickey waited for the chair to fall forward dramatically, but it didn't. It remained, precariously balanced on its back legs, while Lloyd looked up at the ceiling.

'Made her?' he asked, his voice light.

Tasker sighed again. 'I was worried about some nutter in a car.'

'A nutter in a car? Where did he suddenly spring from?' asked Lloyd.

'Well – we're at the old post office, and this bloke comes in a car and just sits and watches us.'

Lloyd glanced at Mickey. 'Ah, that car,' he said. 'We know about that.' Now he let the chair fall forward, but with much less force. 'And that worried you, did it?'

'He'd done it earlier,' said Tasker. 'When we were outside the pub.'

Lloyd frowned. 'When?'

'About ten minutes after we came out – about half past ten, or so.'

Mickey looked at Lloyd, barely shaking his head.

'And he stopped and watched you that time too?'

'He didn't exactly stop the first time. Just slowed right down as he passed us. It bothered Lennie a bit.'

'And then at the post office, you say it happened again?'

'Only he stopped this time. And I didn't want her walking up there alone.'

'And that's it, is it?' said Lloyd. 'That's all you're going to tell me? No make of car, no number, no description of the driver?'

'My client has told you all he knows, Mr Lloyd,' said Mervyn.

'Yes,' said Lloyd, getting up. 'It was her husband, or this phantom in the car. Think about it, Mr Tasker,' he said, indicating with a little jerk of his head that Mickey should also leave. 'And think about Mrs Beale. My colleague will want to ask you some questions about her.'

Mickey met Judy Hill on his way out. Lloyd didn't even acknowledge her, but went striding into his office, closing the door firmly.

Judy shrugged. 'Is Tasker still here?' she said.

'In there, with his brief,' said Mickey. 'But I don't think you'd better go in until Mr Lloyd's finished with him.'

'I won't,' she said. 'I've seen the mood he's in.'

Mickey should have heeded her implicit advice, but he didn't. He left her talking to the desk sergeant, and knocked on Lloyd's door.

Lloyd was on the phone to an estate agent about some property he seemed fairly desperate to see. Presumably all was not well, after all. Perhaps he did stand a chance, he thought. But he was probably too young for her. Pity.

Lloyd put down the phone. 'I take it that it wasn't you who saw them at the pub?' he said.

'No,' said Mickey. 'I was still on watch at the flats.' He suspected that Tasker had invented the first incident, but Lloyd seemed to believe him.

'So someone else was interested in them,' he said.

Mickey frowned. 'Maybe,' he said.

Lloyd rubbed his eyes. 'Well,' he said, 'did I catch sight of Mrs Hill?'

'Yes – she's waiting to talk to Tasker.'

'Then she'd better get on with it,' said Lloyd. 'Mervyn won't let us keep him for ever.'

Mickey gasped. 'You're never letting him go, are you?'

'Don't have much option.' Lloyd stood up, and reached for his jacket.

'But he was there! His prints are all over the place – there's a whole handprint on the phone! He isn't even denying that he stopped her answering it.'

'Quite.' Lloyd banged his own hand down on his phone, making Mickey jump again. 'So when did she answer it? While she was dodging a maniac who was trying to bash her brains out?'

Mickey sat down, and thought about what might have happened. 'Maybe he did let her answer it,' he said. 'Maybe he got angry after that. Or maybe he answered it himself – afterwards.'

'Maybe,' said Lloyd. 'And maybe he didn't. The only motive anyone can come up with is sexual frustration – he'd be unlikely, I would have thought, to call her a whore in those circumstances. There are other much more apt names he could have called her. There is no evidence to suggest that there was any bad feeling between them – in fact there is a lot of evidence to the contrary from the people in the pub.'

Mickey nodded.

'And maybe, as Judy never tires of pointing out, Austin did it. Tasker's suggestion is perfectly valid. Austin's story is weak and uncorroborated, and doesn't even hold up, because the car *was* at the garage. He could well have been in the house all along, with the lights out, watching them. Tasker and Mrs Austin even come in and say a passionate goodnight. It was too much for him, and as soon as Tasker left, he killed her.'

'Do you think that's likely?' asked Mickey. 'In view of his membership of the Apollo?'

'I don't think he would be too pleased to see his wife behaving like that in public – especially in view of his political aspirations.' He closed and locked his desk drawer. 'Perhaps it was Austin who saw them at the pub. You pays your money, and you takes your choice,' he said.

'The neighbours say that Austin's car was there all evening,' countered Mickey.

'And Mrs Hill thinks he used his wife's car. She could be right.'

Mickey nodded again. Austin's behaviour had certainly been strange. And he could have taken his wife's car. And he had also felt that knowingness that had bothered Judy when Austin rang her. He began to see what Lloyd meant.

'Like I said, you pays your money. Reasonable doubt, Mickey. As long as they could both have been there, there is reasonable doubt.'

'Isn't that for the court to worry about, though?'

Lloyd sighed. 'If a jury convicted someone in circumstances that *I* thought constituted reasonable doubt, I would not be happy. I'm not out to get a result. I'm trying to get at the truth.'

Mickey blew out his cheeks. 'But – if it *was* an unsafe conviction it would get overturned. It's not as though they hang them any more.'

'No,' said Lloyd. 'Sometimes I wish they did.'

'What?' Mickey said, startled. 'I'd never have had you down for a bring back hanging man.'

'I'm not,' said Lloyd. 'I think it was utterly barbaric. But we've lost our way since we abandoned it. When a man's life was at stake, reasonable doubt meant something. Now, juries seem to me to convict on possibilities.'

He sat on the desk as he warmed to his subject, and Mickey knew that he had made a fundamental error in bringing the subject up.

'How easy would a bent copper find it to get colleagues to alter statements and plant evidence on suspected IRA terrorists if someone was going to get hanged at the end of it?' he asked.

'Not very,' agreed Mickey.

'No. And the other side of the coin is that without the drama of death being the penalty, some judges seem to have forgotten that murder is a deadly crime. We send people to jail for not paying library fines and give wife murderers probation.' He slid off the desk again. 'If they don't get to put a bit of black cloth on their heads, they can't be bothered doing anything.' He opened the door. 'We abolished hanging, and I for one am heartily glad. But we failed to come up with anything to replace it. Now – I'm off out for an hour or so. If anyone wants me, too bad.'

Mickey watched him go, shaking his head. The day had started out so promisingly, too.

Call him Lloyd? He must be joking.

Steve Tasker sat opposite her, hands thrust in the pockets of his jeans, his face blank.

'I'm investigating the death of Mrs Rosemary Beale,' she said.

'I had nothing to do with that!'

'I know,' she said. 'And of course you don't have to answer my questions. But you're in trouble, Mr Tasker. I don't think you killed Mrs Austin, but there are people here who do.'

'My client wishes to co-operate with the police,' said Mervyn. 'He is as anxious to find the murderer of these ladies as you are, Chief Inspector.'

Judy liked being called Chief Inspector, but her heart felt a little heavy. Lloyd clearly didn't want to know.

'*Are* you anxious to know who killed them, Mr Tasker?'

'Yes,' he said simply, and Judy believed him, if only because it would let him off the hook.

'Mrs Austin told people that you were making a nuisance of yourself,' she said.

191

'She wouldn't have said that,' said Tasker. 'I don't believe that – who told you?'

'Her husband.'

'He's lying.'

Yes, thought Judy. I know he is. But you have to help me, Stephen Arthur Tasker. 'Her friend said she wanted nothing to do with you.'

Tasker smiled, unexpectedly. 'She didn't want anything to do with me,' he said. 'She came to see me once when I was in prison, and that was to tell me what she thought of me. For what I'd done – for using her – she did want nothing to do with me. The trouble was, she fancied me something rotten.'

'Fancied you? Or was in love with you?'

Tasker shook his head. 'I don't go in much for that,' he said.

'But is it true?'

He dropped his eyes from hers. 'I think so,' he said.

'Were you sleeping with her?'

'You mean since I came out?' He shook his head.

'Why not?'

He smiled. 'I know I'm a dead ringer for Tom Cruise,' he said, 'but I don't always get lucky.'

'Especially not with Mrs Austin?'

'Chief Inspector – you did say you were investigating Mrs Beale's murder?' enquired the solicitor.

'Yes,' said Judy, not taking her eyes off Tasker. 'She wasn't into one-night stands, was she? Or cheating on her husband. If she had wanted to go back to you, that's what she'd have told him. Not that she was frightened of you.'

Tasker's eyes widened. 'She didn't say that! I don't believe you.'

Judy shrugged. 'That's what I've been told,' she said.

'By Austin again.'

She didn't answer, but picked up Tasker's statement. 'It says here she was all for it,' she said. 'Arranged a clandestine meeting with you, even.'

Tasker looked desperately at Mervyn, but he seemed to have lost interest in his client. 'She did,' he said. 'I've said why I didn't go.'

'You changed your mind,' said Judy.

'Can you think of any reason why I would *want* to kill her? She was great,' he said, and his shoulders drooped a little. 'She

192

was great. I . . . I can't believe she's dead. I can't believe someone did that to her.'

'But she didn't want to have anything to do with you.'

He looked up. 'She could have said no till the cows came home – I would never have hurt her. But she didn't. She was going to meet me.'

'But she had been saying no,' said Judy.

'Yes.'

'So what made her finally say yes?'

He looked down at the table again.

'Because you told her that her husband was gay? That he was just using her?'

Mervyn looked up sharply, suddenly interested.

Tasker, on the other hand, lifted his head slowly, giving her the blank stare that she knew so well. Which meant she was right.

'But you hardly know the man,' she said, countering his stare. 'Just by sight. You've been out of circulation since before she met him. So how could you have known that?'

His face didn't so much as flicker a response.

'Because you worked as a driver for Rosemary Beale,' she went on, answering her own questions. 'You've seen him. At one of her husband's unsavoury establishments. You didn't just tell Mrs Austin that her husband was gay – you told her that he was a regular at the Apollo.'

She stood up. Tasker's eyes followed her movement, but he himself remained quite still.

'How well did you know Rosemary Beale?' she asked, using Lloyd's trick of looking out of the window. The idea was to turn quickly, to catch a reaction that might escape the witness who was trying hard not to react.

No response.

'Was it when you found out where Mrs Austin's studio was that you went off the idea of meeting her?'

She turned then, and caught him as his eyes lost the blank look, for just an instant. He stiffened slightly, knowing he had given himself away; he wouldn't do it again, so Judy sat down. He was involved with Rosemary Beale.

'Do you know why Mrs Beale wanted to get into Austin-Pearce? Do you know why she wanted Gordon Pearce out? Do you know

193

why she and Jonathan Austin were so interested in lorries?'

He turned to Mervyn. 'Well?' he said. 'Do I still co-operate?'

Mervyn looked from Tasker to Judy, and lifted his shoulders in an elegant little shrug. 'That's what we are being asked to do,' he said.

Tasker held his eyes for a moment, then looked back at Judy. 'I haven't done anything against the law,' he said.

Judy picked up her notebook. 'Then it won't do any harm to co-operate, will it?' she said.

Tasker sat back. 'I saw him go into the Apollo,' he said. 'I was interested, and then I found that he used a false name – and that just means one thing. So I told Rosemary who he was.' He leant forward. 'That's not against the law, right?'

'Right.'

'Then Rosemary comes up with this scheme.' He smiled. 'I don't know if it would have worked – she thought it would. She had contacts, you see. In Europe and the near East – drug suppliers. The big fish,' he said. 'They ship it in from South America, and sell it to smaller fish who import it.'

'And you are one of the scavenger fish who pick up the scraps,' said Judy. 'To sell on the street.'

'I was,' he said, not in the least offended. 'I'm not involved in that now.'

'No?'

'Rosie wanted to bring it in – there's a lot of money to be made.'

Judy's eyebrow suggested that he should tell her something she didn't know.

'They search practically everything that floats – and they take lorries to pieces. But she said it was owner-drivers that they really went for. Because the owners could be bribed, or be drug-runners themselves. They didn't pay so much attention to fleet lorries, with employee drivers. Especially not ones that had been operating for the last twenty years with a spotless record.'

Judy was writing it down, and he was speaking more slowly so as not to leave her behind.

He went on. 'And Austin had a fleet of lorries, the nomination to stand at the next general election, and a guilty secret,' he said.

Lloyd would love this. Judy began to see what Lennie saw in Stephen Arthur Tasker.

194

'But nothing was going to happen until he got elected,' said Steve. 'That was part of the deal. It suited Rosemary – she would have a couple of years to establish her credentials. If anyone was suspicious of her sudden interest in commerce, they'd have given up by the time it really got going.'

Judy looked up. 'She was very sure he was going to be elected,' she said.

Tasker smiled. 'A staunch Tory, our Rosemary,' he said. 'But it didn't really matter if he wasn't. It would all have been very expensive, but she wasn't spending her money on setting it up. It was his, or the firm's. His own, I think. And I don't imagine Rosie's word was necessarily her bond. I think it would have gone ahead anyway.'

Judy nodded. 'And what was your part in all of this?'

'Nothing much. A few presents for tipping her the wink about Austin, the offer of a job – which I wasn't going to take – and being in good with the Beales, which doesn't hurt, as you've probably noticed.' He looked pointedly at Mervyn as he spoke.

I'll bet, thought Judy. She wondered how Stephen Arthur Tasker would have been if his life had taken a different turn.

'And did you tell Mrs Austin all this, too?'

'No. Just that he was queer.' He sighed. 'You won't believe me, but it wasn't just to change her mind. I thought she ought to know. I wish I'd kept my mouth shut now.' He looked at Judy. 'She told him she knew,' he said. 'She must have done. She must have threatened to divorce him, make it public.'

She sighed. 'Thank you for your co-operation,' she said. 'It is very much appreciated. I'll have your statement typed up, and once you've signed it, I'm told we won't be needing you further today.' She smiled. 'You won't do another disappearing act?'

'He won't,' said Mervyn. 'You can depend on it.'

In Lloyd's office, she rang Malworth, and arranged to see the squad car crew who had answered the 999 to the Riverside Inn, complete with notes. That would worry them, she thought wickedly.

She went out to the car she had reluctantly hired that morning. It wasn't too bad, she supposed, as it started first time, and blew refreshingly cold air at her. Perhaps she should get a new one. She drove round the town centre to the hotel, but Austin had left;

195

he had gone home, she was told, so off she went to the Mitchell Estate.

Lennie's car was parked by the garages at the side of the flats; Judy felt a lump in her throat as she pulled in off the road, and parked beside it.

'He's just gone out, dear,' said the next-door neighbour as she prepared to knock. 'He's gone to see about his wife's paintings. At the studio, you know.'

'Ah,' said Judy. 'Thank you.' She was turning to leave when she heard the voices upstairs.

'You could move in on Monday, Mr Lloyd, if you're that keen.'

The footsteps began to descend, and Judy illogically wanted to hide.

'It's much bigger than your present place – these old village flats were never really meant for two people. I'm sure you and your good lady will find the space invaluable.'

Lloyd's good lady sprinted to her hired car, and blessed it for starting like it did as she shot off, back to Malworth, back to get on with her work and to push thoughts of leaving Lloyd's lovely little flat right to the back of her mind.

What was he doing, looking at it without her, anyway? Was it supposed to be some sort of surprise? He had said he could afford one of them . . . he surely didn't think she wanted to live there? But he did like surprising her. And he listened to things she said – if she had ever said she liked the place, or . . . oh, God. A new thought occurred to her.

Was he that upset? Surely not. But he had hardly spoken to her last night, and he was worse this morning. He was still in a filthy mood at the station. But she'd told him that she wouldn't try for promotion if it bothered him that much. Of course that would just bother him even more, she knew that now. Maybe he thought the solution was to . . . leave her? No. No, that was just silly.

But this wasn't the back of her mind, she told herself sternly, and walked into the station to find the two crew of the squad car sitting waiting for her, looking less than pleased at being dragged in when they were off duty.

'My office, please,' she said, and led the way.

She sat behind the desk, and looked up at them. 'Have you got your notebooks with the entries on the call to the Riverside Inn on Monday night?'

196

'Yes, ma'am.'

'What time did you arrive there?'

One of them glanced at the book, as though he hadn't just written it all down when he knew he was being called in. 'Ten forty-eight, ma'am,' he said.

'And how long were you there?'

'About half an hour, ma'am. They took a bit of calming down. All hell was about to break loose – someone had insulted Beale's wife, and you know what he's like.'

'And you prevented it,' she said, with a smile. 'Well done.'

They looked at one another, trusting her much less far than they could throw her, she was sure.

'You called in to say that you were bringing Beale and the other man in at . . . ' She looked at her notes because she could never remember exact times and figures, not for show. 'Eleven seventeen,' she said.

'Ma'am.'

She sat back. 'Were the traffic lights against you?'

They frowned in unison; she liked that.

'Were they?' she said.

'I don't really remember, ma'am,' said the driver.

'Yes, you do,' she said.

'Yes, ma'am, they were.' He sighed.

'And did you run the red light, using your siren, even though it wasn't an emergency?' She tutted.

'Am I getting done for jumping the red?' he asked.

She smiled. 'Just answer the question.'

'Yes, ma'am,' he said crossly. 'Everyone does it. You can get held up forever there – and there's no traffic at that time of night.'

She sat back, her hands clasped behind her head. 'So you used your siren at approximately eleven twenty p.m. on Monday, the 24th of June,' she said.

'Yes, ma'am. And if I'm on the carpet, shouldn't I be speaking to Inspector Menlove rather than you? I don't see why I can't just get done for it like anyone else, anyway. Ma'am.'

'Oh, you won't be getting done for it,' she said, forgiving the usual heavy emphasis on rank, the hostility, in her relief at being given the right answer. 'Inspector Menlove doesn't know or care. And next time we're all in the pub, remind me to buy you a drink. Thanks for coming in – sorry to have spoiled your day off.'

They left, convinced she was off her trolley. The euphoria she had felt evaporated as she contemplated Austin. He was in Lennie's studio, so she didn't have far to go.

Sandwell knocked and came in, ducking under the door.

'You really don't have to,' she said. 'There's a inch clearance, at least.'

'You tell that to my forehead,' he said. 'Some builders like to fool you. I've just been told that one of the latents on the outside of the Beales' front door can't be identified.' He sat down. 'It's not yours, or Drake's, or either of the Beales'. It isn't Tasker's, or Austin's – or Mrs Austin's. They've spent hours trying to match it to any we've got, and it isn't on file, so it's not likely to be one of Beale's band of merry men. Anyway, they think it's a woman's.'

'Yes,' said Judy, a little grimly. At least it put her interview with Austin off for a little while. 'I know whose print it is, Bob. And it's time you and I went to see her.'

Pauline had expected Gordon back; he hadn't wanted to go and look at Lennie's paintings, and she had thought he wouldn't stay. But he must have decided to get it over with. He didn't want to do anything much at all, and mentioning Lennie's name would be enough to make him go into a depression from which it seemed he would never recover. But it would lift a little, eventually, until the next time. He had been much better, until Jonathan had come to get him to pick what he wanted.

It was odd, his attitude to Lennie. It wasn't like before, when Lennie could do no wrong, but it wasn't mourning, either. It was as though he blamed himself for what had happened, and didn't want to think about her. She didn't like him hating Lennie's memory like that. It wasn't natural. Nothing had been natural since Monday night, and she felt as though it never would be again.

She wasn't surprised to see Inspector Hill's face on the security screen; she hit the button with resignation, and left the door open for her, as she would a member of her own family.

'Mrs Pearce – I don't know if you remember Sergeant Sandwell.'

'Yes.' Pauline nodded to him. 'Please take a seat.'

The sergeant sat, but Inspector Hill didn't, and that made Pauline a little uneasy.

'Mrs Pearce,' she said, 'can I suggest that this time we get the whole truth and nothing but?'

The courtroom terminology did nothing to make Pauline feel any better. And she wasn't about to give guarantees.

'You thought, originally, that your husband had done some harm to Jonathan Austin,' said the inspector. 'You wanted to protect him, so you lied to us.'

She nodded, her head barely moving. This woman was moving in for the kill; she could see it in her face.

'But you very soon knew that he had done nothing of the sort; Jonathan Austin was alive and well – Mrs Austin was dead. And not only would you never have suspected your husband of that in the first place, but he was actually with you when it happened.'

Right so far. Pauline sat down, opposite the sergeant, who had taken over the note-taking, she noticed. Or would have done, if she had said anything other than asking him to take a seat.

'So why did you continue to lie to us, Mrs Pearce? Why did you have to wait until your husband had confessed to these murders before you even began to tell us the truth?'

The word truth seemed to echo. Truth, truth, truth. She had never told lies. She had liked that about Lennie. Lennie was truthful. She hung about with people who would cut their grandmother's throat, never mind tell lies, but Lennie herself was honest, and truthful, and Pauline had liked that. Jonathan Austin had said that she had told him she was frightened of Steve; that wasn't true. Lennie wouldn't have said that, wouldn't have let him believe that. It was Jonathan she should be questioning. Who cared who killed Rosemary Beale?

Rosemary Beale had been everything Pauline hated. She lied and cheated and stole. She helped her husband run his sordid clubs and made money out of inadequates.

Truth. It still whispered in the air, as the inspector waited for an answer. Truth. What was so important about the truth? It wouldn't bring Rosemary Beale back, and who would want to, anyway? Jonathan said Beale was cut up about it, but Pauline couldn't believe that. He was just like Rosemary: hard as nails. She had modelled herself on Rosemary when the police had come that morning; it would seem that she wasn't as skilful as Rosemary had been.

'Would you be prepared to let us have your fingerprints for elimination?' the sergeant asked mildly.

Pauline looked up. 'Elimination?' she said. 'But I was just outside. The police were all there when I got there. I wasn't in the Austins' flat. Are you trying to prove that I was? The chief inspector says a woman couldn't have done it anyway.'

'No, Mrs Pearce,' he said. 'We are investigating Mrs Beale's murder, not Mrs Austin's.'

It was a trick. At least she knew not to fall for tricks. But you didn't *find* any fingerprints in the Beales' flat, that's what they wanted her to say. 'If you like,' was what she did say.

'You forgot the outside of the door, Mrs Pearce,' said the inspector quietly. 'Are you still as keen to let us have your fingerprints?'

Don't panic. Stay calm. She stayed calm, but it really didn't seem to get her anywhere. She supposed that was the thing about calm, really. It didn't. They had found her fingerprints. That was almost funny.

'You knew your husband had been hurt dreadfully by the Austins and Rosemary Beale,' the inspector went on. 'You thought he had done something to Jonathan Austin. You came home, you came up in the lift . . . '

'Her door was ajar,' said Pauline. 'I was worried. I didn't know what on earth was happening. And her door was open at almost midnight. I . . . just touched it, pushed it.' She looked at the inspector defiantly. 'I killed her,' she said.

Inspector Hill closed her eyes briefly in annoyance. 'No, you didn't, Mrs Pearce,' she said, her voice as patient as the gesture had been impatient. 'But you cleaned up very thoroughly after the person who did.'

Pauline went to the window when they had gone. No police cars – presumably they wouldn't park obediently in the side-street. But they might; they might want to be discreet, in an area like this. Gordon had been clever without knowing it. Confessing to a murder he hadn't committed made them disbelieve the other confession. And of course he genuinely hadn't known that all possible traces of his presence had been removed.

She sighed, and waited, watching for him being taken away.

200

She hadn't removed traces of her own presence. That really was almost funny.

Gordon couldn't have picked paintings. He had caused all this; he just wanted to die, and Jonathan had wanted him to pick out paintings.

'I really don't know,' he had said.

'It's just that I want to close up this place as soon as possible, and I want to give Beale whatever you don't take.'

Gordon had looked away from the painting he was supposed to be considering, and stared at Jonathan instead. 'Beale?' he had repeated, incredulously.

'I think they should go to someone who appreciates them.'

Gordon drove into the Austin-Pearce car park, thinking about the collection. Beale would appreciate them, all right.

'But you must have whatever you want first,' Jonathan had insisted. 'However many you want. All of them, if you like. I just don't want to have them, that's all.'

He had let his feelings for Lennie blind him to everything; to what was happening to Pauline, to what was happening to Lennie herself. He had seen her with him. And he had known that she didn't want to be with him. She had told him, three years ago.

'Oh, Gordon, save my life, there's a love. If you're with me, he'll just go away.'

And he had seen her, and all he had seen was perfidy and betrayal. He hadn't made him go away. He hadn't saved her life this time.

He had told Jonathan that he couldn't pick out paintings, not yet.

Jonathan had looked upset. 'Oh – of course, I'm sorry. It was thoughtless of me . . . grief takes people different ways, I suppose. I just want to get it all over with.'

Grief. There hadn't been time for grief. Just lies, and more lies, and wanting to die and being afraid to die.

He had barely got into his office when the phone rang to say that Chief Inspector Lloyd was there. He sighed. 'Ask him to come in,' he said.

He swivelled the chair round, and looked out at the sky. Silver grey, with a high blanket of cloud.

'It looks as though the rain will stay off,' Lloyd's voice said.

Weather. Was he supposed to reply? Yes, it does look as though the rain will stay off. Not like last night – eh? Where were you in the thunderstorm? Let's have an animated conversation about how loud the thunder was. Loud enough to waken the dead. And it had. The dead had visited Gordon.

'*Save my life, Gordon, there's a love.*'

'Just a few points we have to clear up about your statement to us,' Lloyd said cheerfully.

Gordon turned. His nonsensical statement? What could they possibly want to clear up?

'You told us that you went to the factory at about five past ten on Monday night,' said Lloyd. 'And left about half an hour later.'

Oh, that statement. The fire. He had almost forgotten that. Had he said five past ten? He couldn't remember all the lies.

'But we know that it isn't true,' he said. 'You altered the time that you went to the factory to accommodate two murders that you didn't commit.'

So? He had set fire to the factory. He might have made a dog's breakfast of it, but he'd done it, all the same.

'Isn't it?' he asked, no longer caring what he was supposed to have done.

'No. You sat in your car in front of the Austins' flat for about twenty minutes, Mr Pearce.'

How did they know that? Gordon sighed. 'Yes,' he said.

'So you didn't storm off from Austin's and set fire to the factory.' He got up, and walked over to the wall.

My God, they didn't even believe he'd done what he had done. 'I set fire to it,' he said. 'I did.'

Lloyd looked at the Queen's Award for Industry certificate for a moment, then turned round. 'Yes,' he said. 'We know you did. You left lots of evidence. But you didn't do it then and there. Something else happened. What made you do it, Mr Pearce?'

Lennie. '*Save my life, Gordon, there's a love.*'

Sorry, Lennie. I'd rather set fire to a factory.

'Something pushed you over the edge, Mr Pearce.'

No. He pushed her over the edge. He left her there with that man. He looked away. 'I saw her,' he said. 'I saw her with him.'

'Who?' asked Lloyd.

'Lennie. With that man.'

'Steve Tasker?'

'I don't know. I never knew his name. She didn't tell me about her boyfriends. But he lived with her for a little while. About three years ago.'

'Where was she when you saw her with him?'

'At the Red Lion — oh, that's not what it's called now. You know where I mean.'

He had had her pinned against the wall. Why couldn't he have seen what was going on? Why did he assume that she was a willing participant?

'He'd pestered her before,' said Gordon.

'When was that?'

The question was sharp; he looked at Lloyd for the first time since he'd started asking about Lennie.

'Then,' he said. 'Three years ago. He left her — or was kicked out, I don't know which. Anyway, he'd gone. But he must have come back, because she kept trying to avoid him. She'd ring me up, ask me to go round there. If he saw my car he wouldn't come in, she said. She was frightened of him. I knew that at the time. But on Monday night, I thought . . . I thought I had been used, I thought she had just . . . I could have stopped. I didn't stop. I saw them, and I drove away. She was frightened of him, and I just left her there with him.'

He could see them again in the headlights. She must have been trying to get away from him, but he had just seen a courting couple, and then seen that it was Lennie. And he hadn't saved her life.

'I . . . I thought she was enjoying it,' he said. 'I got angry. And I came to the factory, and tried to burn it down.' He looked round. 'See how successful I was,' he said.

'What time did you see them?'

'It must have been about half past ten,' he said miserably.

'Thank you, Mr Pearce,' said Lloyd, standing up. 'You should know something, though. Tasker didn't leave Mrs Austin. He wasn't thrown out, either. He was arrested at dawn one morning.'

'Oh. Might have known.'

'He was taken into custody, held on remand, and served a prison sentence. He was released two months ago, Mr Pearce.'

At first, Gordon didn't see the significance, then his eyes widened. 'He was in prison?'

'All the time. Tasker wasn't pestering her. She wasn't scared of him, Mr Pearce.'

'Perhaps she should have been,' Gordon said.

'Perhaps. But she wouldn't have thanked you for intervening. She probably was enjoying it, and you couldn't have prevented what happened.'

Gordon could have kissed him. He contented himself with standing up, and grasping warmly the hand that was being offered to him. 'Thank you, Mr Lloyd,' he said.

'And Mr Pearce,' Lloyd said, 'you and your wife could try telling one another the truth.'

Gordon waited in his office, looking down on the car park until he saw the chief inspector drive away, then he told his secretary he wouldn't be back, and followed suit, driving back to Malworth.

He keyed in his number, and pushed open the door. Hadn't he told Pauline the truth? He thought he had. 'Pauline?' he said, almost afraid, as he entered the flat. Please don't be Barbara Stanwyck, he thought. Please. Please, jus' be Pauline.

She didn't answer; he walked through to the sitting-room, and found her looking out of the window, as she had been on Monday night. A lifetime ago.

She looked round. 'Did you miss her?' she said.

'Who?'

'The inspector. She knows, Gordon.'

That's it, Gordon, old son. That's where telling the truth comes in. All this cryptic chat about who's done what and what who knows. Try asking, Gordon. Try talking to the woman. She's your wife.

'Knows what?' he asked.

Pauline seemed almost startled by the directness of the question. Flustered – embarrassed, even.

'Knows what, Pauline?' he asked.

'She knows I cleaned up next door after you.'

'Cleaned up after *me*?' he said.

Pauline's eyes were blank. Slowly, he could see them come back to life, realise her mistake.

They stared at one another.

'You thought I'd killed Lennie,' she said, in self-defence.

He flushed. My God. What had they done?

'Oh, Gordon,' she said, after a long, long time. 'We're in terrible trouble. They'll charge us with God knows what all.'

'Yes,' he said, finding himself smiling for the first time in what seemed like years. 'Arson.'

'Whatever you call interfering with the scene of a crime,' said Pauline.

'Interfering with the scene of a crime, I think,' said Gordon.

'Making false statements.'

'Wasting police time.'

'Accessories, maybe,' she said.

Gordon blinked. 'Accessories to what?' he asked.

'I might be an accessory to murder.'

Gordon thought about that. 'Yes,' he said. 'You might be. I think we should talk to a solicitor.'

Pauline smiled. 'I think we should,' she said, coming into his arms.

The desperation was gone. The hurting was gone. Barbara Stanwyck was gone. Poor Lennie was gone, but it hadn't been his fault. He still had his business, his wife and his baby. And he would gladly go to prison as long as they were all there when he came out.

She had caught him just as he was going to leave the studio. Appeared from nowhere. She had offered her sympathies, talked a little about Leonora. But a detective sergeant had come in with her, so it wasn't a duty call by a friend; it was a duty call by a police officer.

'You know,' he said, 'I'm sure Leonora would have wanted you to have a painting – if there's one you particularly like . . .'

Judy shook her head. 'Lennie knew I was a philistine,' she said.

Jonathan put down the one he had been holding. 'Oh,' he said. 'So am I, I'm afraid.'

Judy was very withdrawn, very cool.

'I was sorry to hear that you and Michael had split up,' he said.

She smiled coldly. 'I think we're both better off,' she said.

'Probably.' He cleared his throat. 'Have you found this man yet?' he asked.

'He's been interviewed,' she said.

Jonathan couldn't believe what she had said. 'Interviewed?' he repeated. 'Does that mean you've let him go?'

She walked a little way into the room, looking at the paintings round the walls with the same slightly puzzled attitude that he did himself; Beale hadn't been like that. His eyes had lingered, as they might over a beautiful woman.

'*Have* you let him go?' he asked angrily, walking up to her, catching her arm, making her turn towards him.

The sergeant took a step towards him, but she shook her head very slightly, and he stepped back again, close to the door.

'We have interviewed him,' she said. 'And we'll interview him again, if necessary.'

'And meanwhile he kills someone else?'

'We can't prove anything,' she said.

Jonathan felt his face grow red. 'You could charge him anyway,' he said. 'At least you'd have him while you got proof!'

'It doesn't work like that, Mr Austin,' said the sergeant.

Jonathan let Judy go and turned towards him.

'If we charge someone, we can't ask him any more questions,' Sandwell said. 'And asking questions is how we get answers.'

'No! He'll just lie to you – for God's sake, you must know that.'

'All the better, sir. When people start lying, that's when they're vulnerable.'

Jonathan knew that. 'But he's a maniac,' he said. 'Did you see my flat?'

'No, sir.'

'Did you?' He turned back to Judy.

She dropped her eyes; she didn't have to answer.

'He's a maniac, Judy!'

She looked up again. 'Whoever did it, yes,' she agreed. 'But we don't know that it was Tasker.' She walked over to another painting, and was looking at it when she spoke again. 'It could just as easily have been you,' she said.

Jonathan nodded. 'That's what you've thought all along,' he said. 'That's why you just walked away that night.' He took out his cigarettes. 'You don't like me, do you?' he said.

'It's hardly relevant, sir. Mrs Hill isn't investigating your wife's murder,' said Sergeant Sandwell.

'No?' Jonathan lit a cigarette. 'Then she can answer the question.'

Judy turned. 'I've never thought about it one way or the other, Jonathan,' she said. 'I don't know you very well.'

'No. You don't. And you think I didn't care about Leonora, and you are wrong.' He made to put the packet away, and then remembered that she smoked. 'Sorry,' he said, offering her one.

She shook her head.

'You think I did it,' he said. 'You think I could do something like that to Leonora. Whoever did that hated her!' he said, his voice rising.

'Tasker didn't hate her,' Judy said.

'No – but if he *loved* her – don't you see?'

'I don't think he loved her. She loved him.'

She said it like a statement of fact. Loved him? No. No, she was wrong.

'But I think you're right about one thing,' she said. 'I think it was someone who loved her.' She took a step towards him. 'Maybe loved her enough to block it all out,' she said.

Gordon? Was that what she meant? Oh, no, surely not. No. Gordon's love was devotion, not passion. It was passionate love that turned to passionate hate, not Gordon's kind of love.

'Perhaps we're dealing with someone who simply doesn't know he did it.'

Jonathan frowned. 'Who?'

'Someone who isn't certain what he was doing at the time. Whose story doesn't really make much sense.'

Slowly, he realised. 'Me?' he said, aghast, jumping to his feet. '*Me*? You can't believe that!' He brushed away the sergeant, who was attempting to restrain him. 'I'm not going to attack the woman!' he said. 'But don't you think more attention should be being paid to what Leonora was doing?'

'You've been very keen on that line all along, haven't you, Jonathan?' said Judy. 'There was a belief that you might even have known what she was doing. Seen her doing it. But that wasn't it at all, was it? You just didn't want us to enquire too closely into what you were doing.'

'Because I'd lost my reason and killed Leonora without being aware of it?' he said. 'That is sheer nonsense. And I know exactly what I was doing when Leonora died.'

'So do I, Jonathan,' said Judy. 'So do I.'

He froze, just for an instant.

'You left the flat at ten thirty,' she said, 'and went to fetch Lennie's car, like you said.' She walked slowly two paces to the next picture, and looked at it as she spoke. 'But what you didn't say was that you did pick it up. Using the key that's on your key-ring right now.'

His hand automatically went to the pocket with his keys in it, as though he could magic the key away; she turned just as it did so. Michael had once told him that he mustn't be fooled by the big brown eyes. Those eyes looked frankly into his now.

'You thought Lennie was in her studio – that's where she went before when you'd had a row. Or perhaps visiting Pauline Pearce – you told Chief Inspector Lloyd that you thought she might have been doing that. You got a bit confused about what you thought.'

He drew on the cigarette, and sat down again.

'You went to pick her up. You felt badly about not doing what she'd asked, and about what you'd just done to Mr Pearce. You thought if you picked her up, that might help smooth things over.'

Jonathan tried to look relaxed, being reminded idiotically of the selection interview; he'd sat back then, answering their questions about why he'd be good for Stansfield, winging it a lot of the time when it got down to local issues of which he knew very little. He could do that; he could. And he hadn't even been able to smoke in front of the selection board, so this shouldn't be so difficult.

'I think you probably got stopped at the traffic lights,' she said. 'But I'm just guessing about that. And what I think you saw was Rosemary Beale, walking home alone. Alone. No Frank, no minders, no driver. Alone, and vulnerable, just like any other woman is when a man is determined to kill her.'

He flicked ash to the floor. 'Kill her?' he said. 'Do you still believe these ridiculous rumours?'

'No, Jonathan. I know they're not true. I also know about David Morris.'

At the selection interview, they had asked him if there was anything in his background that could embarrass the party. No, he had laughed. Nothing that he could recall. He laughed now.

'Who?' he asked.

'I know how she forced her way on to the board, and I know

208

why she did. I've got a statement from a witness, Jonathan. And I know what it did to Gordon Pearce when she forced you to kick him out of his own company, his own business – his life. And so do you. That was what was in your mind when you saw her. Gordon Pearce.'

She could be crediting him with a little more compassion than he possessed, he thought. Yes, Gordon had been in his mind. Yes, it had been the most difficult thing he had had to do. But what had been uppermost in his mind was the certainty that it would not end when he got into parliament. Then Rosemary would have an MP in her pocket, and she'd think of some good use for him. The endlessness. That was what was in his mind. More Gordon Pearces, more and more.

'You drove to the flats, and you saw the light on in here, so you knew where Lennie was, you thought. You parked in the private car park, using one of the Beales' spaces, since they only needed one. No danger of being moved along, or creating trouble. You got out, and waited in the shadows. I expect that's when you worked out what you were going to do afterwards.'

He dropped the cigarette to the floor and stood on it, simultaneously reaching into his pocket for the packet.

'And she arrived, in due course. But things started to go wrong there, really. Because she turned and walked back out again.'

His hand paused for an instant with the cigarette halfway to his lips. *Had* they been watching him? How did she know that?

'You've only visited these flats once before, Jonathan,' she said. 'Gordon Pearce brought you here. They don't like cars parked in their spaces, and Frank Beale's Rolls needs two. Rosemary did what any right-thinking Andwell House tenant would have done. She came marching round here to tell Lennie to get her car out of Frank's space.' She moved again, to the next picture. 'If I have a favourite,' she said, 'this is it.'

It was called Self Portrait, but it didn't look remotely like Leonora; it was a strange, double image of a woman with wild hair. Judy could have it, if she wanted.

'But she found that this place was empty. So then she was probably very puzzled. Lennie's car in the car park, the light on in the studio, and no Lennie. She went back, and let herself in with her card. That door takes a long time to close, and you took advantage of that to slip in behind her. No camera, no record of your presence.'

He lit the cigarette, and blew the flame of the lighter out.

'Then she made things very easy for you. She left the door unlocked, and she went straight to the phone. She phoned Lennie, not unnaturally, to find out what had happened. An opportunist murder,' she said. 'That's what it looked like to one of my colleagues. He was right.' She smiled. 'He always is,' she added. 'He was right about a lot of things.'

He had had to do it. She would never have stopped. He couldn't have borne to be Rosemary's performing monkey for the rest of his life. And the other option was just too dreadful to contemplate. Disgrace; prison, quite possibly. He released smoke into the room, on to the paintings. He would have to contemplate it now.

'You left. I don't think you bothered about fingerprints. What you were going to do was establish that you were somewhere else altogether, so it would never occur to anyone to ask for your fingerprints.'

But they had, because of Leonora, and he had thought it was all over. He hadn't understood why it wasn't, but he hadn't given himself away. And he wasn't so sure that any of this actually constituted a case against him.

'You had my new telephone number,' she said. 'And I was perfect. A police officer. A reasonably senior police officer of good character. So you rang me, asking if I'd seen Lennie. She wasn't home yet, you said. I would assume that you *were* at home. You knew Lennie wasn't – she was in her studio, or so you thought. So she couldn't mess up your alibi.'

Had she actually said anything that she could *prove*, that was the thing. Jonathan wasn't convinced that she had. And she hadn't even cautioned him.

'While you were on the phone, a police car ran the red light, using its siren. Remember? No police car did that on the Mitchell Estate, Jonathan, or anywhere in Stansfield. No traffic lights. But one did it here. While you were in the phone-box. I heard it. Then you drove the car back, left it where you had found it, this time taking care to wipe its surfaces, and walked home. To find that Lennie hadn't been in her studio at all. She had been murdered too.'

He brushed some fallen ash from his jacket. He didn't want to think about that. Not any more. Thinking about it didn't bring her back, it didn't get that lunatic off the streets. And Judy Hill wasn't even interested in Tasker. Too busy trying to get him.

'I don't know that that constitutes proof of murder,' he said.

'It's enough to take you in for questioning,' said Judy. 'Just as my information on Rosemary Beale's blackmail is enough to take Beale in for questioning.' She looked over at Sandwell. 'I think you should make arrangements to take Mr Beale in, sergeant,' she said.

'Yes, ma'am.' Sandwell left.

Judy smiled at Jonathan. 'I'll have to let him go, of course,' she said, with a rueful smile. 'I'm assuming that I don't need squad cars and uniforms to take you in, but I can soon get them if necessary.'

Jonathan rose slowly. 'No, no,' he said. 'I'll come quietly. But I think you'll probably have to let me go too,' he said.

'Probably. Unless you make a statement of your own accord. We do have forensic evidence – it might place you at the scene, or it might not. But you'd be better making a statement. She was blackmailing you, which should be a quite powerful plea for mitigation. Shall we go?'

Jonathan stared at her. They couldn't go now; Beale would see him. And they would have questioned him about the blackmail. He would know. He would *know*.

'You can't do this!' he said.

'Can't do what? I'm not doing anything except taking a suspect in for questioning.'

'You'd have to give me some sort of protection!'

'Who from?' She looked puzzled.

'You know damn well who from! Beale! He'll see me – he'll know she was blackmailing me!'

'But if you didn't murder his wife, why would you need protecting from Frank Beale?' she asked.

He sat down again, the prospect becoming clearer and clearer.

'He'd have me killed,' he said, his voice hardly audible. 'You know he would.'

'All I can guarantee, Jonathan, is that the state won't have you killed.'

211

My God. Don't be fooled by the big brown eyes. He stood up again. 'Isn't this duress?'

'I didn't say Frank Beale would kill you,' she said. 'You did.'

Jonathan ground out his cigarette. 'I just hope you're as clever at finding Leonora's murderer,' he said.

'People keep making that mistake,' she said. 'I'm not investigating Lennie's murder, Jonathan. I never was.'

'That's all right, Mrs Sweeney, we'll see ourselves in.'

Steve heard Beale's voice, and wondered a little about the plural. He didn't have to wonder long, as the door opened with a rush, and Frank plus two heavies stood in the doorway.

'Stevie,' he said, walking in.

Stevie was bad. The other two came in behind him, one of them closing the door quietly.

'Frank,' said Steve. 'Mervyn said to tell her. She knew it all anyway – she just had to have it in writing, that's all. I knew you'd be well out of it. They wouldn't have anything on you.'

'They didn't, Stevie. As you see, I'm here. Free as a bird.'

'So why the visit?'

'I owe you money, Stevie. A fat bonus I said, and a fat bonus it is. You co-operated, and she got him. I told you I had faith in her.' He reached into his pocket, and drew out a bulky envelope, tossing it on to the bed.

Steve picked it up gingerly, as though it might contain explosives. But it didn't. Just at least a hundred used twenty pound notes.

'That counts as small denomination these days, Stevie,' he said. 'I thought it would be more useful than larger notes.'

Steve put it back down on the bed, still moving carefully, still unhappy with the tone of the proceedings.

'She had me taken in for questioning,' Beale said, with a smile. 'I knew she was good. Keeping me out of circulation until she had Austin safely tucked away where I couldn't get at him.' He took a huge cigar from his breast pocket, and bit the end off. Then he spent some moments lighting it. 'Can't smoke them too often,' he said. 'Heart, you know.'

The expensive smell filled the room.

'But I'm having one now because that young woman got him, even if I didn't. Rosemary would have liked her,' he said. 'She's got it up here.' He tapped his temple. 'But pulling a stroke like

212

that left my boys here at a loose end,' he said. 'So we thought we'd visit you.'

Steve's heart began to beat faster. Outside, there was just a chance of running. Here he stood no chance. But there was Mrs Sweeney, he thought, relieved. She'd call the police as soon as she heard anything going on.

'Very nice woman, your landlady,' said Beale.

Dear God, he could read minds.

'Said to tell you that she was on her way over to her friend's, but she'd be back at teatime. A young lady friend of mine is giving her a lift over there in the Rolls, as it happens.'

Steve didn't speak, didn't look at him. He breathed in cigar smoke, and waited.

'See, Stevie, there was a good reason why they couldn't tie me in with this crazy blackmail and drug-smuggling business. I didn't know anything about it.'

Steve looked up then. 'What?'

Beale shook his head. 'No,' he said. 'Nothing. Or I wouldn't have made a fool of myself accusing Austin of having it off with Rosemary, would I?'

Steve hadn't thought of that.

'The brain, Stevie. You should use it now and then. I didn't know about Rosemary's plan – I'd have talked her out of it. She knew that, so she didn't mention it. Thought she'd just show me how clever she'd been. Or maybe she wanted to be financially independent. Crazy. It would never have worked. But you knew, Stevie. She told you. Pillow talk, Stevie.'

Cigar smoke was puffed into his face as Beale bent down towards him. 'Clever girl, Rosemary,' he said. 'But she always wanted more than I could give her. Funny – a lot of women from her background get turned off, but I think with Rosemary it was a labour of love, if you see what I mean. She did stray, too often. So, when I take someone on to keep an eye on her, and she can't stray without my knowing about it, she just has it off with him. I should have guessed. I really should.'

Steve didn't dare breathe as Beale straightened up. A horn sounded, and he smiled. 'That's my friend back with the Rolls,' he said. 'I'm sorry, Stevie, but I really must be going now. I'd love to stay and chat, but you know how it is. My friends will be pleased to keep you company, though.'

Beale was gone; all that remained of his presence in the room was a pall of heavy, sweet smoke, two men whose combined ages didn't reach his, and an envelope containing payment for their services.

'Are you still worried about the reasonable doubt?' Drake asked, as they turned into Queens Estate.

'No,' said Lloyd, slowing down at the turn into Lady Jane Avenue, glancing at the numbers of the houses.

'Well, he is the only one left in the frame now,' said Drake. 'It may be circumstantial, but Allison's quite happy about it.'

'He's very strong on not having to prove motive,' said Lloyd. 'I'm happier when I understand why someone has done something.' It had its number on the gate, nice and clear. He indicated to the following car.

'She led him on, then didn't want to know.'

Lloyd pulled up outside the little semi with its neat garden, and released his seat-belt. 'No,' he said. 'That wasn't the motive.'

Drake frowned. 'You've got some new information?' he asked.

'No,' Lloyd said. He looked back to see the squad car pulling in behind him, and two constables get out. 'Old information. Information we've had all along. Let's go,' he said, looking at the young man's puzzled face.

They trooped up the narrow path; his finger was just about to push the bell when he heard sounds coming from the curtained room. He tried the door, but it was locked.

'Round the back!' Drake shouted to the other two, and then applied his shoulder to the door. It took several heaves, but the lock broke just in time to see one disappear down the corridor. The other, not as quick off his mark, was within grabbing distance.

'Stop,' said Lloyd, catching hold of him. 'We're— '

A fist smashed into his face, and sent him reeling backwards. He saw a boot, and closed his eyes, but the blow never landed. He got to his feet as Drake overpowered the youth, and bundled him towards the squad car, while the other two caught up with the one who had at least had the sense to give in gracefully rather than assault a police officer.

Drake was supervising their arrest; Lloyd rather shakily made his way into Tasker's room, aware that Judy wouldn't have been just as useful as Sergeant Drake had been on this occasion.

214

Tasker was kneeling on the floor, his hands on the bed, as he pushed himself into a standing position.

'Do you need a doctor?' Lloyd asked.

'No,' he said, checking his rib cage. 'Where did the cavalry come from? They'd hardly got started.' He was breathless, bleeding, and smiling. 'I never thought I'd be glad to hear the police smashing down my door,' he said.

Drake came running back up the path, and into the room. 'Lloyd? Are you all right?'

'Yes,' said Lloyd. 'Thanks to you.'

'You'll have a black eye,' said Tasker, then smiled at Drake. 'Oh, it's you,' he said. 'You've had a lot of experience of smashing doors down, of course.'

'Do you want to be seen by a doctor?' Drake asked.

Tasker frowned. 'Now that sounds official,' he said. 'No, I don't, thank you.'

'What's this?' Drake picked up the envelope.

'A present from Mr Beale,' said Tasker. 'For helping the lady chief inspector to get Austin.'

'He gives you money and then has you beaten up?'

Tasker shook his head. 'This had nothing to do with Mr Beale,' he said, indicating his battered face.

Lloyd sighed. Beale was protected by some sort of guardian devil. 'We could take you to the out-patients,' he said. 'Have your ribs checked over.'

'No thanks, Mr Lloyd.' He took his money from Drake, and pulled a bag out from under the bed, wincing as he bent down. 'I'm grateful for the rescue, but I'll be on my way.' He frowned. 'Why are you here anyway? Did the old girl get suspicious and call you?'

'Something like that,' said Lloyd, ignoring the look that he knew he was getting from Drake. 'Thank you for your help, Mr Tasker. Might I suggest that you look for less hazardous employment wherever you do go? And you will of course let the police and your probation officer know? It is a condition of your parole, and you may be required to give evidence.'

'Already done, Mr Lloyd,' he said. 'Just didn't get on my way soon enough, that's all.'

'You'd have missed out on Mr Beale's present,' said Lloyd.

Tasker smiled.

Lloyd went out into the grey afternoon, and his face began to throb now that it understood that someone had punched it. No one had punched it since he had been on the beat, and it didn't care for it at all.

Drake got into the car beside him, and Lloyd pulled away, on his way back to the station.

'Lloyd,' said Drake. 'Don't you think Mr Allison was expecting you to make an arrest?'

'That's all right, Mickey,' said Lloyd. 'I am making an arrest. You're not obliged to say anything, but anything you do say will be written down, and may be given in evidence.'

He was concentrating on the road. He couldn't see the young man's face.

'I couldn't understand,' he went on, 'how you had ever got on to the special course, never mind succeeded. Trying to revive a woman whom a child of two would have known was dead, touching things at the scene of the crime, being knocked for six because you'd seen a dead body. But you were knocked for six because you'd killed her, Mickey.'

'Is this a joke?'

'The last time your work went off it was a woman. A woman who made you give up smoking. Mrs Austin didn't like her husband smoking.'

'Lots of people don't like smoking!'

'True. But you know what was odd, Mickey? Pauline Pearce stopped seeing Mrs Austin – or Miss Hovak, as she then was – after Tasker was arrested. Because every time she went there, there was a police car outside the house. But we weren't interested in Miss Hovak, were we? We didn't charge her, we didn't question her – Jack Woodford said if she hadn't been in bed with the man when we went in, she would never have figured on the paperwork. So why was there always a police car outside, just when you started giving cause for concern? Just when you got involved with another woman?'

'Coincidence.'

Lloyd prayed there would be no traffic hold-ups. He could feel the tension in the car; Drake would make a run for it if he had to stop, for all his bravado.

'And the crack factory,' said Lloyd. 'Everyone told me it was impossible. There wasn't any crack in Stansfield. And if

216

there ever was, it wouldn't be being made in an area like that. Oh, but I said, he's been with the force drugs squad – he's got good contacts. Let him try. If he spots anyone, then we'll set up surveillance and all the rest.'

He was coming to the roundabout. One car, approaching from the right, but a reasonable distance away. He pressed down on the accelerator in a way that was foreign to his nature, approaching a junction, but he got on to it without having to stop.

'I saw that flat today, Mickey,' he said. 'No crack factory.'

'No – they'll have moved out. I was spotted, that night. I was going to tell you, but all this . . . in fact,' he said, 'I wouldn't be surprised if it wasn't Tasker who spotted me.'

'It very probably was, Mickey,' said Lloyd. Two more round-abouts, and two pedestrian crossings, as he recalled. He'd just have to keep his fingers crossed. 'He recognised you straight away today, didn't he? As soon as you walked into the interview room. He has a better memory than you, it would seem.'

Drake didn't speak, and the pedestrian crossing was winking in the distance.

'You go to Crown Court to give evidence that's going to send a man to prison for five years, and you don't remember what he looks like?'

This time he slowed as he saw someone approach the crossing, and moved slowly towards it. Get on to it if you're going to, for God's sake, he thought. The pedestrian crossed, and Lloyd's foot went back on the accelerator.

'I found that very hard to believe, Mickey. So maybe Tasker did spot you – he was in the area. But that flat has never even had squatters in it. Developers these days look after their properties – they want to sell them, and it's a buyer's market. They can't run the risk of squatters, and they don't.'

Roundabout. Cars. If he could just edge his way on, just push out enough to inhibit the one with the right of way. A horn sounded angrily, but he'd made it.

One more roundabout, one more crossing, and he'd be at the station. He wasn't convinced he'd hang on to him there, but he could park with the nearside tight against a wall.

'No, you made it all up, so that you could spend time up there watching Mrs Austin. Talking to her. Calling on her. Alarming her enough for her to tell her husband. And to tell you that she

217

knew your boss, and she could get you into trouble. Mrs Hill was your boss at the time, Mickey.'

Roundabout, empty. Almost there.

'You wanted to be there in the evening. Three nights, you said. And the third night would be Wednesday, when she would be alone in the house, because her husband went to Barton on Wednesday evenings. But you didn't make it to Wednesday.'

Silence, now. Just silence.

'Tasker's almost fifty – it wasn't him she was afraid of. The one she was afraid of was young. She told Austin that she would have thought he would have grown out of it by now.' He sighed. 'But you hadn't, because you're an obsessive, aren't you, Mickey? Sixty cigarettes a day, then you give them up because she asks you to, and become obsessed with her instead. When that gets too much for her, she starts avoiding you, and you throw your obsessive soul into your work, apply for the special course, come through it with flying colours. But then you came back here, and the old obsession took over again.'

Pedestrian crossing, people. He had no option. With great reluctance, he stopped the car.

Drake didn't run. Lloyd didn't look at him.

'If there's reasonable doubt about Tasker,' Drake said, 'then there's reasonable doubt about me.'

'No,' said Lloyd, moving off again, the station in sight. 'Because in your case, we have a witness.'

'Witness? Where did a witness come from all of a sudden? There's only the next-door neighbour, and she saw nothing at all.'

'Quite,' said Lloyd, almost scraping the car against a wall as he brought it to a halt. 'She saw nothing at all until the police car came.'

There was a silence.

'But she should have done, Mickey. She should have seen you.'

He looked at him now; his face was deathly pale under the red hair, and he wasn't looking at Lloyd.

'She was at the window while the noises were going on, and she stayed there after they had stopped. According to you, you were walking towards the flats, getting the radio message. And you told them you were right outside, and ran into the flats. She couldn't not have seen you, Mickey.'

He didn't speak.

'You were inside before the message ever came. It probably stopped you hitting her again. You answered the radio, then opened the balcony windows with the tissues you used to get your prints off the murder weapon. Then you scattered the others round. You had to say you had tried to revive her to account for the blood on your clothes. You had to say you'd pulled the furniture away, because you had. So that you could get at her.'

Drake wouldn't look at Lloyd as he continued. 'It's your story that doesn't bear examination, Mickey. You left the flats at a few minutes after eleven, and you saw them at ten past. You were worried, turned round and came back. So how come a five-minute journey took you twenty minutes? If it had been Tasker – why would he wipe the murder weapon and not the phone? Whoever cleaned the murder weapon wanted Tasker's prints found. We'll ask the right questions this time, Mickey.'

He lifted his head slowly. 'It wasn't my fault,' he said slowly.

Lloyd switched off the engine.

'She wouldn't have anything to do with me,' Drake went on. 'She was married, she said. I had to go away. She would tell her husband, she would tell Judy Hill – she couldn't have anything to do with me, she was married now!'

His eyes blazed again, as his voice grew louder. 'And then I see her with that . . . that scum. Someone who sells poison to school-kids, someone she said she would never have anything to do with again!'

His head dropped down.

'I wasn't sure, I wasn't sure,' he said. 'That's why I went back. The door was open. I could hear her.' He was shaking. 'I picked up the ashtray, and went in. I saw them. I saw her. She was in there with him – I could hear her. Promising to meet him, saying she couldn't wait! And the phone ringing all the time – she just let it ring while she let him— ' He shook his head. 'It rang and rang . . . then he went, and she answered it, but there was no one there. I watched her. Looking at herself. Looking in the mirror at herself. Undoing her blouse, looking at herself. Pleased with herself. It wasn't my fault. It was her own – it was . . . '

He broke down, and Lloyd waited for a moment before getting

219

out of the car, and beckoning to two sergeants who were leaving the station.

'Mr Drake is under arrest,' he said, and went to report back to Allison, who would be less than pleased with his methods. A short wait, and a long, long interview. Partly on the carpet, partly being told he'd done a good job. A lot of stuff about the image of the force, a lot of mutual sympathy and regret.

At last, it was all over, and he could go home. His eye ached, and he felt weary and stiff, but he refused the offer of a car, and drove himself.

Judy met him at the door, examining his eye, making him sit down. She handed him a very large whisky.

'I've got steak,' she said.

'I don't think it does any good.' He sipped the whisky.

'It does if it's rare, and served with onion, chips and peas,' she said. 'My speciality.'

He smiled.

'Lloyd, why didn't you tell me?'

He shook his head. 'I couldn't. I couldn't tell anyone. I kept hoping I was wrong, though I knew I wasn't. But I couldn't accuse him of something like that, not even to you. I thought if we went out to Tasker's, if he really thought someone else was going to get the blame, he might . . . ' He shrugged. 'But he didn't. Wishful thinking.'

'When did you realise?'

'Almost straight away.' He took a much larger gulp of the whisky. 'But it was just last night that I knew for certain.' He smiled at her, a little sadly. 'That's why I was in a bad mood,' he said. 'He called her Lennie. Pauline Pearce called her Lennie – that was the first time I'd heard anyone call her that. But Drake wasn't there, and he had never heard anyone call her that. He'd only ever spoken to Austin, and he always called her Leonora.'

Judy nodded. 'I always wondered why,' she said. 'Lennie hated it. But then Lennie's a boy's name – maybe he . . . ' She smiled. 'I'm getting as bad as you,' she said.

'I used your method. I looked at the facts we already knew in a different light. I stopped wishing the next-door neighbour had seen something, and realised what she hadn't seen.'

'Lennie took risks,' Judy said, after a moment. 'She liked people who weren't all that safe.' She looked at him. 'I'm glad,

220

in a way, that it was that risk that killed her. Not just because she happened to pick up a telephone.'

He knew what she meant.

Two hours later, they had finished their leisurely meal; Judy's speciality had done the trick, as she had said it would, and Lloyd felt much better, as he tipped the last of the brandy into Judy's glass.

'I've lost my temporary promotion,' she said.

'I thought we didn't discuss that at home?'

She smiled.

'Still, it was a good way to lose it, from the career point of view,' he said. 'I owe you an apology. I really thought you'd lost your way.'

'I owe you one. I really thought you were going to buy one of those flats.'

'It was you, was it, speeding? I nearly took your number, but you were moving too fast.' He took her hand. 'I suggest we leave the washing up and go to bed.'

'What a good idea.' She got up from the table. 'You can talk to me in French,' she said.

'No I can't.'

'Your mother was half French, and you don't speak the language?'

'My father's wholly Welsh, and I don't speak that either. I speak the most wonderful language in the world. English.'

Judy laughed. 'Isn't that treason, or something?'

'Oh, yes. They'd probably blow me up. But English doesn't need an Academy to make people remember to speak it, like French does. As for Welsh roadsigns – if you have to plug a language into a life support system, forget it.'

He put his arm round her as they walked into the bedroom. 'A language should live,' he said, kissing her ear. 'It should breathe . . .'

'Why did you never tell me?' she said.

'It should be pliant and responsive.' He pushed her down on to the bed, his lips touching her temple, her eyes. 'But complex, and not too easy to master.'

'You talk about everything. All the time. Nineteen to the dozen. And you never told me you had French blood in your veins.'

221

'You should want to explore it.' He kissed her hair. 'The deeper you delve into its mystery . . . '

'You, the romantic, keep quiet about being one-quarter French, as though it was something to be ashamed— ' She broke off, and stared at him.

'What?' he said, sitting back. 'You look so like a gun-dog that I want to give you a biscuit. What?'

'It's French.'

'Forget it,' he said. 'I told you there would be no supplementary information given. You produce names, and I will tell you if you are right, I promise. But no— '

'How did you know I was talking about your name?' she asked, interrupting him in full flow.

He couldn't believe he had fallen into so simple a trap. It was the blow on the head that had done it.

'It's French,' she said smugly, then frowned. 'But I'd have thought you would have liked a romantic French name. Michel, Jean-Claude, Pierre . . . so, it must be a dreadful French name.'

He started to undress.

'But how would we know what sort of name qualifies as dreadful in France?' she said. 'It must be a name that means something in English. Or a name that we use in a quite different context from— '

'I do the talking,' he said, turning to her, kissing her before she could get any further with her exploration of language. It occurred to him, later on, that he had never made love to a chief constable either.

Perhaps he had that to look forward to.